LOATHE GRAY

LEIGH DONNELLY

To Bekah, my real life Sam. Ignore that bit in the copyright about how any similarities to real people are coincidental. Sam's totally you, and Smitty's a bit of you, too. Sorry about that.
And to Lauren, my smutty book bestie. What a wild and crazy year it's been. Here's to many more.
Thank you, ladies.

CHAPTER 1: SAM

"Fuck, fuck, fuck," Sam muttered as she killed the engine, turned off the audio on her phone, and rummaged around for a sweatshirt or something, anything, to cover up with. The beat-up 2004 Corolla she loved and refused to replace blasted heat regardless of how much she messed with the temperature controls. Now that she was getting pulled over in a tank top and daisy duke shorts while there was a foot of snow on the ground, she could see what a mistake it had been to put off that repair.

Tap, tap, tap.

Sam plastered her best smile on her face then hit the button to lower the window. She was well aware how suspicious she looked: scantily dressed in the middle of winter in a car full of all the possessions she could cram into it. Candy wrappers, evidence of her emotional eating thanks to her impending divorce, glistened around her feet. Since she'd never, ever broken the law or been pulled over, she didn't know what to expect and likely looked excessively nervous or guilty. She hoped it was the former.

The officer leaned down and peered into her car. He had

reflective sunglasses on so she couldn't see his eyes or tell what exactly he was looking at at any given time. "Good evening, I'm Officer Hoffman. Do you know how fast you were going back there?"

"Um…yeah. I was going thirty-seven, thirty-eight max?" She was confident in her answer, but it came out as a question in the end once she properly took in the officer. His face was clean shaven, revealing a chiseled and striking jaw. The hard lines and angles of his face fit his demeanor. From what she could see from his waist up, tall, dark, and handsome didn't begin to describe the towering stud outside her car.

His sunglasses came off, and his dark brown eyes narrowed at her response. "You were going thirty-six."

She smiled back, relieved to hear she'd only been going one mile-per-hour over the limit.

"The speed limit is twenty-five. You just passed the sign." He was exasperated already, though that hardly seemed fair given how little he knew her.

She turned and strained to look behind her as if she could see the sign now facing the other direction. As a child, Sam had vacationed with her family in Deep Creek Lake for three weeks each summer. A few years ago she could have easily rattled off every street, store, boat ramp, and speed limit in the tiny town.

She'd returned now for the healing powers of the great lake. She could already see herself on the back deck of the vacation house with her feet propped up on the fire pit as she settled into an Adirondack chair. Her books, the gentle lapping of waves from the boats passing by, and the occasional splash of a fish jumping out of the water was exactly what she needed to reset her life. Getting pulled over on the way to said new life had not been part of that plan.

"Twenty-five? It's always been thirty-five. Did they change it?"

"For safety reasons we lowered speeds throughout the area back in August." She could see his eyes making a sweep of the inside of her vehicle though his face gave no indication of what he thought of the dumpster fire. "I suggest you keep a better eye on the road so you're aware of the changes."

"Yes, absolutely. I'll do that." Her shoulders slumped in relief. She was only getting a warning. A ticket on top of her already chaotic life—mainly the impulsive move across the state to get away from a failed marriage regardless of having zero job prospects—could very well have pushed her over the edge of the cliff she was currently toeing.

"I'll need to see your license and registration, please."

"You're giving me a ticket?" Her smile vanished and her tone dripped with indignation. She was cautious almost to a fault when it came to driving, and after this one little mistake he was going to give her a ticket? Couldn't he see her grip on life and sanity was down to one little pinky finger poised to slip at a moment's notice?

His voice remained even and unaffected as he repeated the command, "You were going more than ten miles over the speed limit. License and registration. Please."

Sam pursed her lips to keep from saying anything further. She could tell he didn't want to hear it anyway. Jerk. But if she was honest with herself, he wasn't wrong about her not paying attention to the road. As a side hustle, she'd started a smutty book review blog. She *had* been distracted when her phone's PDF reader, an emotionless narrator set at twice the normal speaking speed, hit the big climax of the book.

Sam had scrunched her face in confusion and strained her ears, unable to fathom what was happening in the scene. Someone was kneeling in the kitchen, then suddenly they were bent over on the bed in another room. Seconds later, yet another magical character was simultaneously pleasuring four different people—how many hands did the woman have?

The monotonous, robotic voice from the phone's default audio reader had said, "She kept pumping more and more orgasms from him," and Sam had lost it.

"He can't have four consecutive orgasms! That's not even how that works!"

Her attention darted back to her driving when she noticed the flashing lights behind her. At the time she couldn't help feeling the sirens were actually sounding in solidarity. WEEooo...WEEooo...WEEooo! Sex violation: That's not how that works.

Still fired up about the impossible sex acts from the book and from the impending ticket, she said through gritted teeth, "Of course, officer. They're in the center console. Give me one second."

Sam went to move her phone from the top of the console, but her thumb must have hit a button on the screen because without any warning her car reverberated yet again with the robotic voice speaking so quickly it sounded as though she was on speed while she narrated the worst orgy ever written. Since her car's heater roared with effort and her ancient engine was deafening, she'd kept her phone volume on the loudest possible setting to hear it. But there with Officer Hoffman at her window and her car shut off, it was ear-splitting and competing against nothing to be heard.

The unexpected sound startled the phone from her hands, and she watched with utter horror as it slipped from her fingers down between the seat and the center console.

Sam had too much pride to let him witness her panic during what was sure to be a botched rescue mission for her phone, so she let it be. The fast-paced voice continued to assault their ears with a barrage of poorly selected adjectives and adverbs, all conveying a filthy, though physically impossible, happy-ever-after sex scene. Ignoring it all, she retrieved her license and registration and handed them over.

"Here you go, officer!" she shouted as nonchalantly as she could given the circumstances.

His left eyebrow cocked halfway up his forehead as he sized her up. Then he took her cards and glanced down at her license.

"You live in Milton, Maryland?" he yelled as her phone described one of the characters shooting ropes and ropes of cum all over the main character's waiting and heaving bosoms.

Clearly he wanted to play erotica audiobook chicken with her—which one would be the first to acknowledge they were screaming over an audiobook porno. Normally she would have jumped at the challenge, but at the end of a four-hour car ride from the Chesapeake Bay to the mountains of Western Maryland, she was too tired for games.

Sam held up one finger to request a minute, then she turned and shoved her hands down between the seat and console as she groped around for her phone. Someone was commenting on the beauty of the "gaping flesh tunnel" in front of them when she finally found her phone. Sam killed the audio and turned back to the officer.

"Yes, but I'm temporarily moving out here while I sort out a divorce and an early mid-life crisis." She disgusted herself with her blatant manipulation of his emotions as she innocently twirled a lock of her blonde hair around her finger. *Look at me,* her eyes pleaded. *I'm the biggest disaster of a human you've seen today. I'm sure of it. Just give me a warning and let me on my way.*

"I'm sorry to hear that. Excuse me for a moment."

In her rearview mirror she watched him walk back to his car and tried to size up the likelihood of her getting a ticket. The minutes ticked by and as her assurance that she was indeed getting a ticket increased, so too did her irritation with the heartless officer.

"Mrs. Thornton, I have a citation for you today," he said when he returned. "Your arraignment date is on the bottom right corner of the citation. If you can't make it on that day, the back of the citation lists out your next steps. There's also a number on the back that you can call if you have questions."

Sam gave an irritated huff as she took the citation and cards and stuffed them haphazardly into the center console.

"Perhaps if you weren't listening to... *that*," he said as he pointed to the phone in her lap and she looked down to see the amateur-porn looking cover and the title, *She Had All the Kings' Men*, by B.J. Queene, clearly in his view, "while you were driving, you'd be more attentive to the road."

"Noted, officer." She didn't owe him any sort of explanation about her preferred reading genre, so she provided him with none. If he wanted the satisfaction of shaming her, he wouldn't get it. Even though she herself *was* embarrassed to be listening to the erotic abomination B.J. Queene was attempting to pass off as literature, she wouldn't let him know as much.

Just as he was about to turn back to his car he added, "I think you should know that's not how that works with the whole -"

"I know, I know," she said, cutting him off.

Officer Hoffman raised his eyebrows and lifted his hands in defense as if he wasn't fully convinced she knew, but also didn't want to argue it any further.

"Ma'am," he said as he tipped his hat and walked back to his vehicle.

The familiar roar of her engine and the blast of warmth from the heaters settled her once more. One ticket would not break her, and that whole incident with the cop would not start her new life on a negative note.

The phone went back to the center console but stayed silent. Her review of the book was due tomorrow, but she would not be listening to the end of the story. She didn't have to. It was becoming increasingly obvious Sam should have stopped listening somewhere around Baltimore when she realized it would never get better and the characters would not be developing beyond their basic descriptions and cringeworthy sex-scenes. Sam turned on the radio and slowly made her way through the last few miles of her journey to her parents' vacation house which she'd be sharing with her friend Lexi for the foreseeable future.

Her father's vet business had been good for the family, and they'd been periodically escaping life to enjoy the tranquility of the cozy, two-bedroom chalet on the lake for as long as she could remember. She'd nearly cried tears of relief when Lexi had agreed to let her move in with her. She pulled into the drive and took in the wrap around porch and snippets of lake beyond the house and tress. She could almost see herself along with Lexi, back there with their wine glasses, winter or not, enjoying the healing powers of the water and letting their problems fall into the pitch-black depths of the lake.

The next morning, Sam was roused from a nightmarish dream by someone knocking on the front door. She rolled off the couch, caught the book she'd fallen asleep reading, and flung open the door dressed only in a pair of Lexi's pajama pants and the tank top she'd worn the day before. No bra. Her nipples rose to full attention with the rush of the cold winter air.

"What are you doing here?" she demanded.

7

CHAPTER 2: GRAY

He blinked a few times, trying to make sense of why Samantha Thornton was answering Lexi's door at six in the morning. Before he could stop them, his eyes traveled down her long blonde hair, no longer in a ponytail, cascading around her shoulders and down to her chest. In his defense, his blatant, lingering gaze at her boobs had started as an innocuous appreciation of the gorgeous honey color of her hair that he'd missed during the traffic stop. She was in the same tank top, but this time he could tell she wasn't wearing a bra.

He also couldn't help but notice she had a death-grip on a book with a half-naked male on the cover and a hot pink title in a fancy font he couldn't read. The book was filled with neon colored sticky notes poking out here and there.

When he snapped out of it and finally looked up again to meet her eyes, her head tilted and her eyes narrowed, as if daring him to comment on what she was wearing or reading.

He didn't bother defending himself since she'd clearly caught him shamelessly checking out her tits. "Mrs. Thornton—"

"Smith, not Thornton," she interrupted.

"Smith. Sure. I didn't expect to see you here."

"*I* live here. What are *you* doing here?" Like an animal puffing herself up to demonstrate dominance and aggression, she stood up straighter and pushed her chest out. He forced his eyes to remain on hers, even if it gave off the impression that he was accepting her animal-dominance challenge and was ready to do battle with her. In reality, he was not ready to battle anyone. He was barely awake without his morning coffee and workout.

"Well?" she pressed when he didn't immediately answer.

Where to start on how he'd ended up at Lexi's door one morning each week for the last year or so with a box of doughnuts?

Lexi and her fiancé Paul had been renting the house together. Paul was out for a run one evening when he was hit by a car and killed on impact. He'd been the first to arrive on the scene that day and the one to inform Lexi about what had happened. The aftermath had been brutal, and he'd stayed with her and held her for over an hour until her family arrived.

He made it all of a few days before he broke down and stopped by unexpectedly to check up on her. As far as he was concerned, stopping by once a week with comfort food was the least he could do for someone who'd experienced something so tragic. Not to mention that her long dark hair and large brown eyes made her look eerily similar to his kid sister, Bea.

Rather than go into any detail about all of that with Samantha, someone he barely knew and mostly disliked, he held up his box of doughnuts as an explanation for his visit.

Her eyes lit up at the sight and she gave a wicked grin as she reached out to grab the box. "Doughnut DoorDash? Lex is too perfect. Thanks, Hofferman." With a whoosh, the door slammed in his face.

"It's Hoffman," he said to the bright red door.

Before he could piece together what had just happened, Lexi opened the door. "Gray, sorry about that. Come in, come in. It's freezing out."

He looked over her shoulder and into the house to see Samantha at the island, helping herself to the doughnuts he'd brought for Lexi.

"Lexi, how've you been?" He stepped into the living room and noticed a stack of books on the coffee table. All with covers like the one Samantha had been holding at the front door. A few steps closer revealed the mess of sheets and pillows on the couch. She'd been heading to Lexi's the day before when he'd pulled her over?

"Good, really good. Mostly due to my new roomie, Sam." Judging by the empty wine bottles next to the sink and the bags under their eyes, they'd had a long night. Though it wasn't as obvious with the extra-pep-in-her-step attitude Lexi was sporting.

Sam turned to Gray and raised a doughnut to him as if she were toasting in his honor. "Yup, we're doing just fine. Thanks for your concern, Hofferman. And thanks for the doughnuts."

"Your new roommate?" He didn't acknowledge Sam or her obvious attempts to annoy him by messing up his name. He fixed his gaze on Lexi as he waited for any other answer that would make more sense than Sam being her new roommate.

"For the time being, yes," she answered.

"Sorry about the door, Gray," Sam added. "Thought you were delivering a DoorDash." Her flat voice and the smirk on her face said otherwise. She took another large bite of doughnut and went to the couch to continue reading the dirty book she'd been holding when he first arrived.

"Sam…" Lexi started to say. She looked from Gray to Sam, then back to Gray again as she tried to read whatever was happening between them.

"It's fine," he said. "She's just bitter about the speeding citation I gave her yesterday."

Lexi's mouth opened to speak, but Sam beat her to it. "I'm not bitter. You were in the wrong. You're supposed to give me a warning first. I've never gotten a ticket in my life."

Lexi again opened her mouth to speak but Gray snapped back, "The ticket *is* your warning. I'm *warning* you to slow down or you could kill someone."

Shit. He'd been too annoyed with Sam to realize what he was saying. Within minutes of his arrival, he'd pissed off Lexi's new roommate with his existence in general, and he'd reminded Lexi of her fiancé's death. Smooth.

"Want a coffee, Gray?" Lexi offered, seemingly unaffected by the mention of a fatal car crash. Sam went back to her reading.

"No, thanks. I'm running late today. Got held up by an accident. Likely someone going too fast on the road," he called in Sam's direction.

"I can make it to-go." Typical of her southern roots, Lexi would not allow a guest to leave without something.

"Yeah? Sure. That'd be great. Thanks." He followed Lexi into the kitchen and lowered his voice. "Is she really living here with you? On your couch? You didn't find her on Craig's List or anything, did you?" Lexi had been making progress getting over the loss of Paul and getting back out into civilization, but this was extreme. A random roommate she barely knew sleeping on her couch, of all places. A woman who was obsessed with erotic literature and way too caustic for Lexi's sweet personality and precarious recovery.

She dismissed his comments with a flick of her wrist, then poured his coffee into one of her traveling mugs with the words, "Don't you wish your coffee was hot like me?" written in flowery letters.

"Technically, she'll be living in the apartment above the garage, but yes, she'll have full access to the house as well. And she's not some Craig's List stranger, she's the daughter of the owners of the house, and she's my friend. She's going through some stuff, too. We're a perfect match."

She laughed when she looked up to see his face registering complete disbelief.

"I'm serious. And I know I've mentioned her to you before. Remember my book buddy? We've been sending letters and books back and forth since the accident."

"Her?" He gestured to Sam as if there could be some misunderstanding as to whom she was referring. Because as far as he could tell, there was no way *this* woman was the same one who sent Lexi the care packages of biographies and historical fiction books, and other carefully curated items that Lexi inevitably loved and gushed to him about. The most recent being a metal crab ornament along with a few lines in the letter about how Lexi should put up a Christmas tree that year, even if almost no one would be there to see it. To Gray's surprise, she had put up a tree, and it had made her feel better.

"Yes, her. Clearly you guys got off on the wrong foot yesterday, but once you get to know her, you'll see she's lovely. Just going through a bit of a thing. You can understand that."

Lexi turned and gave a mournful look over at Sam, like a mother fretting over a sick or injured child. Gray wasn't going to win the argument, so he let it go before it turned into a two against one with him on the losing side. He didn't want anything coming between him and Lexi. He'd never had a close, platonic female friend before. It wasn't something he was willing to risk.

"Okay. If you're sure…"

"Positive. But I appreciate your concern."

He looked back at Sam. Maybe she could see him in her periphery, or maybe she sensed him glance in her direction. Either way, her eyes still glued to the book, she raised a middle finger in his general direction before putting it down again to turn the page.

Thanks to his run-in with Satan that morning, he was late for his workout with Ronan. They'd first become friends when they had assigned seats together in Mr. Connor's sixth-grade homeroom, and the friendship only got stronger as they kept falling into the same interests: lacrosse, Frostburg State University, a career in law enforcement. Both born and raised in Deep Creek and likely staying for the long run.

The end of the era started when Ronan met his girlfriend, Mel, a few years back. He'd had it bad for her since day one, but recently it had only gotten worse, to the point where he rarely wanted to go out with the guys without Mel in tow. Even though he and Ronan were roommates since college, they hadn't seen much of each other the past two years outside of work, the gym, and their poker nights.

"What's with you?" Ronan huffed. They were both on the treadmill, finishing out a five-mile run. Gray had his speed up beyond his normal setting with an incline on top of it. His muscles burned from exertion.

"Nothing."

"You're killing yourself on the treadmill. You know today's leg day, right?"

"Shit… leg day." He lowered his speed and went back to a

flat run for a few seconds before raising the speed back up again. His mind was racing, and his limbs were wired. A hard workout was the only thing capable of keeping his sanity.

"You see Lexi this morning?" Ronan asked, making conversation. He loathed running and needed to watch something on his phone, listen to music, or talk to someone to distract him from it. Since Ronan forgot his headphones, again, it was Gray's job to keep him entertained. Whether he was up for talking or not.

"Every Tuesday."

Gray could feel Ronan scrutinizing him. "No shit," Ronan said.

Confused, Gray turned and found Ronan looking at him with a shit-eating grin. Ronan's lips curled up into a twisted smile.

"You finally hit that, didn't you?" Ronan practically shouted in the middle of the packed gym. "That's why you're all jacked up this morning. Why you were late getting here." He wiggled his eyebrows in approval while Gray shook his head as if Ronan were impossible. "Don't be embarrassed, man. I mean, it took forever, but you got there in the end."

"About damn time," someone chimed in from the stair climber a few feet away.

"See? That guy knows what I'm talking about." Realizing they had an audience, Ronan lowered his voice. "So, what happened…" he prompted after he stopped his run and stood by Gray's machine.

"I told you it's not like that. She's like a sister to me."

"Seriously? I figured you were only saying that to cover up her rejecting your ugly ass."

Gray laughed. Ronan, like most of the guys he knew, could not understand how two single straight people of the opposite sex could enjoy each other's company but not want to sleep with each other. Ever. He and Lexi had even gotten drunk a few times, and not even a flicker of a spark had ever presented itself. At least not on his end.

"No, still nothing but mutual platonic love and respect between Lexi and me."

They moved from the treadmills to the free weights to begin the torturous reps that made up leg day.

"What about you? You were already a mile in before I even got here. What's got you going this morning?" Whenever Gray was sick or out of town, Ronan would skip his run. Similarly, Gray would skip leg day unless Ronan was around to hassle him about it.

"I got lazy over the holidays, put on a few pounds. Just making sure I can still fit into the tux." The wedding. Yet another friend was taking the plunge and getting married while he was starting all over again.

Jessa, Gray's girlfriend of three years, dumped him right before the holidays. She said they both wanted different things, and it wasn't a good fit. He saw her a week later walking hand-in-hand with another guy. It wouldn't have surprised him to hear Jessa had been screwing around before their split. Hindsight's twenty-twenty and looking back he could see all the red flags had been frantically waving as if they were being beaten by hurricane winds: secretive texting, late nights at work, and zero sex drive.

His determination to settle down and get married had clouded his judgment. Made him think he could have a happy future with Jessa even though they had little in common once the initial attraction had faded.

But memories of Jessa weren't all that was bugging him that morning. It was mostly Sam. He increased the weight and reps to see if he could at least focus his attention on his posture as he lowered down into the perfect squat rather than why he couldn't get that horrid woman out of his mind.

Gray desperately wanted to know what each of those

little dirty-book notes said, wanted to know what she and Lexi had confided to each other after a few glasses of wine, and he really wanted to know what that smart mouth of hers felt like against his. He pushed it out of his mind before his body could react. He was too old for random boners out in public, and his flimsy gym shorts would do nothing to hide it.

In between reps, Ronan jabbed a finger into Gray's gut. "You working off a few extra pounds, too? Your squats are aggressive."

"No," Gray said as he smacked Ronan's hand away. They both picked up the weights for another rep. "Annoyed is all. This woman was a nightmare yesterday when I gave her a ticket, complaining about how I should have given her a warning instead. Then she answers Lexi's door when I showed up this morning and was just as irritating. They're roommates now."

"Why didn't you give her a warning?" Ronan looked perplexed.

Gray didn't want to get into how he'd found one of Jessa's old t-shirts in the back of his closet before his shift and how he'd taken his residual Jessa anger out on Sam. He didn't think he wanted Jessa back, but it was still a harsh reminder of how he'd had someone, and then he didn't.

"We lowered the limits for a reason. It's life or death out there and she's going to kill someone not paying attention to the road and the road signs."

"Fine. She deserved the ticket. What was wrong with her being at Lexi's?"

"Everything. She answered the door like she owns the place, snatched the box of doughnuts from my hand, and then slammed the door in my face. Claimed she thought I was DoorDash at six in the morning. And she flipped me off behind Lexi's back before I left."

"DoorDash." Ronan snickered at him. "Didn't recognize you in your street clothes, huh?"

"She knew who I was. She's a bitter, angry person. I'm telling you. And now I'm going to have to keep seeing her since she's living with Lexi."

"She's hot, isn't she?"

Yes, but Gray refused to answer.

"Yup. She's hot if you're all worked up over a door slam and a middle finger."

Gray stopped his rep and turned to face him.

"We've seen a million times worse from people we pull over and you never bring those up outside of work. She's under your skin because she's hot."

Gray looked at his watch. "Shift starts in thirty. We better get going."

"Oh, I see. We're doing that thing where you don't want to talk about it anymore, so you change the subject."

"I got an extra doughnut for you. But you probably shouldn't have it since you're porking out." Gray poked his gut the same way Ronan had done to him earlier.

Ronan swatted his hand away. "You're a dick, you know that? I bet you two would be perfect together."

CHAPTER 3: SAM

"What was that all about?" Lexi asked Sam as soon as Gray left.

Sam lowered the book she'd been pretending to read while Gray was there. "I don't know what you're talking about." She did her best to look innocent with big doe eyes. She wasn't sure if Lexi caught her middle finger to Gray.

"He's not your boyfriend, is he?" Sam prepared herself to be supportive if that asshole turned out to be the one Lexi gave her heart to after the sudden death of her fiancé.

Lexi rolled her eyes as if she'd never heard of anything so absurd. "He's my closest friend." Her smile turned down when she added, "He was the first one on the scene... with Paul... He's been stopping by every week since. When he's not working, we hang out a bit and catch up."

"*Him*? *He's* your closest friend here?"

Lexi looked down into her coffee. "I shut down for a while afterwards. Things got difficult with friends. It felt easier with Gray."

Sam wanted to kick herself for being so insensitive. She

needed to tread lightly with the conversation. "He's never pressured you or—"

Lexi's head shot back up. "No, never. He's not like that. *We're* not like that. Just friends."

Sam believed that was how Lexi saw the situation, but she didn't believe Gray was some nice guy who befriended her at her lowest moment, and then, for over a year, continued that friendship solely because he liked the company. Lexi was great and all, but guys didn't function that way.

"Is he gay?"

Lexi shook her head. "He was dating a woman for a while, but they split last month. I think she broke up with him."

"Someone dumped Gray? But he's so charming." Sam feigned a look of shock and put her hand to her chest.

Lexi was not amused. "Enough about Gray. I need to log into work at eight, so we have just enough time to get started on our new-year-new-us plans."

The night before they'd made a pact to help each other get their shit together. With the wine flowing like water, they were in no shape to tackle such an undertaking and had sworn they would do it first thing the next day. With the sugar rush from the doughnuts and the promise that the sun would rise yet again, the seemingly impossible task of getting their lives in order appeared somewhat more doable in the morning.

Within minutes Lexi came up with four solid goals: attend grief counseling, something she felt comfortable doing once Sam promised to go with her; join the local book club, which she'd been meaning to do for the past few months anyway; and take up hiking. Maybe learn to water ski in the summer. A final goal, clearing out what was left of Paul's things from the guest bedroom, was on the list, but she wouldn't be tackling that one until she had a few sessions of grief counseling.

"Your turn," Lexi said as she turned the pad and pen towards Sam.

The fresh sheet of lined paper looked both promising and daunting.

She'd been the one to leave Jeremy, partially because she felt she'd lost herself with him. The boyfriend turned husband she'd been with since she was fifteen—during her most formative teenage years and all her adult life—had been stifling her growth. Sam wasn't the person she was supposed to have grown into because she'd felt trapped with Jeremy. Right?

She wasn't so sure once she'd walked away from him and had yet to have anything close to an epiphany about who she was without him.

The sense of freedom she'd been sure she would feel as soon as she'd crossed the Chesapeake Bay Bridge never hit. Instead, she was Molly Ringwald looking into the mirror on her sixteenth birthday and wondering why she hadn't changed a bit.

"I like your book club idea, and I would like to meet more people in the area. Do you mind if I go with you?" she heard herself ask. For fuck's sake. Jeremy had accused her of taking on his interests instead of finding her own, and there she was doing it again. But with her brain giving her absolutely nothing to work with, she didn't see any way around it.

"I'd love that!" Lexi squealed. "It's called Blue's Clues Book Club and they read mostly mysteries. They're meeting in a few weeks at Paging All Bibliophiles. Should be enough time to read the book before the next meeting."

Sam had fond memories of Paging All Bibliophiles. She and her childhood friend Jackie would always stop in to buy a few dozen books the first day of their vacation each summer.

"Blue's Clues? And it's for adults?"

"The guy who runs it is nicknamed Blue. But he's a great guy once you get to know him."

Sam thought about it for a beat. Did she really want to commit to a book club called Blue's Clues that read nothing but true crime?

"Some of the books I've been sending you have been books they've read for the club," Lexi added.

"Were those his comments in the margins?" As much as Sam prided herself on not jumping to conclusions about gender, the first thought she'd had when she read the notes in the margins was that Lexi had decidedly manly handwriting with her blocky, all caps writing. The second thought was that the person who wrote the notes was pretty damn smart, and funny, too.

"Yup. That's all Blue. I'm one of those people who can't write in books or even dog ear a page."

Sam nodded. It had been difficult for her when she'd first started writing her own notes in the margins. It seemed criminal even though it was with books she'd bought and owned outright.

"The books were pretty good. I could get into some discussion about them. But they seemed to lack…" Sam wasn't sure how to say sex without sounding like an addict. With the nudes on her covers covering Lexi's coffee table and their previous discussion about her book review website, it wasn't a secret what Sam's preferred genre was. But Lexi wasn't in the same steamy boat she was in. Much like her personality, she was a sweet romance kind of gal.

"Sex," Lexi said, finishing Sam's sentence. "I think it's because Blue wants everyone to enjoy the books and some people get offended by sex and foul language. Not me," Lexi was quick to add when she saw Sam's reaction. "But some people do."

Sam let the sexy talk fall to the side while she focused on

a more pressing question: "Why are you so knowledgeable about a book club you've never attended?"

Lexi's face turned scarlet. "Blue's invited me to join the last few months. He gave me his old copies as a bribe." She held up a hand as Sam's eyes widened. "Before you jump the gun and assume there's anything to this, I assure you, there's not."

Sam stared her down, waiting for her to cave and admit she had a thing for this Blue guy.

"He's married; they have seven kids."

Seven? Sam mouthed, unable to even say the word aloud. She did not want to have kids—yet another obstacle that had come between her and Jeremy. It's not that she didn't like babies or kids; they were fine. In small doses, and always with the caveat that she could dump them back on their parents when she tired of them. Seven dogs? Now that she could do.

"Seven," Lexi confirmed.

Sam shook her head in disbelief. How did he even find time to read?

"Anyway, like I said, he's always on me to attend a meeting. He'll be even more excited when I show up with a friend, too. Now," Lexi said while Sam scribbled down her first goal of joining the Blue's Clues Book Club, "let's focus on jobs."

"Right, jobs." Sam's parents did well for themselves and were always generous with her regarding money. Her first job was as a vet working in the clinic her father owned. She'd never had so much as a job interview or a nervous handshake with a new boss. Finding a new career made her stomach flip and her palms sweat.

"What, exactly, are you looking for here? Something long term? Something that pays well? Flexible hours? Room to move up?"

Last November Sam had had an epiphany of sorts when

she realized she'd only become a vet to please her father (she loved animals, but her stomach couldn't handle the surgeries and her heart couldn't handle the ones that didn't make it) and that her marriage wasn't working. That day last fall when she'd walked away from, well, everything, she'd imagined her next steps would be clear once she'd had distance and time to think.

Sitting at Lexi's table, her dismal though not yet depleted bank account displaying on her phone, she didn't know what her priorities were or what she wanted.

"I still have some money. My parents are throwing me a bit of cash, I have savings to pull from, and I'm starting to make decent money from ads and affiliate links on my blog. So I'd like to make something, hopefully more than minimum, but I'll take what I can get."

"Good, good."

"I'd love to still work with animals."

"Yeah? There's a pet store in town. They might be hiring."

Sam jotted down *pet store* below her underlined heading of *Jobs*. "Maybe... Except the vet job was too much of an emotional drain. Not sure working at a pet store would be much better with all those homeless animals stuck in tiny cages all day long." She scratched out the words *pet store*.

Lexi's shoulders slumped. "I never thought of it like that. No, not a pet store."

"I can weld. I'm not officially certified since I only did it as a bit of a side hobby. But I could probably get my certification easily."

"You want to be a welder? That won't involve animals. Will it?"

Sam crossed off the word *welding* as soon as she finished writing it. "No, and I don't have any of the equipment either. It's all back home... My old home. Most of it belongs to Jeremy, anyway. He's the one who made a career out of it."

She'd merely taken it on as a hobby in a failed attempt to reconnect with her husband.

"Let's go back to the animal angle and focus on that."

"Dog walking?" Sam wrote it down on the paper, sure that it was the best idea yet.

Lexi's mouth scrunched in what Sam had learned was her classic tell when she had something to say but didn't want to say it. "That's not really a thing around here—paying people to dog walk, that is."

"Yet? Or in general?"

"In general? Most people send their dogs to Bark Sniff Wag Doggy Day Care. It's like a summer camp, but for dogs."

"Year round or only in the summer for the tourists?" She'd already begun writing out *doggy day care* before Lexi could answer her. With her vet background she'd be a shoo-in for a job like that.

"Year round. Paul and I thought about getting a dog… You know, for the kids to play with one day. Guess we got a little ahead of ourselves when we looked up dog day care options before we even had a dog or any children…"

Sam reached out and placed her hand on Lexi's. Her neon pink nail polish and usual bubbly personality contrasted against the deep anguish which had permanently settled below the surface, threatening to rise whenever they least expected it.

"You didn't get ahead of yourselves. No one could have predicted what happened with Paul."

Lexi nodded and squeezed Sam's fingers.

"Doughnut?" Sam offered. It would be Lexi's third but there was great comfort in dough and sugar.

"Any strawberry left?"

"Yes. Because strawberry icing is gross, there are three strawberry left." She walked over to the island to get Lexi's strawberry doughnut and grabbed a cholate one for herself before returning to the couch.

"I disagree. Strawberry is the best. That's why Gray makes sure at least half have some sort of strawberry flavoring. He's great that way."

Sam reached out to cup Lexi's chin and turn her face towards Sam. "Are you blushing?"

"Probably," Lexi moped in response. "I blush all the time. It's resulted in more than a few weird miscommunications."

"So you're denying that mentioning what a great guy Gray is, is making you blush?"

Lexi turned her head to free her chin from Sam's tenuous grip. "Not at all. And I know I'll blush even more when I tell you that yes, I know Gray is a handsome man."

"I knew it!" Sam raised her fist, doughnut and all, in enthusiastic triumph.

"But…"

"No, no buts. He's hot and you think he's great. That's all you need."

Lexi's expression changed. "Excuse me, did you just say Gray's hot?"

Sam rolled her eyes. "His hideous personality almost ruins it for him, but yes. He's a certifiable stud. Now back to you."

The blushing was back at full force, but she said, "I one hundred percent know with absolute certainty I don't feel anything romantic for Gray."

"He kissed you?" Sam guessed. Her stomach was full, but she shoved another glorious hunk of chocolate frosted chocolate doughnut into her mouth anyway. Chocolate paired wonderfully with sexy stories from friends.

"No. And before you ask, he's never tried." Lexi's lips pressed together as she assessed whether she should share with Sam her deepest thoughts and secrets.

"I won't let it go until you tell me," Sam assured her.

"No, you won't let it go. Will you?" She sighed and set down her doughnut. "A few months ago, I had an unsexy sex dream about him," she said before burying her face in her hands and dropping her head down as if trying to disappear into herself. It was adorable. She'd never be able to read the smut Sam read.

"What?! What happened? Tell me everything."

"No, no. I can't. It was weird and not sexy at all even though we were both in the shower together."

Without Sam's consent, an image of Gray popped into her head. He was in *her* shower with hot water streaming down his sinewy body. Sam obviously had no idea what he looked like under his clothes, but thanks to her preferred reading genre, her imagination excelled when it came to picturing sexy naked men. Sam squirmed in her seat as an ache formed between her legs.

Nope. Unacceptable. She (somewhat reluctantly) shoved naked Gray out of her mind and returned to the issue at hand: "How is a shower dream with Gray not sexy?"

Lexi's eyes peeked out from between her fingers. "I was washing him… all of him… like I was his mother. And… we were singing a nursery rhyme together."

Sam cringed. Yup, that was without a doubt the unsexiest shower dream she'd ever heard. A much-needed bucket of ice water to her libido.

"I woke up in a cold sweat and couldn't look him in the eye for a month."

Sam eased Lexi's hands from her face. "Everyone has random naked dreams, Lex."

"They're supposed to be about showing up at school naked or about naked people you actually want to sleep with."

Sam nodded. "Usually." Lexi wasn't convinced. "I once had a dream where I had sex with a client. We weren't just naked; our parts were doing their thing. But not sexy because I was in no way attracted to him, and the whole time we were discussing his dog's gastrointestinal obstruction and how he'll need to check the dog's feces to verify that it passed."

Lexi took a sip of her coffee. "That's…"

"No, let's not discuss it anymore. I'll start remembering it all over again and I can't. Not this morning."

"Agreed. No more mention of sex dreams." Lexi's fingernails tapped against the table. "But I've started to wonder…," more tapping of the nails, "what if the dream meant something? Not that I wanted to do anything with Gray, but maybe something with someone else…"

She'd caught Sam mid-drink so she couldn't respond.

"Paul would have wanted me to find someone. To have kids," she managed as a tear trickled down her cheek, "just like he and I had wanted."

Sam handed her a napkin for the tear. She'd left Jeremy but she still couldn't imagine the pain she'd experience if he unexpectedly died, and she could never see or talk to him again.

"But I'm terrified to do it. Dating, kissing, loving another man… It will only put more distance between me and Paul, and I can't spare another inch." Lexi's single tear turned into a flood complete with hiccups that jerked her frail body. Even with the excess of doughnuts each week, Lexi was clearly missing meals here and there as she vacillated between being okay and hanging on by a thread.

Sam held her while she heaved gut-wrenching sobs and drenched her tank top with tears and snot.

Then it was over. She wiped away the last of her tears and dried her runny nose. "Sorry. Every now and then I try a bit too hard to keep it all together and then it's like a dam bursting and my emotions are everywhere."

"No, no apologizing."

"It's just... I'm lonely, Sam. I Googled 'Why am I so lonely?'"

"Oh, no. Bad idea."

"Right? Especially since it was four in the morning. But I ended up down this rabbit hole of online quizzes, Ted Talks, and Reddit forums, and it's not just losing Paul that's killing me." Her fingers were back to their tapping. "I'm touch starved. I'm single and working from home and basically a hermit. So I never touch anyone and that's an actual health issue—not having physical contact with other people."

"Aw, Lex," Sam said as she reached out to rub Lexi's arm.

She placed her hand on Sam's. "Thanks," she said with a lopsided smile. "But it goes beyond the friendly touches. I miss having a warm body next to mine in bed, holding hands, and someone rubbing my ankles and calves during a movie while my legs are in his lap."

"Yeah." Sam nodded as a lump formed in her throat. She refused to let the lump turn to tears though since she'd left Jeremy while Lexi had had zero say in Paul's departure. "I understand."

Lexi took a deep breath and moved the paper back in front of herself to add *Go out on a date* to the bottom of her list. She slid it over to Sam and asked, "What about you? Is it too soon?"

Sam shook her head no. An ankle rub during a movie sounded fabulous. She was lonely, too. She had been long before she and Jeremy split up. While she wasn't ready for anything serious or long-term, she wouldn't say no to a goodnight kiss or lay depending on the guy. They were already going to grief counseling and book club together; they might as well start dating together, too.

In all caps she added to the bottom of her own list, "HAVE EPIC SEX WITH EVERYONE." It wasn't true, but she loved seeing Lexi blush.

"Wow... everyone, huh?... that's... that's a lofty goal."

"I'm fucking with you, Lex,"

"Yeah, yeah, I know that." She let out a sigh of relief and checked her phone. "I need to get changed and log into work."

"Sounds good. I'm going to pick up our book club books, grab lunch at Dick Murphy's BBQ, then stop by the dog place to see if they have any openings. Wish me luck."

CHAPTER 4: GRAY

"Smitty," Gray called as he entered Bait Me, a local-owned convenience store on the north side of the lake known for their endless supply of bait and suspiciously cheap, yet delicious, foot-long hot dogs. Gray hadn't been in for either since his twenty-first birthday when he and Ronan engaged in a drunken hot dog eating contest that ended with them projectile vomiting in the bait case.

Unfortunately, his current visit was business, not pleasure. He'd received yet another complaint about Smitty, and he had a feeling the conversation wasn't going to be a good one.

"Hey, Gray." He never called him officer, and because Gray had known him long before he donned the badge, he didn't push it. Though to be fair, he didn't care regardless of whom he was talking to.

"Wanna hot dog?" Bert Smith asked, his tobacco-stained mustache pulled up into a curl. Well over a decade later and Smitty still offered him a dog every damn time he saw him, in or out of the store.

"Still not funny." Gray walked over to the counter, ready

to engage in the predictable and tired conversation he frequently had with Smitty. For the first few months Gray was on the force, these confrontational conversations about Smitty's antics around town had turned into shouting matches with Smitty all worked up and threatening to have Gray's badge, or at the very least, to stop paying taxes since that was paying Gray's salary.

But the more he got to know Smitty, the more he caught on to what a semi-predictable creature Smitty really was. He dressed for the day's mood: a comfortable flannel shirt or t-shirt with flannel print in the summer when he woke up feeling light as air, or a t-shirt with a kangaroo on the front for days when he wanted everyone to eat shit. It was almost imperceptible given how faded the shirt was, but coming out of the kangaroo's pouch was a hairy, grown man's hand with his middle finger sticking up. Disturbing on so many levels, but largely overlooked by the tourists who flowed in and out of the store without a second look at the people who served them throughout their vacation. Lucky for Gray, Smitty was decked out in his finest flannel shirt and appeared to be in good spirits.

"We had another call at the station," Gray said.

Smitty crossed his arms and stepped up on the stool he kept behind the counter. No one that worked there needed a stool at the counter. Smitty kept it there solely for this purpose. It was a quick and easy way to look down on whomever Smitty needed to look down on.

"I don't know what you're talking about. Did something happen?" Refusing to step down from his stool, he leaned forward and pretended to straighten the meat sticks and lighters on the counter. His thick fingers fumbling about and accomplishing nothing.

A few good inches shorter than Smitty on his stool, Gray leaned on the counter anyway as he leaned into his purpose for stopping by. "Another flat tire. This time at Mulligan's Grocery."

"Hardly seems worthy of a call to the police." Satisfied with whatever it was he thought he'd accomplished with the meat sticks, Smitty locked eyes on Gray. "But we sure are lucky to have you here, keeping us all safe with flat tires and cats in trees and such."

"They have you on tape, Smitty. Mulligan's security tapes have a clear visual of you letting the air out of a customer's tire in their parking lot"

"Don't see how that's possible since I wasn't there."

"I didn't tell you what day."

"I've never been there."

Tired of inhaling Smitty's signature scent of stale cigarettes, and tired of the games Smitty always played, Gray straightened his back and said, "I helped you carry your groceries to the car last week."

Smitty raised one hand to cup his chin and looked up to the ceiling as if he were replaying the events of last week to see if Gray or Mulligan's had made an appearance.

"I don't recall..." he said, letting it trail off as though the memory might come back to him at any minute and so he couldn't say with any certainty one way or the other.

"Smitty... they have you on camera letting the air out of the customer's tire."

Smitty's hand dropped, and he fiddled with the buttons on his flannel. "Sorry, Gray, but you've got the wrong guy." Relieved of its buttons, his flannel opened to reveal the angry, furry hand with a middle finger sticking up. Gray was flipped off for the second time that morning.

"This can't keep happening," he said with all the patience he had left. Life hadn't been kind to Smitty for the past few years, and Gray tried to keep that in mind each time he interacted with him.

At last, Smitty broke down. "It was *his* fault. Mulligan's stocks the dairy-free ice cream for me, and I had my hand on it first! He bought it, but it was meant for me."

Gray nodded his head, relieved that Smitty at least acknowledged he was a part of the incident. Occasionally, he'd denied it until the bitter end, usually with success since he wasn't the type to exact revenge on the spot. Rather, he'd let it sit for a night or two—sometimes even a few weeks. He was usually more careful about being caught on tape.

Gray inhaled deeply, buying them both a moment to calm down. "He bought an ice cream, so you let the air out of his tires?"

"He bought *my* ice cream. And just one tire. And you're making me sound petty. I have a routine, Gray. He ruined it."

It always came back to Smitty's routine and love of soap operas. As they spoke, there was a rerun of one on the tiny TV behind the counter. But as Gray knew from countless years of interacting with Smitty, the reruns were for during the day while he'd save current episodes to catch up on each night after work. The ice cream part of the routine Gray hadn't been privy to, but it didn't surprise him.

He softened his expression. "You can't keep doing this. There are crazy people out there. One day you're going to piss off the wrong one and they'll do much worse than taking your ice cream or calling me."

Smitty looked down at the counter as he buttoned his shirt back up and stepped down from his stool. "Won't happen again, Gray."

"Can't you just stock the ice cream here at Bait Me?"

"It's doesn't taste the same."

Gray nodded. It was no use trying to change Smitty's mind once he was set on something.

.   .   .

After spending the morning dealing with a serial package thief and then a disgruntled Smitty, Gray skipped his usual lunch in his cruiser at one of the scenic rest areas. Instead, he headed over to his favorite store: Paging All Bibliophiles.

An old firehouse renovated into a bookstore, the giant red-brick faced building was near the halfway point between the lake and downtown Oakland. The giant rolling doors that once let the fire trucks in and out of the building had been converted to large glass windows that allow plenty of natural light in. The tiny winding staircase was still in use, but the pole had to be decommissioned to keep liability costs down.

Marcy and Buck Diggins, co-founders and co-owners of Paging All Bibliophiles for the past thirty-two years, graciously allowed him to have his book club meetings at their store each month. On top of providing a roof over their heads, she set up a monthly book club display in one of her windows, along with information about upcoming meetings.

"Hey, Blue," Marcy called out when he entered the store and the bell chimed. She'd come up with the punny police officer moniker the first time he'd walked in wearing his uniform, and she refused to call him anything else since.

"Marcy, how's everything going?" And by everything, he meant business. It was his go-to question whenever he entered the store. He was genuinely concerned with their ability to keep the place going considering how book sales, and sales of everything, really, were moving away from brick-and-mortar stores to online platforms.

Lucky for them, ties in the Deep Creek community ran deeper than even the seemingly bottomless sections of the massive lake that made up the center of their town. "Shop local" wasn't a one-day-of-the-year motto for them.

She flip-flopped her hand to show sales were up and down, but then said, "We're doing okay. Same as always. I will say we've already sold eight copies of *What They Found Below*." Her dark red lips turned up a wide smile as she pointed behind him to the book club display table in front of the middle window.

"Eight? Sounds like we should have a pretty good turnout." He turned towards the display. "Did you draw this yourself? I didn't know you were an artist." She had a chalkboard display with a hand-drawn image of the author on one side and a quote from the book on the other side. He walked over and marveled at Marcy's work. If they ever went out of business, it wasn't for a lack of trying or talent.

"A little something I whipped up. Thought I'd try something new. You know that old saying about doing the same thing and expecting different results."

He could see the hidden concern in her eyes and hear it in her voice. "It's amazing, Marcy. I'll have to check it out from the street. I bet it brings in a few new customers."

She waved her hand in his direction. "Oh, stop. It's not that good."

She would never take the compliment, so he let it go and instead said, "You know, I really appreciate all you do for the club. And for me." He picked up a book and absentmindedly thumbed through the pages, taking in the sound of the pages fluttering and the smell of the fresh print.

"Aw, shucks, Blue. You know we love having you. You have March's book picked out?"

He put the book back on the display just as he'd found it. "*The Last Memory of Me*. It's Shelly Fulton's latest, and everyone's saying it's her best yet."

"Better than *That Was Before the Rain*? Impossible," she scoffed.

"Better. Wait till you read the blurb." He made his way back to the counter.

"You're basing this on biased PR from the publisher and a blurb?"

"Which *you* haven't even read yet, so how can you be so certain I'm wrong?"

"Doesn't matter," she said, shaking her head. "I know Fulton and I know I've read the best of what she has to offer."

"I see… So it's come to this…" Gray said as he stepped forward, so only the counter separated himself and Marcy. "Another friendly wager between friends."

She paused only a moment before extending her hand out to shake. "Poor naïve Blue. You're on."

"A lot of confidence for someone who's lost three bets in a row to me."

Marcy leaned in towards him, their hands still together but no longer shaking. "I've been playing you, sweetie." Her eyes narrowed as they shook. "And now you're right where I want you."

His eyes widened. "More than confident. Downright haughty, even. Care to up the stakes from our usual five bucks?" Gray had been waiting for another bet to present itself; had been dreaming of upping the stakes. "A week before the meeting we'll have the book clubbers vote on which Fulton book is best. Loser comes up with and supplies a fancy drink to accompany March's book."

As obvious as Blue's Clues sounded for a book club run by someone nick-named Blue that read nothing but murder mysteries, it had taken them months to come up with it. Doing the whole "fancy drink with a catchy name that perfectly matches the book they were reading" thing was appealing in concept alone. They both loved the idea of it but going through the mental work wasn't worth it. Most months, they offered a house red and house white wine with a store-bought platter of cheese and crackers to go with.

"Clearly, you're going to lose this one and I'm warning

you now, no mind erasers as the fancy punny drink to go with *The Last Memory of Me*. It's too on the nose for one— you're better than that—and everyone would get hammered for another."

Gray held his hands up. "I promise to never let a repeat of the infamous *Vodka Murders* book club meeting happen again."

"I'll hold you to that, Blue." A customer off to the side caught Marcy's attention. "I'll be right with you, hon," she called to the customer. "Anyway, I think you and I are squared up for the next meeting, but Buck has some questions for you in the back."

"Let me guess: A missing woman in her twenties last seen somewhere in the Midwest?"

Marcy cracked a smile at the slight jab to her true-crime-loving husband. "Tonya, twenty-two, missing since New Year's Eve, and last seen outside of Vegas."

"I was close." Out of habit, Gray tipped his head to Marcy and then meandered through the bookstore on his way back to see her husband, Buck. Marcy was the brains and brawn behind the operation, while Buck did more of the administrative tasks of inventory and bookkeeping. When he wasn't knee-deep in crunching numbers for the store, he liked to play detective with various true crime social media groups. That meant Gray was often his go-to resident expert whenever he had detective questions.

On his way back to Buck, Gray pulled his cookie-dough flavored protein bar lunch out of his pocket and ate as he took his time perusing his favorite sections of the store: true crime, biographies, and contemporary fiction.

He was thoroughly engrossed with the blurb of a novel about the Villisca, Iowa, axe murders of 1912, when he heard Sam's now-familiar voice coming from the front of the store. How was it even possible that he was running into her for the second time that day when it was barely noon?

He was tallish at six foot four. The bookshelves in the center of the store came up to his chin, and the tops were lined with book displays, obscuring Sam's view of him. Hidden or not, he found himself walking to the end of the aisle to make sure he was out of sight while remaining within earshot of her.

"And what about this one?" a woman asked.

"If you hated *Chasing Miles McCovey*," Sam told the customer, "I don't think you'd like that one either. Similar writing style and somewhat similar plot now that I think of it."

The woman sighed. "No, I didn't like the McCovey story at all."

"Here, take a look at this one."

Gray poked his head around the shelf a smidge further for a glimpse of the front of the store to confirm what he thought was happening. Sure enough, there was Sam Thornton or Smith or whatever the hell she went by in all her annoying glory, offering recommendations to what he could only assume was a stranger based on the body language and conversation between the two.

The woman read the blurb and then shook her head and handed it back to Sam. "I don't think so."

Gray smirked as he watched Sam pretend she was some sort of book whisperer, handing out advice to random customers. There was something immensely satisfying about watching her fail at it.

"Looking for something a little spicier?" Sam asked.

The woman leaned in and said something Gray couldn't make out.

Sam handed the book back to the woman. This time she'd opened it to a specific page. It was quiet again as she read the section Sam had pointed to. Then the woman looked up at Marcy and said, "I'll take this one and everything else you have by this author."

"I thought you'd like that one," Sam said, not bothering to hide the victory in her voice.

Marcy rang up ten books for the customer and Sam gave her a business card in case she ever wanted future recommendations. Gray closed his eyes and shook his head. Had that really just happened? Sam sold ten books to some random customer *and* whipped out a business card? What kind of egomaniac had business cards for recommending books?

After the customer left, Sam and Marcy chatted at the front of the store, but their voices were lower, and Gray could only make out a few words here and there. He couldn't follow any of the conversation. He leaned against the bookshelf, thoroughly annoyed at Sam for interrupting and essentially ruining his time at Paging All Bibliophiles.

"Blue? You around?" he heard Marcy call out in his general direction.

He had no intention of speaking with Sam. He stayed put where he was and tried to convince himself that hiding from his problems didn't make him any less of a man.

"Guess not," Marcy said, her voice remaining loud enough for him to hear. "He and I were just talking about *The Last Memory of Me*; I bet he'd love to hear your take on it."

Gray rolled his eyes and slipped into the back to see Buck. Sam had already won over Lexi and there she was intruding on his favorite store in town, too. His haven.

By the time he re-emerged from the back, she was gone, and he once again had the store to himself. He paid for his copy of the book club pick, as well as a few others he'd found. At the register, he noticed a small stack of her business cards sitting on the counter.

It was white with dark-pink flowery trim around the border. Her name was nowhere to be found on the card, but her blog name was written in bold at the top and there was a QR code he was certain would lead to her book reviews.

"I tell you what. That woman is something," Marcy said, seeing his eyes trained on the business card. "See the name, Cat the Great? As in the Russian Empress, Catherine the Great? Very clever."

Gray gave a noncommittal nod, as if he could give or take whatever information Marcy was throwing his way.

"Catherine was known for her... Well, at the time it was considered promiscuous behavior. Fitting name for a blog about racy romance novels."

Marcy handed him his books and his credit card; she was waiting for some sort of response from him. "Very clever," he offered. Sam wasn't there to hear it, but he could tell that somehow, she felt it in the depths of her soul that Gray had said something nice about her. He pulled out a piece of gum to eliminate the sudden foul taste in his mouth.

"I knew you of all people would appreciate that."

He gave her a quizzical look, wondering what it was about him that made her think he wanted to read smutty romance books.

"A fellow bibliophile," she said. "She had some great insight into *The Last Memory of Me*."

Gray couldn't wrap his head around Sam. There was the woman listening to Alexa narrate poorly written erotica on her phone, and there was the woman appreciating and catching all the subtle nuances and brilliance of an author like Shelly Fulton. It didn't seem possible the two women could actually be one and the same.

With all the sincerity he could muster, he said, "Really? It's a shame I missed her."

"She might still be here if you have a minute." Marcy's

eyes were shining with excitement. Before Gray could protest, she was calling out to the front corner of the store. "Sam, you still here? Come meet Blue!" To Gray she said, "I wanted to introduce you earlier, but you were back with Buck and then I just plain forgot when we got to talking about getting her a display in the front window."

A display table in the front window? The woman had been in town less than twenty-four hours. How did she have a personalized display at Paging All Bibliophiles? It had taken him years to get his own book club display.

Gray slowly turned around, reminding himself to play nice in Marcy's presence. First Lexi, now Marcy. It was as if Sam had some supernatural ability to hone in on every person and place Gray treasured, and slowly take it over as her own, nudging him to the side in the process.

When he finally turned and Sam realized Blue was actually Gray, he noticed a stutter in her step before she recovered.

"You stalking me, *Gray*?" she asked with a cocky smile.

"Not possible considering I got here before you and generally dislike everything about you."

Oblivious to their words and the negative energy surging between them, Marcy lit up. "You two know each other? Well, actually, that doesn't surprise me given how alike you two are."

As if Marcy had slapped them in the face, they both turned and gave her a look.

"*Him*?" Sam said at the same time he said, "I don't know about that."

That was proof enough of how different they were. Sam's first reaction to the comparison was blatant surprise and disgust. Incredibly rude, though not out of character for her. Someone needed to call her out, and Gray was just the man for the job.

"Tell me, Marcy, can you look up a book for me to see if you have it?" He shot a smug look at Sam.

Marcy furrowed her brow at the confusing turn of the conversation. "Yeah, sure. I can look something up for you."

"It's a romance novel. *She Had All the Kings' Men* by B.J. Queene. Spelled with an 'e' at the end of Queene."

"The author's name is B.J. Queene?" Marcy asked as her fingers flew over the keys. "I see... Is this book for you, Blue?"

Sam narrowed her eyes at him.

"For Sam, actually. She was listening to the audiobook yesterday. I bet she'd love to have a hard copy if you have any in stock."

"I don't know we could keep anything like this on the shelf. Mitsy and the others would have my doors shuttered up faster than a cat lapping chain lightning."

Sam stepped forward. "Gray's mistaken. I was listening to my phone's text to speech feature to quickly get through a novel I needed to review for my blog. It was not a good book, and I do not want a copy."

"You looked hot and bothered by the book to me. Speeding and wearing nothing but a tank and shorts in the middle of January."

Marcy finally caught up to the hatred that permeated the air. "Coming, Buck!" she called towards the back, fooling no one. "I'll just let you two chat a bit while I help Buck with some accounting issues." She shot Gray a look, warning him to be nice to her new friend, then she turned and left them at the counter.

"I have a busted heater, and it really was only for a review they contracted me to give," she hissed at him.

"Sure, okay."

Sam rolled her eyes as if to say he was hopeless, then she

glanced down at his hand. "Are you married with seven children?" she asked.

"No…" He let the word hang, unable to think of what else to say to such a question that was apropos of nothing at all.

His response irritated Sam. As if his single, childless status somehow offended her. "Lexi," she said with a sigh. Then she turned and walked back to her display table.

That was his cue to leave. He'd parked in the lot behind the store and had two options to get to his car: turn right to pass the displays or turn left to round the corner without traveling across the front of the store.

His curiosity was stronger than his feelings of annoyance, and so he turned right to catch a glimpse of Sam's in-progress display. The cover images were tamer than what he'd seen on Lexi's coffee table and certainly much tamer than B.J. Queene's book, but it was still clearly romance. Then his eyes caught the chalkboard display on the table: *Personalized Romance Book Recommendations Every Tuesday at 6 pm.*

His jaw dropped for a split second before he realized Sam had caught him gawking. She looked thoroughly amused by his reaction. Gray clamped his mouth shut and got back to work.

That night at his apartment, he found Ronan abandoned him yet again to crash at Mel's place. At least he still had Daisy to keep him company. The small, brown, cuddly-sweet mutt often hung out with him on the couch, her head resting on Gray's leg so he could scratch behind her ears as he read a book, or they both watched TV.

He took a sip of wine, then set the glass on the coffee table and cracked open *The Last Memory of Me,* ready with his notebook and pen at his side for potential discussion questions and notable scenes. But his head wouldn't allow him to get into it. Every few paragraphs or so he would think about Sam: Did she, too, think the opening paragraphs were cliché and too similar to Fulton's previous novel? Had she assured Marcy she would win their bet?

He tossed the book onto the coffee table and pulled out his phone.

"Wanna see what all the fuss is about, Dee?" As if he was only Googling *Cat the Great Reads Smut* to ease Daisy's curiosity and not his own.

He clicked on the link—which, impressively, he found on the first page of the results—and his screen lit up with the image of a man's naked torso holding the same book Sam had been clutching that morning. He wondered if the man in the picture was her ex-husband or current boyfriend, and why the thought of her having a boyfriend who looked like a male model bothered him.

But the craziest part of it all happened when he scrolled through her site and read a few of her reviews. Even though he'd never read any of the books, he found the reviews to be witty and well-written. He momentarily forgot how awful she was as he chuckled at some of her commentaries and bought a book she'd rated as one of her top ten reads. He bought it as an ebook, of course.

Just twenty-four hours after meeting Samantha, he'd turned into someone who secretly read smut on their phone. What was she doing to him?

CHAPTER 5: SAM

Two weeks into her life at Deep Creek Lake, Sam had mostly settled into her new routine. Unfortunately, that routine included her waking up each morning on the couch with a sore back. Before the move, she had given Lexi almost a month's notice that she was coming. In that time, Lexi being Lexi, she'd splurged and upgraded the garage loft's queen bed to a king, installed two large bookcases, and put down new area rugs.

A sweet gesture, to be sure, but one that also caused a bit of an issue when it came time to crash at the end of the day. Right after her split with Jeremy, her friend Jackie had come to the rescue offering her room and board in Milton, but Sam always ended up sleeping on her couch. It was comforting, and temporary, and tiny. The massive king Lexi got her, with its endless cold sheets and extra-long pillows, would swallow her whole. Would smother her with constant reminders that it was frigid and roomy because it held only her.

But even her back problems from her couch-sleeping habit couldn't diminish her good mood. For one thing, the pain was quickly forgotten once she stretched out her neck and back in the morning. For another, she'd just completed her first week of work at Bark Sniff Wag and she was thoroughly in love with the company, her coworkers, the dogs, everything. It was quite possibly her dream job if she allowed herself to jump to quick and outlandish conclusions, which she absolutely did on the regular.

That evening she pulled into their driveway after work sporting her favorite jeans—the ones that hugged her ass just right and didn't give her muffin tops—and her work polo a little before six. She had thirty minutes to get changed before the card game. Lexi was hosting a night of poker for a family friend whose power went out that morning and had yet to be restored.

With the heat cranking and her window down so she didn't turn into a sweaty mess, she remained in her car to finish rocking out to "High Hopes" by Panic! At the Disco. Life was good. She could feel it in her bones that she was going to meet some hot guy at poker. Preferably one with a bunch of tats and a motorcycle. Suddenly single, Sam had a long list of things she found attractive in men, and she wanted to hit every single one of them. Not all in one night, of course. She'd need to ease into it despite what she'd written on her list of goals with Lexi.

Tap, tap, tap.

Sam let out a few expletives and would have jumped a mile high had her seat belt not kept her firmly in place. What's the only thing that could ruin her otherwise fabulous mood? Officer Hoffman at her car door, yet again. This time tapping on the back window since her front window was down.

She gave him the stink eye, rolled up her window, and

killed the engine. Panic at the Disco! was tragically cut off before the song was finished. Gone too soon.

Once she stepped out of the car, she cut straight to the point. "What do you want, Gray?"

He wasn't in his uniform this time. No hat, either. If only he didn't speak or do anything, she'd be drooling all over him. Man-in-uniform was definitely on her list of guys to do.

"There's that winning personality. Just wanted to let you know your back tire looks flat."

"Looks flat" was a gross understatement. She couldn't believe she'd even made it home. The thumping of rubber on the pavement must have sounded awful as she'd driven on it. But with the music, heaters, and engine drowning everything else out, she hadn't heard a thing.

"Yeah, I know," she said, using the same tone she'd have used if he'd told her the sky was blue.

"Have you been to Bait Me yet? Or seen Smitty around? About yay high, salt and pepper full beard?" He moved his hands about, showing how tall and how bushy of a full beard he was referring to. "Wears flannel or a kangaroo t-shirt? Sometimes both?"

She eased her head back slightly, wondering where the hell Gray was going with his line of questioning.

"No?" he pushed.

"No," she said as she continued to size him up like a feral animal she needed to evade. "Smitty a friend of yours? A fellow stalker?"

"Funny." His brows furrowed, and he looked over her shoulder in the direction of the garage. "Did you salt your steps? Did you even clear them?"

She stepped to the side to intercept him before he could make his way over there. "What are you doing here, Gray?" When he didn't stop walking, she put her hand up to physically stop him. Her palm hit the hard wall of his chest and their faces were inches apart.

Finally pulling his eyes away from the steps, Gray looked down at her and backed up just enough so that her hand fell back to her side. "The poker game. I'm early to help set it up." His eyes went back behind her. "You guys need to be salting your driveway and—"

"Nope, no, no." Sam shook her head and turned to walk up to her apartment. How was it even possible for one person to be such a wet blanket? Gone were her daydreams of some tattooed stranger giving her multiple orgasms after she'd robbed him blind during poker. Instead, her only visions of the future included Gray with his no-nonsense attitude and overabundance of caution at every turn. Would he even allow them to play poker without an official gambling license? Or perhaps they would play for M & M's or some other nonsense.

Annoyed, she turned back to give him one last piece of her mind. The only word to come out of her mouth though, was "Shit!" as she felt searing pain shoot through her knee when it slammed onto the icy, unforgiving driveway beneath her.

Before she got her bearings or even realized what had happened, Gray was crouching down beside her. One hand reached for her arm while the other went to her leg just above her busted knee. He grimaced and asked, "Are you okay? That looked bad."

Behind him, Lexi emerged from the house and rushed over. "Did you fall on the ice? I'm so sorry. I rushed through salting this morning to get a head start on work. I wanted to finish early."

Sam bit her lower lip, trying to take in and overcome the fiery pain coming from her left knee. "I'm fine," she practically grunted at them. "Just hit my knee."

Lexi looked down at her knee, then turned her head to the side and dry heaved. "Oh, that's gross."

"What?!" Sam's eyes widened as she took in the panicked expression on Lexi's face and her state of near vomiting after she'd glanced at her injuries. "What's gross?"

Gray cupped Sam's chin and commanded her attention. His dark brown eyes bore into hers. "Sam, you're going to be okay." It was the first time he'd spoken to her using a voice that wasn't brusk or demanding. It was confident and yet empathetic.

"Is she?" Lexi called from behind him. She wouldn't even look at them. She had her eyes scrunched closed and had her head turned towards the street.

Gray turned Sam's gaze back to him and ignored Lexi. His voice remained calm. "You've dislocated your knee cap. Happens all the time. It's an easy fix, and you're gonna be just fine."

Sam slowly nodded. This was not the same Gray she'd spoken to before. This one was pleasant and soothing. Worthy of her trust.

"I have a thing with joints." Again, she bit her lip at the physical pain of the wound and the emotional pain of sharing something personal, especially since she was in a vulnerable position and sharing it with him, of all people. "It's my biggest fear, jacking one up." She trembled as she said it, and she couldn't bring herself to look down at her knee.

"It's jacked up, Sam," Lexi blurted out.

"Lex, you are the least helpful person ever right now," she called over Gray's shoulder.

"Oh, god. You're right. Sorry… You're doing great. Gonna be just fine."

Sam caught Gray trying to stifle a laugh. Any other day it would have enraged her. Maybe it was his warm, comforting hand cradling her face that caused her to find his chuckle endearing and cute. But it was impossible to say for sure with the abject pain rushing through her leg.

"What do I do now?" In a bizarre turn of events, she put herself completely in his control.

"We need to elevate and ice your knee. Let's get you into the house." He hooked one of his arms around her back to help her up when Lexi chimed in yet again.

"What about her kneecap? Aren't you going to pop it back in first?"

"You can see it? Is my bone sticking out?" Sam's eyes widened in complete terror, and she fixed them up towards the sky. Her head tilted way back lest she see even a fraction of what was making Lexi freak out.

His voice grounded her once again. "Trust me, Sam. Okay? Can you trust me?"

With her head permanently pointed as far away from her knee as possible, she couldn't see his face when he'd said it. But based on his words and the soothing tone of his voice—not to mention her compromising position where she was incapacitated on the slick driveway—she found herself nodding that she did indeed trust him.

"Good. We stand on three. One... Two... Three." Without even a grunt or any sign of straining, she was effortlessly in his arms: one under her legs and the other behind her upper back. The position had her knee front and center in her field of vision. There was a bulge under her jeans, like a golf ball was lodged a few inches to the side of where her knee should have been. Before the sight could thoroughly freak her out, she felt and watched it slide back into place as he repositioned his arms a bit and jostled her legs.

Sam and Lexi simultaneously dry heaved. Sam had been a vet for the past ten years and she still never got over how the blood and gore of it all made her queasy. Especially when it was happening to her own body.

"I figured it would pop back once I moved you a bit. Do you feel any better? You still look a little pale." His eyes were studying her face, and she did the same in return. Though in fairness, he was assessing her health while she was not. There were a few crinkles in the corners of his eyes, and she guessed he was somewhere in his mid-thirties. Just a little older than she was. There was a scar on his right cheek. It was the size of a quarter and looked like a half circle. She almost reached up and traced it with her finger. Then his eyes shifted, as if he realized she was scrutinizing him as well.

The pain in her leg immediately subsided to a dull ache, but mentally she was still in a bad place with the image of her knee cap off to the side permanently branded onto her brain, along with her new, conflicting thoughts about Gray.

"I'm fine. I'm okay." She suddenly had the urge to be out of his hands and anywhere except in his presence. She didn't like the way her fingers wanted to rake through his hair, and she didn't like the way his eyes glanced down at her mouth.

"Good. Let's get you inside." Gray turned to Lexi's house and walked with Sam still in his arms.

"No, I need to get to my room. Above the garage." She was still wearing her work polo, and her hair was in a ponytail. It had been a while since she'd actively tried to garner the attention of the opposite sex, but she was sure her current look would not cut it.

He didn't even slow his pace, much less stop walking. All warm and fuzzy thoughts about Gray fell away as Sam saw the controlling, thinks-he-knows-best version of him reappear.

"You fell before you even made it to the steps. There's no way you're getting up there before—"

"It's not up to you, Gray." She impressed even herself with her commanding voice, given that it was coupled with her inability to do much of anything beyond allowing herself to be carried by him.

"You can't walk; I'd say it is up to me."

"Like hell it is." Using the only weapon she had, she pinched his neck. Not her best moment, but she didn't do vulnerable and trapped well. Feeling both at the same time, along with the pain in her knee, had caused her lash out.

"Argh fuuuuu…" He winced as she twisted the sensitive skin between her fingers. He jerked his head away, but it was pointless since she was in his arms and within striking distance regardless of how far he strained in the opposite direction.

The assault must have been the last straw. He carried her into the living room and unceremoniously dropped her onto the couch.

"Ouch."

"You're welcome." He kneeled and began untying the laces on her sneakers. "I need to take a closer look at your knee. I'll turn around while Lexi helps you out of your jeans."

"I'm *not* taking my pants off for you." She jerked her good leg out of his reach before he could get the second shoe off.

Gray exhaled in exasperation, put his hands up in surrender, and stood. "Then you should see a doctor. It could be more serious than just popping it back into place."

No way was she going to spend her Friday night at an ER and miss out on a potential rebound. "I'll take my chances," she said through gritted teeth. She knew he'd be a killjoy that night. She just hadn't realized it would happen before the game even started.

"Fine. Good luck with that." Like a flip of the switch, his nasty attitude was gone when he turned to Lexi. "Are you okay getting started on setting up without me?"

Lexi was a civilian stuck in the middle of a minefield. She'd watched it all play out and wasn't sure what wrong

CHAPTER 12: GRAY

Gray always arrived thirty minutes early on book club days. It took only ten to fifteen minutes to set out wine, the store-bought cheese and crackers platter, and cups, plates, and napkins. The extra time was spent settling his nerves and doing a cold run-through of everything he wanted to discuss.

He'd originally thought book clubs were relaxed events that often ran themselves to a degree. After all, plenty of people read and casually discussed books. Most were well versed in the task: discussing books casually with friends over dinner or while on a drive. His book clubs were a whole different beast. Perfect strangers (at least for the first meeting before everyone got to know each other better) were all coming together with insights and inspirations from what felt like entirely different books once they put their own takes on them.

His first meeting had five people in attendance, and they'd read a book about the hunt for a hit-and-run drunk driver who'd killed three people. One member had offered to bring the drinks, to which Gray was much obliged. Not only was it nice to have someone else taking on part of the event, but he'd also wanted everyone to feel like it was their book club, too. Another member, supposedly an up-and-coming social media influencer, asked to take pictures throughout for their social media pages. Not seeing any reason to deny the request, Gray allowed it.

Looking back, he realized his many mistakes. He should have clarified what drinks the person was bringing, and he should have put out some limits on the online photos.

The drink for the night was called Road Rage, and it had a hefty dose of vodka in it. The other members found the name to be insensitive. They'd had connections to drunk driving themselves and didn't find anything humorous or cute about sipping Road Rage drinks while discussing road rage and booze-fueled fatalities.

The twenty-something wanna-be social media influencer went from holding up the meeting for impromptu selfies to taking pictures of book club members arguing and posting about how horrible the meeting was. She proudly Tweeted about it in real time.

Afterwards, he and Marcy sipped Road Rages as they dissected everything that went wrong with the meeting. At the time, Marcy said she could only afford to give Gray one more chance to get the book club thing right before he had to find a new business or location to host. Fair enough. The social media influencer started a whirlwind of shit for Paging All Bibliophiles. They literally could not afford to have the bad press that came with irate, online book clubbers.

Going forward, Gray carefully selected the books before-hand to make sure they had the least amount of triggering content possible. He provided everything: drinks, food (gluten and nut-free), and discussion questions. He opened it up to other commentary as well, but he always had safe content to redirect with in case shit got ugly.

word or move could set off the next argument between them. "Um, yeah. I have everything we need for the night. I'll start setting up now."

"Great. Thank you. I'll go out and see what I can do about the ice so no one else falls." Gray turned back to Sam. His tone was still pleasant when he said, "I'll take care of the steps; you can go up to your room when I'm finished." Without waiting to hear her reply, he left.

Going upstairs before he gave her the green light to do so wasn't up for debate. And as much as it pained her, Sam had to agree with him. The drop to the couch had irritated her knee; she couldn't imagine trying to walk upstairs or how much it would hurt if she fell on it again.

Lexi set Sam up with some pain relievers, an ice pack, and an old knee brace she still had from her days as a cheerleader. Then Sam watched helplessly from the couch as Lexi set everything up.

"Lex… Is Gray is the family friend who lost power today?"

She didn't look up as she added the last ingredients to the buffalo chicken dip and popped it into the oven. "He's like family to me…"

"And he's Blue, too. From Blue's Clues book club?"

Sam knew Lexi hadn't meant any harm from the white lies. It wasn't her fault Sam and Gray didn't get along, and it shouldn't be her problem either. That wasn't fair to Lexi.

She looked up at Sam and said in a low voice, "Oh… I was going to tell you about that… At some point."

"Does he even have one kid?"

She busied herself with the dip. "No. I have no idea where the seven kids idea came from. I'm really sorry. I panicked. I thought you wouldn't want to go with me if you knew it was Gray's book club."

Sam couldn't handle the look of guilt and shame on her

face. "It's fine, Lex. Really. But there will be other guys here, right? Hot, single guys with tattoos and motorcycles?"

That got a smile from her. "That's oddly specific."

"Fair enough. At this point, I'd settle for anyone with a penis. Anyone besides Gray."

"Eww. Too broad. Get some standards, Sam. Gross."

She chuckled. "You know what I mean. I want to flirt tonight with single guys. That's all."

"Me, too. That's why I jumped at the chance to host. You and I are the only women that I know of. Ronan's engaged, and I'm not sure about Leo and Jon."

"Leo and Jon sound hot."

"Maybe," Lexi said. "I haven't met them yet."

"Can I borrow one of your tops and some makeup?"

"Aiming to get a goodnight lay after poker?"

Sam winced as she eased herself up off the couch and hobbled over to Lexi so they could make their way to her room. "Probably not with the bum knee. I don't even think I can get my pants off without shedding a few tears from the pain. But I wouldn't mind getting a bit of action above the belt."

As far as she could tell, it was safe to assume Gray would be his usual anal self about getting the driveway and steps cleared, meaning she had about twenty minutes before he'd be back in. She wanted to be changed and fixed up before then. And for some reason, she didn't want Gray to see her unable to do it on her own, or to come back in before she was anything less than one hundred percent ready.

CHAPTER 6: GRAY

The driveway wasn't that bad. As someone who'd experienced Deep Creek's mountainous winters before, Lexi did a decent job clearing out the snow and laying down salt so it didn't freeze into a deadly sheet of ice.

Sam, however, had done nothing to treat her steps the night before or that morning. He silently cursed her as he broke up the ice with a shovel and then spread out the salt he'd found in the garage. It was a wonder she'd made it down the steps earlier that day.

Satisfied no one would break their neck on their way into either residence, he put the tools back and went inside to help Lexi set up before the guys arrived. And even though Sam was a pill, he'd check on her as well to make sure it wasn't anything more serious than a dislocated kneecap.

Earlier that day, he'd casually mentioned to Lexi his power went out, and he'd need to cancel his poker night at the last minute. At the time, her quick text back that she'd love to host if she could join had surprised him. He thought they'd lucked out since Lexi's house was ideal for entertaining: a large circular table (perfect for poker), a massive bay window overlooking the lake, a wood-burning fireplace in the living room, and cathedral ceilings. Some houses made him feel claustrophobic, but he never felt that at Lexi's place.

Her less than altruistic intentions became clear when he entered the house and found Sam with fresh make-up, her hair down, and a shirt more suitable for a club than a poker game. Her red tank top dipped down low in the front to accentuate one of the nicest sets of tits he'd seen in a while. He looked back at Lexi and noticed she'd changed outfits as well. They'd turned his poker game into a blind date.

"Driveway's cleared."

"Thanks, Gray. Sorry you had to trouble yourself with it. We'll do a better job next time."

"No problem, Lexi. Happy to help." He turned to Sam and kept his eyes carefully trained on hers so they wouldn't wander to her cleavage. "You should be able to make it up to your room now if you want me to help you get up there."

"So sweet of you, Gray. But I'm good. Thanks."

Her bright red shoes caught his attention, and he didn't bother trying to hide his look of disdain. "You should elevate your knee, and you shouldn't be in heels."

Sam got up off the couch and shuffled over to the kitchen to get a drink. He could see her gritted teeth through her smile as she cracked open a beer and leaned against the island to help take some of the weight off her bum knee.

"I'm fine."

"Did Lexi give you anything for the pain? It's not safe to mix pain relievers with alcohol."

"Nope," Sam said, her eyes throwing daggers at Lexi as a warning not to contradict her.

Gray wasn't sure who Sam thought she was hurting by ignoring his advice. What did he care if her leg took twice as long to heal and caused her insurmountable pain? He smiled thinking about how much he could torment her throughout the night pushing the new button he'd found.

His smile faded a few hands into the game. There was no time to come up with ways to torture Sam when he was getting his ass handed to him in poker. They all were. Based on the stacks of chips in front of the women, it was clear they'd all underestimated Sam and Lexi. Or maybe not. It was hard to say given the erratic hands they were playing with sheer luck as their only discernible strategy. The only other possibility was that they were impeccable poker sharks and worthy of a trip up to Atlantic City, or at the very least, a higher stakes game than their quarter chips.

"What happened to your leg, Sam?" Jon asked as he shuffled the cards. According to Gray's baby sister, Bea, Jon was a cross between Mathew McConaughey and Keanu Reeves, but with the body of a marine and the charisma and charm of Tom Holland. Whatever the fuck that meant.

"Dislocated knee cap. It's fine."

Funny, it didn't seem fine when she was freaking out in his arms an hour earlier.

"Ouch," Jon sympathized. Sam threw out her ante, and the table followed suit. Jon dealt the cards. "Have you seen a doctor yet? I'm an EMT; I can take a look if you'd like."

Sam's interest was obviously piqued. She sat up straighter and leaned in toward him. "It just happened tonight. I may go see one tomorrow."

"I offered to look at it and I offered to take her to the doctor," Gray interjected, unable to let it remain unsaid that he'd already tended to her.

Sensing the tension between Gray and Sam, and looking to cash in on it, Jon teased, "Good call, Sam. I wouldn't let him near me, either."

Gray looked at his cards: a four of hearts and a seven of hearts. The flop was a six of hearts, an ace of diamonds, and a three of diamonds. Feeling cocky about his three hearts and potential flush—along with the fact that the flop was probably shitty for everyone else—he decided to call Jon out on his bullshit.

"Really? Because I clearly remember sewing up your back last summer after the infamous throwdown between you and Ronan."

"There was a fight?" Lexi asked, looking slightly uncomfortable at the idea of grown men attacking one another.

"Like a fistfight?" Sam asked. She, on the other hand, seemed even more intrigued by Jon at the mention of a brawl.

"An epic battle, really," Ronan said, his interest in his cards waning by the second. "Tell them all about it, Gray. I never get tired of hearing about the time I kicked Jon's ass."

Jon rolled his eyes which Gray took as encouragement to continue. The guys were there when it happened, so he directed his story mostly at Lexi with a few cursory glances at Sam.

"We had a guy's weekend out in the woods for a bit of drinking and other manly activities." Ronan grunted his appreciation at the manly-men comment. Predictably, Sam rolled her eyes impressively high and took a long swig of her beer. She was almost too easy to annoy.

"Trying to lighten our load of what we had to carry back, we all drank too much. And these two," he said as he pointed to Jon and Ronan, "got into a debate about something… D'you even remember what you were fighting about?"

Ronan shook his head, his brown hair swishing back and forth across his forehead before he combed it back with his fingers for the hundredth time.

"Not a clue," Jon said, his eyes set on Sam.

"Nothing important, I'm sure. But at the moment it was, and we were drunk, so they settled it with a wrestling match."

"No, not we. I wasn't there for this part," Leo said, his dirty blonde hair hanging over his forehead. He stroked his neatly trimmed beard while his green eyes remained focused on hers.

Lexi beamed at her knight in shining armor, impressed that Leo wasn't present for the caveman-like solution to their disagreement. "Where were you?"

The game continued as they threw down their discards, and Jon dealt out the new cards.

"I was in my tent. I called it an early night," he said to Lexi. She almost swooned in her seat, likely thinking he was a perfect gentleman and above their primitive antics.

Not liking the vibes between them, Gray donned his big-brother hat to set the record straight. "He met someone on the trails earlier. What was her name? Amber Lynn, Ray Lynn? Something like that. Right, Leo?" He could see Leo's jaw clench at the cock block. "His early night was spent entertaining her in the tent he'd relocated out of earshot of us." That did it. Lexi turned back towards the table and to her cards.

She and Sam had no poker face whatsoever, but it didn't matter since they had such little understanding and skill. What they thought were good hands mostly weren't, and vice versa. Lexi sulking at her cards while Sam looked elated meant practically nothing. It could have been disappointment at Leo's past indiscretion, or Lexi could be looking at a royal flush and pouting because she didn't have any pairs.

Leo mouthed "What the fuck" to him. He'd been asking about Lexi for months and Gray knew he'd be looking for an in during the game. He also knew it wouldn't be a good match—at least not on her end. Leo didn't date, and the last thing Lexi needed was someone who was going to disappear on her. She craved stability and long-term commitment. Leo was allergic to both.

"Anyway," Gray said, bringing the conversation back to the night of the infamous fisticuffs. "These two threw down for the wrestling match, but as soon as Jon hit the ground, he landed on the jagged end of a broken stick and almost impaled himself."

Jon nodded. "But I didn't."

"No, you're lucky it only split your skin open half a foot."

Even though no one at the table requested to see his scar, Jon jumped at the opportunity to strip off his shirt and show off his ripped chest, abs, and back.

"I would have stitched it up myself if I could have reached it."

"Jesus, Jon," Leo said. "We're not playing strip poker. Put your shirt on and show the turn."

Sam leaned in for a closer look at the scar, so he remained shirtless and turned to give her a better view.

Leo repeated his request with more bite to it in hopes of compliance. "Jon. Shirt. Turn."

He flipped the card first, a five of hearts, so everyone could get to their bets while he took his time getting his shirt back on and covering up his well-maintained physique. It wasn't a secret Jon went to the gym twice as much as any of the other guys there. How could it be when he was always finding a reason to take off his clothes or mention his workout routine?

The table chatted about bets while Jon and Sam shared a quiet conversation to Gray's right.

"But seriously, I can take a look at your knee if you'd like."

Out of the corner of his eye, he saw Sam's cheeks redden, and he wanted to vomit. Was she really falling for all of it? Even though Leo had been the one in the story with a woman in his tent, it was usually Jon who was the most active one in the group. With his perfectly toned body, gelled hair, and boyish charms—his words, not Gray's—the women found him irresistible. Present company included it seemed. And Jon was often indiscriminate about who he took to bed. If they had a pulse, they met his standards.

Gray was pulled into a debate about bets between Lexi and Ronan, so he missed the next part of their conversation. But when he turned back to them, he found Sam's injured leg across Jon's lap while his free hand rested on her ankle. His thumb grazed over her skin as if they were lovers and not strangers.

"Everyone still in?" Jon asked when his attention turned back to the game.

A murmur of confirmation went around the table as they impatiently waited for the river—the last card of the hand. It would come close to making or breaking some of them. Himself included. The odds of the card being a three or eight of hearts were slim, but for whatever reason, he was feeling lucky.

"Ready for the river?" He paused mid-flip to taunt Leo. "This might be your last hand if you don't win this one."

"Turn the card, asshole," Leo said. Of the three of them he was the actual poker player. The one who would watch the World Series of Poker, and the one who desperately trying to arrange a trip out to Vegas. His pissy attitude came from his dwindling chip pile and Lexi's rejection.

"Two of diamonds," Ronan said. "What shit community cards. Alright, let's see what everyone has."

Jon and Ronan both had a pair of aces and Lexi had a pair of queens, while Leo smoked them all with three sixes. With a flourish, Sam presented her king and queen of diamonds.

"Royal flush, bitches!" she said as she reached out for the relatively large pot given their crappy hands, but Sam had kept upping her bets, and they'd refused to back down, so sure she was holding nothing of value.

"Actually, that's not how that works..." Gray said, unable to resist hinting at their first conversation about the physically impossible orgy she was listening to when they met. He touched her wrist before she could slide the pot into her own pile of haphazardly stacked chips, forever mixing the wins that weren't hers with the sizable winnings she'd already accrued from nothing more than dumb luck.

"Why not? It's all the same suit and all in a row."

Jon winced. "Sorry, love. Flushes can't cross the ace."

"Sorry, love," Gray mocked as he released her wrist.

"Pot's mine, bitches!" Leo said as he gathered his winnings. "And what a fine pot it is. Thanks for that, Sam."

Just before midnight, they finally called it for the night. The guys were off their game, and it didn't look like they'd ever have a definitive winner as long as Sam and Lexi were playing. They cashed out all the chips and helped to clean up before getting their coats and heading out the door.

"Mel just got back to the apartment. Says the power's back on." Ronan looked up from his phone to Gray. "Want a ride home?"

Gray hadn't meant to drink at all that night, but something about Sam's leg in Jon's lap had pushed him over the edge, leaving him too drunk to drive himself home. He contemplated his options: back to his apartment where Ronan and Mel would likely be a sickeningly perfect couple complete with loud, passionate sex, or crash on Lexi's couch.

When Gray didn't immediately respond, Ronan added, "We'll need to drop Jon off at Heather's on the way. Isn't that right, Jon?"

Jon didn't respond, but Ronan and Leo were practically

giddy at cockblocking Jon's attempts with Sam. Not that Jon minded much considering he was about to meet up with one of his many friends with benefits.

Sam tensed. Her leg was still in his lap with his hand around her ankle. His fingers had slid under the bottom of her jeans. She forced a smile at him. "It was so nice meeting you, Jon. Have fun tonight with Heather."

Gray could tell it must have killed her to move her leg so quickly, but she removed it from his lap with grace and didn't let on how painful it must have been to jerk it back from his grip.

It wasn't until after they'd all said their goodbyes and were out the door that Gray realized he wouldn't have a ride back in the morning for his car. Everyone else had carpooled with Ronan over, but Gray had opted to drive himself so he could get there early to help set up.

"I'll bring you back in the morning," Ronan offered.

"Nah. I don't want to put you out. I'll just crash here; Lexi won't mind."

Ronan made the same face he'd made at the gym a few weeks back.

"Just friends, Ronan."

Jon grabbed the keys from Ronan so he and Leo could start warming up the car.

"Oh, I know," Ronan said. "I'm talking about Sam, now."

"Drive safe. Better get going. Don't forget to let Daisy out."

"Just admit that I was right all along. You've got some weird   hate-you-but-also-want-to-fuck-your-brains-out thing going with her, and you've plotted this whole thing out tonight hoping for a bit of passionate hate sex."

Gray turned and walked back to the house.

"Your silence admits guilt. Just saying…"

Gray threw his hand up behind him as a goodbye wave

and then walked back into the house, knowing the three of them would talk shit about his intentions towards Sam on their drive home. He silenced his phone, anticipating the obnoxious text messages and dirty gifs they'd soon be sending. Right on cue, Leo was the first to send a rather filthy suggestion as to what Gray should do with Sam. He included a picture for reference because he was thoughtful like that.

"Hey, Lex, mind if I crash here tonight?" he asked as he walked back into the house.

"Not at all."

"You'll have to take the floor. I already called the couch." Sam was so smug when she said it that Gray could finally pinpoint the attraction. It was her confidence. She was still one of his least favorite people ever, but at least he could understand why she'd started to get under his skin and why Ronan was right. He had some small, minuscule hope that somehow he and Sam would end up in bed together.

He shook his head. "You have a king-sized bed waiting for you above the garage. Your stairs are clear. I'll even help you get up there if you want."

"I don't need any help; I'm fine here."

He wondered if maybe he was a tad too optimistic thinking that Sam was feeling anything towards him as well. But he'd seen the signs that night; he was sure of it. Had caught her stealing glances at him, felt her body melt into his when he'd carried her in, felt the connection when he'd held her face in his hands and promised her she would be okay. He stood next to the couch, assessing the situation and her.

"I'm not moving." She crossed her arms and looked at Lexi for support, so Gray did the same.

Lexi smirked back at them. "I'm not getting in the middle of this. It's between you guys. Good luck. I'm going to bed."

CHAPTER 7: SAM

E ven though her leg had been in Jon's lap most of the night, her mind had been on Gray. Watching his guard drop as he cut loose with his friends and had a few glasses of bourbon was like seeing a whole new side of him. He had a sense of humor buried underneath his non-nonsense exterior.

"Did they ever find out who that flasher was last week?" Lexi had asked Ronan and Gray mid-way through their poker game. The summer tourist town was slower during the winter months. A drive-by flasher was the hot topic at Bark Sniff Wag, Paging All Bibliophiles, and every other local business Sam had been in over the past few days.

"Since Ronan's face is buried in his phone, probably texting Mel, again, I guess I'll fill you all in on what happened at the last community meeting. You know, since you all couldn't be bothered to attend."

Ronan paused his text to flip him off and her approval rating for Ronan went up three levels. Various groans went around the table, Sam included. Only Gray would complain about a lack of community interest during a poker game.

"I don't need to go. I already know what happened," Leo said. "Milly's convinced this is the first step towards complete anarchy and public orgies," Gray nodded his confirmation, "and Buck insisted he was on the case and would have it wrapped up in no time once he involved his online detective group."

"Obviously," Gray confirmed. "But that wasn't even the worst of it." He downed the rest of his bourbon and rolled up his sleeves. Sam couldn't help but notice the bit of black ink at the top of his forearm that disappeared under his sleeve. It was the slightest hint of a tattoo, and for all she knew it could be something cliché, like an infinite knot. Even worse, it could be something crazy, like a button collage creating the form of the Queen of England.

Regardless, she was on some sort of tattoo kick and that little tease, along with the beer, had her wondering what else Gray had to offer under his black quarter zip top and made-for-his-perfect-ass jeans.

While Sam let her mind drift to dirty thoughts about Gray, he regaled them with the antics of the various community members—most of whom she'd yet to meet. "And then Mitsy got in on the action…"

Groans and chuckles went around the table. Even Lexi rolled her eyes and said to Sam, "She lives about a half mile down the road. I don't think you've met her yet, but once you do, you'll never forget her."

"That's the one," Gray said. He pushed his chair back and got up from the table. "She marches to the front of the meeting and sides with Milly saying she saw a prostitute on her road a few days prior."

"Someone was hooking on Lake Shore Drive?" Jon asked, his voice a mixture of disbelief and intrigue.

"According to Mitsy. She said, 'I just about ran my car off the road when I saw a woman with cheap blonde extensions, six-inch heels, and the shortest skirt I've ever seen on the side of the road with her knee out like this,'" Gray posed dramatically with his knee cocked out à la *Pretty Woman*.

Lexi and Sam's eyes widen with realization and Sam shot Lexi a look that warned, "Don't you fucking dare."

"You know who Mitsy's talking about?" Gray asked, picking up on their silent conversation.

"No way. Who is it? I have to know," Jon demanded, looking back and forth between Sam and Lexi.

Her lips loosened from the bottle of red wine she drank that night, Lexi laughed as she said, "It was Sam."

She could feel the men assessing her, their eyes inspecting every detail as they made up their own minds as to whether she could really be the now infamous Lake Shore Drive hooker.

"It was a joke," Sam explained. "Lexi was out running errands when we decided to go out for dinner. Since she was already out and not too far from the house, she offered to pick me up on the way to Ace's for a bit of food and drinks. My skirt was not that short, and my heels were not that high, but yes, I did jokingly strike a pose at the end of the driveway when I saw Lexi's car. Except that it wasn't Lexi's car; it was the same color and model, but some other woman was driving. Mitsy, apparently."

Sam was sure Gray would get on his soapbox yet again with how dangerous something like that was, and how she could have been kidnapped and cut up out in the woods somewhere or weighted down and chucked into the enormous lake.

"I knew it was you!" Gray said as he pointed to Sam. Then he turned to Ronan, "You owe me ten bucks. I'll take it now, in chips."

Sam felt her mouth involuntarily drop open at the

thought that Gray had heard there was a hooker in town and immediately assumed it was her. Would bet on it even.

After collecting his winnings from Ronan, he finally looked back to her and noticed her reaction. "Mitsy said it was around this house and a blonde. No offense, but it was a no-brainer that it was you."

"Did you tell her it was me?" She did not want her new life in Deep Creek tainted by Mitsy's misguided accusations.

He set half the chips in front of her. "Hell no. She'd be out here with torches trying to burn you both at the stake. Remember what she did to Sally Hopley?"

As he told the animated story about poor Sally who'd held a sex toys house party that went horribly wrong, he bent over with laughter with one hand on the back of his chair for support. His forearm tattoo inching out more to show her an intricate pattern of black swirling lines that begged her eyes to follow them up under his sleeve. A sense of humor, a toned body, tattoos… Gray was checking off more and more qualities on her to-do list.

He was also sweet and loyal. Not just with the way he'd tended to her in the driveway, but she could sense it in the camaraderie he had with his friends. The way he didn't like her, but he still hadn't outed her to Mitsy, and the way he'd shared his Ronan bet winnings with her.

But his love of books was what really did it for her. Ever since she bumped into him at Marcy's store, she couldn't stop thinking about how he ran a local book club and was an avid reader.

Jeremy didn't read much. *Shit.* She hated that she was already comparing Gray to Jeremy, but there it was, again. Not only did she want to dip her toe into the dating pool with tattooed, motorcycle-riding hotties, she wanted to shag readers, too. Another box Gray checked off.

· · ·

It seemed just about everything that had happened before and during the poker game had put her in an impossible position as she sat on the couch waiting for Gray to make his next move. If he made any sort of advance, she already knew she didn't have the willpower to turn him down. She didn't want to turn him down. Her body craved him regardless of everything that had happened before.

"You're not sleeping on the couch when you have a bed just next door." There he was again, being all bossy. Except once the switch flipped in her mind, it was irresistible. It was take-charge, and with her life in shambles, she kind of liked that in a guy.

Not that she had any plans to show her cards to Gray just yet. She still had a part to play in their tit for tat arguments.

"Actually, I am, Gray." Lexi's guest room was a holding space for the last of Paul's things that Lexi couldn't bring herself to part with. The only other option was the floor, or for him to saddle up with her on the couch.

"We can do this the easy way, or the hard way." He moved towards the couch. The tiniest hint of a smile pulling at the corner of his mouth.

"I'll take the easy way. The blankets are in the closet by the bathroom. Enjoy the floor."

"Hard way it is. Brace yourself, Sam. I'm taking you up to your room." He held a hand up to stop her from protesting. "And if you fight it, you'll only make it worse for yourself."

"No!" she said louder than she meant to. Loud enough even that Gray stopped in his tracks and went from looking amused to concerned. "I can't," she continued at just above a whisper. "I'm scared it's going to pop out again."

He carefully stepped over her extended leg, her ankle propped up on the coffee table, and sat next to her on the couch. "You can't live on Lexi's couch for the next few days."

She'd been too scared to look up anything about her

dislocated kneecap, treating it more like a minor and brief inconvenience rather than something to be concerned about beyond that night.

Tentatively, he rubbed her back. It helped until he said, "Maybe longer…"

"Have you dislocated your knee?"

"No. But I was an EMT for a few years before I joined the force."

She gave a slight nod, as if that information did nothing for her even though she almost came when he said it. A man in uniform was stunningly hot, and this guy potentially had a closet full of them.

"You've already alleviated some of the pain with your booze and ibuprofen cocktails, so we might as well move you now while I'm here and can help."

"That's all you're going to say? No long, boring lecture about how I shouldn't be mixing pain meds and beer?"

The corner of his mouth slid up in a half smile. "Maybe another time. For now, let's get you upstairs."

She nodded in agreement, and Gray placed her arm around his broad shoulders. Then she felt his other arm go behind her back, his hand curving around her waist. She felt the warmth of his fingers on her skin where her shirt pulled up and revealed the tiniest bit of her midriff. In a sensory overload she was suddenly aware of each fingertip gripping her side, the feel of his muscles in his shoulder and back as they flexed in anticipation of carrying the majority of her weight, and the smell of him—some sort of cologne mixed with bourbon—as they stood and leaned into one another.

The pain, the booze, and the hot (though occasionally jerky) cop had almost made her forget what a war zone her apartment was. Aside from the corner of the room where she kept her bookshelves and did all the photos for her social media and blog, the rest was nothing but dirty dishes, clothes, and papers everywhere. Binders of to-do lists and checklists for her book-review side-hustle, spicy romance books, and her divorce paperwork were spread out on the kitchen table like an invitation for her guests to skim through while enjoying their coffee.

There was no way she could let him into the apartment when it looked like that. His own apartment was probably meticulous with everything in its place and all surfaces bleached and disinfected each day. Safety first and all. A few hours ago, the thought would have annoyed her. In his arms, it was kind of sexy.

Not even the frigid air could cool her down as he escorted her down the walkway. Especially as he became more protective of her, overprotective even—surprise, surprise coming from Mr. Safety himself. But it felt good to be the center of his concern. To feel his grip tighten as his body moved closer to hers. Their sides completely flush and his hand clamped over hers on his shoulder.

"Did you skip the doctor just to play poker?" he asked as they shuffled along the walk towards the driveway and her stairs. They were taking it exceptionally slow in an abundance of caution or to prolong the walk. Maybe it was both.

"No." It wasn't a lie. She didn't want to go to the doctor because she wanted to flirt. She needed to feel a man's hands on her skin and to feel his eyes looking her up and down in anticipation and animalistic desire.

"That's good, because you suck at poker."

It was more playful than malicious, so with her free hand, she threw a light jab to his solid gut. "I was kicking your ass at the beginning."

Both of his arms were full making it impossible to fight back, though she doubted he would have, anyway. Even a playful tap on a potentially icy driveway was probably not the best idea given her current state and his somewhat drunken state.

He went with a verbal attack instead. "You were lucky at the beginning. But what did you leave here with? Fifty cents?"

Did he just sneak a whiff of her hair? She hoped not. Sam was in no condition to wash it after work, and she'd had limited time for grooming before the game started. All she could manage was a spritz of something Lexi had in her bathroom which she was almost certain left her with a flowery canine scent given her tendency to get down in the thick of it with the dogs at Bark Sniff Wag. She tried to move her head away from his general direction, but there was nowhere for it to go.

"My pockets are lined with a buck twenty-five," she said.

Then, to her horror, she gave the unsexiest grunt to ever come out of her mouth as she accidentally put all her weight on her injured leg while stepping over the minuscule rock wall that separated the driveway from the grass on the front lawn. She didn't have a walkway to the stairs yet. Another item on her parents' vacation house renovation to-do list that would realistically not be done any time in the near future.

"That's it," he said as he adjusted his hold on her. "I'm carrying you."

CHAPTER 8: GRAY

A little ways off from Lexi's house was the two-car garage, and above the garage, was Sam's apartment. The garage was tight and could barely fit two regular-sized cars, much less an additional set of stairs. The only way into her apartment was a set of stairs on the side of the garage that led up to a small landing with what appeared to be a semi-stable railing surrounding it.

He was only slightly drunk, somewhere on the spectrum of beyond tipsy but not ready to make a fool of himself just yet, so he trusted that carrying Sam was safer than allowing her to navigate the steep steps on her own. They were too narrow for them to go up side-by-side, and he didn't want her to risk hurting herself more than she already had.

"Fine," she conceded.

He relished the sweet victory of her finally agreeing without arguing or throwing out any snarky comments. But before he could pick her up again, she put a hand against his chest to stop him.

"Just up to the door. I can handle it from there," she said.

His feet still firmly planted, he leaned his body back from hers and sighed. She made it sound like he was some sort of opportunistic pervert preying on a drunk, injured woman. As if he was helping her home only with the hopes of getting into her pants. Yes, he was semi-guilty of that since the thought had crossed his mind, but he wouldn't act on it or push her in any way unless she made the first move. Besides, he was only thinking of kissing her and maybe sharing her bed—to sleep in. That was it.

He huffed out a laugh and employed his thickest layer of sarcasm when he said, "You are incredibly sexy right now." He took a long, exaggerated sweep of her body with his eyes. "Those ridiculous heels, the 90s looking knee-brace, and that bit of dried mud on your ass." He paused for effect and to fan himself. "But I think I can control myself. No need to get out the pepper spray just yet."

She pursed her lips as if holding back whatever it was, she wanted to say to him. He couldn't believe she had the nerve to be offended by his comment when *she* had been the one who had started the argument with *her* preemptive rejection of him.

They stared at each other, going back to their familiar looks of disdain until she blinked first and said, "Well? Let's get this over with," as she crossed her arms and impatiently tapped the foot of her good leg.

"I'll need to carry you over my shoulder this time since the steps are only wide enough for one person."

"Fine. Whatever, just do it."

And so he did. Gray tried to be gentle with her, but she stiffened in his arms and made sudden movements as he walked, almost throwing them both off balance each time she did. At the top he'd wanted to drop her on her ass again and retreat to the warm couch in Lexi's living room, but instead he eased her onto the platform and made sure she had her bearings before he fully released her. It was just wide enough for them to both stand outside of her door.

"Thanks," she said.

"Yeah, no problem." Why wasn't she going in? He shoved his hands into his pockets and bounced on the balls of his feet to keep warm.

"I can take it from here."

He nodded. Of course she could unlock her front door and let herself in. Except that she wasn't. Was she waiting for him to leave so that she could get a secret key from under her welcome map? Because if so, he wasn't holding back this time on a lecture about safety. How did she even survive this long in life? Her driving was erratic, she had super-power abilities when it came to pissing off perfect strangers—he had no doubt her flat tire was a product of Smitty's vengeful personality, and she lacked common sense when it came to hiding the house key.

"You're not coming in," she nearly shouted at him, startling them both as her words pierced the previously quiet night.

"Still don't want to come in… I can't leave until you're safely inside."

She rolled her eyes at his chivalry, pulled a key out of her pocket, and hobbled in without giving him another glance. The door slammed in his face, and he made his way back to Lexi's.

On the walk over, he couldn't get it out of his mind that she was hiding something up there. His cop senses were tingling, and he had to know what it was. A secret drug ring? She did have some unusual tendencies, and they all barely knew anything about her. He shook his head at the thought. She wouldn't survive in the seedy underbelly of the drug business. He hoped that whatever it was, it wasn't anything illegal; he did not want to deal with the paperwork that would accompany that.

When he reached Lexi's front door, he found the decision on where he'd sleep that night had already been made for him. He'd locked himself out of Lexi's house.

Gray knocked on Sam's door and winced as he heard her swearing and hobbling about on the other side.

"What," she snarled when she opened the door.

"I locked myself out. I need to crash here."

Her left eye twitched, and he wondered if it was a natural tick or if it stemmed from the fury he could almost see coursing through her veins.

"There's a key under the gnome with the gardening can."

"It's covered in ice."

"Uncover it."

He dropped his head and then looked up at her with desperation. A plea not to send him out to the front yard to dig around in the icy mulch for a key.

"Please, Sam."

She looked back at her apartment, seemingly assessing something behind her. She turned back to him and sighed. With a bit of maneuvering, she opened the door for him. "I only made it to the couch, and I'm not moving. You can have the bed; just push all the books to the side or throw them on the chair. I don't care."

"Such generous hospitality. Much appreciated." By the time he was inside with the door closed behind him, she was already on the couch again, right next to the door, with her nose in a book. The same one his club was reading.

"Book any good?"

"Shhhhh, I'm reading."

As he looked around, he sheepishly realized the only

thing Sam had been hiding was how messy she was. He took in her apartment, which was more of a loft since the only walled up room in the space was a bathroom in the front right corner of the long, narrow open floor plan. Along that front wall sat Sam's bed, neatly made but covered in books, with a meticulously kept far corner that held a few bookcases, some plants, and what looked like a box of photo props. Not that he'd found her on Instagram and looked through all her photos and recognized some of the props he was seeing. The left side had a kitchenette and a sort of living area with a couch and a small table.

Shit. It was much more intimate than he'd expected. In his mind, she would be locked up in a far corner room while he poked around a bit before crashing on a couch, not sleeping in the same room with her—and definitely not in her bed while she took the couch.

"I can't take the bed. I'll help *you* to the bed, and then I'll sleep on the couch. I practically lived on Jon's for a few months. I don't mind."

Her eyes remained on her book as if she wasn't going to answer him. Without looking up, she said, "Or we can both sleep in the bed. It's big enough."

When she lowered her book and raised her eyes up to his, he struggled to read her ambiguous expression. There was a stern look that dared him to say anything or to read too much into it, but he could sense at least a small part of her was nervous. As if more was riding on the request than she was letting on.

His eyes widened in surprise as his alcohol-muddled mind tried to keep up with hers. Throughout the night, her attitude towards him vacillated between aggressive and flirty. On the one hand, he probably had a mark on his neck that resembled a hickey thanks to her hostile pinching, and then on the other hand, he was almost positive he caught her in his periphery eye-fucking him during the poker game while he'd been pretending to listen to a conversation between Lexi and Leo.

"Never mind, just forget—"

"No, that's fine."

She continued to glare at him.

"You surprised me. Considering…" He didn't quite know how to explain the mixed signals without pissing her off further since he wasn't exactly sure what he did to piss her off in the first place. Aside from the initial traffic ticket, though even that felt like water under the bridge by then.

"You didn't want me here at all, and now you're being overly nice to me by offering the bed. It caught me off guard is all."

"Yes or no, Gray."

"Yes. We'll both take the bed. Thank you." He held his hand out to help her off the couch, and she took it. But when he went to help her over to the bed, she shooed him off and shuffled over there herself. In a belated attempt at being a gentleman that night, he averted his eyes when she started to take off her jeans.

Something caught in his throat, and he had to clear it before he said, "A glass of water?" Was his voice an octave or two higher just then?

He let his eyes dart back to her. She was leaning against the bed with her back to him, one leg helping to shimmy her pants off without irritating her hurt knee.

"Please. Glasses are in the cabinet next to the fridge."

He got two glasses and filled them with water, taking his time to give her the time she needed to get ready and to get under the sheets without his watchful eyes on her.

"Here you go." He set the glass on her nightstand.

"Thanks."

"Thank you for letting me crash."

She shrugged as if it wasn't the big deal they both knew it was.

"Wow, that's a whole lot of tan, man flesh," he said, taking in the couple dozen smutty romances that covered most of the bed. She'd slipped in on one side of the bed—perched precariously close to the edge so as not to disturb the books or to keep as far from him as possible.

"Yeah, well, it's how you know they won't fade to black when it's time for the good stuff." Zero apologies and zero shame. He liked that. A lot.

Gray cleared her bed of the shirtless men and pulled a Jon move by taking off his shirt and his undershirt before stripping down to nothing but his snug boxer briefs. It was too cold to be sleeping in next to nothing, but he wanted to see what her reaction was. He needed another hint as to how she wanted this to play out—if she wanted it to play out at all.

Gray kept his back to her so she could freely take in what he knew was a well-chiseled body. In case she was enjoying the show, he took his time making his way over to turn out the light by the front door.

No luck. Even though she'd left her book on the couch, Sam's eyes remained glued to what he assumed was an ebook on her phone as he climbed into the bed, equally careful to keep to his side. He pulled up one of her dirty ebook recommendations on his phone. It only seemed right given the circumstances.

In the middle of the night, he woke up to take a leak and get another glass of water to curb the morning hangover he'd already felt coming.

When he first glanced at the table of paperwork in the kitchen area, he expected to see notes about the myriad of books she was reading, including the one for his book club. He wanted a quick peek at what she thought about it.

He hadn't meant to see everything else. The table was awash with personal documents and information. There was a to-do list that included the line, "*HAVE EPIC SEX WITH EVERYONE.*" Given her unabashed preferred reading genre, it was difficult to say if that part was private or not. But the divorce paperwork, the to-do lists about finalizing taxes with the ex and getting the rest of her belongings—he knew that was.

The divorce wasn't a secret. She'd told him as much when he'd pulled her over. What he hadn't known was that she'd been married for ten years. It almost seemed impossible to him when she looked to be in her mid-twenties. She must be a few years older, but it still meant she'd married young and had been married most, if not all, of her adult life. A divorce like that had to be traumatic. He looked up at Sam, still asleep in the bed. Maybe he had been a bit of a dick to get her a ticket that day. Maybe he should be a little more forgiving of her occasionally bitter attitude.

He refilled her water glass as well, and then read for another hour before he fell back to sleep.

In the light of the morning, his pity for Sam diminished as he sat up in bed and took in her cocky smirk from across the room.

What a horrible idea it had been to read *Fire Down Below* while sleeping in the same bed as Sam. The main character, Mercury, had long blonde hair, and his mind wouldn't stop picturing Mercury as Sam. When he woke up in just his underwear and a flimsy sheet, his cock was rock hard from all the dirty dreams he'd had. It stood shamelessly like a beacon for all the apartment to see. And there was Sam, just beyond it—he literally had to peer over his cock to see her—on the couch, reading as she had been the night before when he'd insisted on spending the night.

"Morning, Gray." The words rolled right off her pretty pink tongue, the same one that had done such dirty things to his body in his mind the night before. "How did you sleep?" She was smiling, but he could tell her question was not altogether innocuous; there was much more beneath it, though he couldn't see it at the moment.

She'd noticed his morning wood; of that he was certain and generally not embarrassed by. He was a guy and that's what guys did. Besides, he had reason to be cocky when it came to his cock.

But had she heard him talking, too? More than a few friends and girlfriends had told him he talked in his sleep. Usually it was unintelligible murmurs or a few meaningless words here and there, but given his choice in late-night reading, the alcohol, and his confusing feelings towards Sam, it was hard to say what could have come out of his mouth that night.

He sat up straighter, giving her an eyeful of his toned chest and the tattoo which covered his right pec. It was an intricate piece with bold black lines designed and given to him by his baby sister, Bea. During his late-night or early-morning drink of water, he couldn't help but notice that under the words *HAVE EPIC SEX WITH EVERYONE*, in all caps, was a list of qualities (if that's the right word for it) she was looking for in said mates. One happened to be a man in uniform, and another was a tattoo. Wasn't he morally obligated to put it on display as she eyed him up from the couch?

With no way of knowing where they stood once they

LEIGH DONNELLY

were both sober and in what appeared to be much better spirits, he played along.

"Just fine," he said, flexing his muscles.

"Yeah? Good dreams?"

"Maybe. I never remember my dreams."

She nodded and smiled sweetly back at him. "I can remind you."

CHAPTER 9: SAM

S am heard the faint snores of a man next to her and almost reached out for him the way she'd done with Jeremy for all those years. She'd slept so deeply the night before—with Gray's warmth and soothing masculine scent filling the bed—that it took her a few minutes to remember where she was and why.

She'd been hesitant about having him in her personal space when it was such a clear picture of how disheveled and disastrous her personal life was outside the illusion of perfection she presented to everyone except Lexi.

Even so, when he'd returned claiming he'd locked himself out of Lexi's, she couldn't resist the allure of having someone else in the loft with her. Another presence to help diminish the abject loneliness she'd been feeling since the night she left Jeremy. In the light of day, she knew it had been the right choice. The perfect way to ease herself back in the habit of using an actual bed. She even toyed with the idea of easing herself into it further by not washing the sheets for a few days. It would be nice to have Gray's scent helping to lull her to sleep in the upcoming week.

Well, it had been the right choice as a benefit to her. She wasn't sure how Gray would interpret the whole thing. He'd told her flat out the night before she'd been sending mixed signals.

She didn't know how to explain it though. It wasn't like she and Gray knew each other well enough for that sort of conversation about how the night before she'd thought she could have sex with someone—had even considered Gray as that potential someone—except once he was there in her apartment, she freaked out. She hadn't had a first kiss since she was a teenager. Aside from Jeremy, no man had seen her naked body.

When she invited Gray to sleep in the bed with her, regardless of what she'd thought earlier that night, it had been only a courtesy for them both. He needed a bed to sleep in, and she couldn't sleep in one without someone else there with her.

She'd been relieved when he took the hint and kept to his side. Like an old married couple, they'd read their books silently in bed before drifting off to sleep. His body radiated heat, so the sheets were no longer like ice against her skin, and his overall presence kept those deep-rooted feelings of intense loneliness at bay throughout the night.

Fully awake early the next morning, she carefully rolled out of bed and went back to the couch. Her leg was stiff from the injury and immobility during sleep, but she found it felt a tiny bit better with each step. It was the perfect environment for reading with the relaxing rhythm of his breathing taking off the edge of what was usually too quiet of a space.

Her ears perked up when she'd made out a syllable or two hidden in those deep breaths.

"The car... No... Okay."

She set the book on her stomach to hold the page while she shamelessly stared at the half-naked man in her bed.

"Mercury, do that thing… With your tongue… Mmmmm…"

He moaned, and she almost covered her eyes with her hand, but she was too mesmerized. Gray's hand lazily ran a few fingers up and down his shaft. It was under a sheet, and in his sleep, he couldn't quite figure out how to get to it. The scene was immensely intimate and private. And yet since he'd barged in the night before and insisted on sleeping under *her* roof, she absolved herself of any guilt as she watched him lightly go to town on himself.

Did she hear that right? Was he talking to Mercury? As in Mercury D. Stalla from L. C. Holmes's super-smutty trilogy, *Fire Down Below*? If it was, she couldn't blame him for the wood he was sporting. Sam knew exactly what tongue thing he was referring to. She herself would try it, eventually, if she ever got up the nerve to put herself out there again.

When his eyes fluttered, she snatched her book back up and pretended to read while he woke up and got his bearings.

"Morning, Gray. How did you sleep?" She eyed him up, trying to determine if he was the kind of person who woke up and immediately remembered his dreams or not.

"Just fine," he said, stretching in a way that displayed his god-like body and the large black and gray tattoo that covered the right side of his chest. It was geometric but difficult to fully take in since she refused to allow her eyes to travel around his body like a lost tourist. That's what he wanted her to do, and she wouldn't allow herself to take the bait.

"Yeah? Good dreams?"

His eyes locked on her hers and a flicker of guilt flashed through them. "Maybe. I never remember my dreams."

His eyes looked away from hers and he pressed his lips firmly together, causing them to disappear into his mouth.

All signs he was lying to her based on what she'd learned from the spicy detective novels she'd been reading. A bit of research for her latest blog post: "My Fifteen Favorite Filthy Novels About Dicks."

She nodded and smiled sweetly back at him. "I can remind you."

"Hmmmm?" He cocked his head to show he wasn't sure what she was talking about.

"Something about Mercury and that thing she does with her tongue…" Sam wished Lexi could have been there to see someone blush even harder than she did.

Gray cleared his throat and shook his head. "Nope, nothing." In his haste to get out of bed, he twisted up in the sheets and fell to the floor with a thud in a tangled mess of sheet and limbs.

Sam stifled her laugh and said with as much sincerity as she could manage, "Are you alright?" Her neck strained as she tried to get a proper glimpse of him half naked and a flustered mess on her floor.

His back to her, he grabbed his pants and shirt from off the chair by the bed and quickly got dressed. Then he snatched his phone off the nightstand, ran a hand through his mussed-up hair, and said, "I have to meet Ronan at the gym. Thanks for letting me crash."

Still the rule follower—this time it was social etiquette rules he couldn't ignore—he paused at the door and said, "Can I get you anything before I go?"

She beamed back at him, thoroughly amused at how easy it was to run him off. "I'm good, thanks." A few beats after the door closed, she peeked out the curtains. He'd hauled ass down the steps and then across the lawn as he repeatedly ran his hand through his hair. Too sensible to take out his frustration on the road, he eased out of the driveway and cautiously turned out onto Lake Shore Drive.

Sam allowed herself a few minutes of peaceful bliss before getting started on her various to-do lists. Her kitchen table was full of them: divorce tasks, blog tasks, social media tasks, welding certification tasks.

It would have been nice to have had Gray stick around for a while. If only to keep her apartment from feeling so empty and lonely, but she couldn't risk him seeing what a cluster-fuck her life had become. It was bad enough that he'd seen the chaos of clothes and books thrown around. She didn't want him to be privy to the current feud she was having with Jeremy about who got what in their divorce.

With a deep breath, she put her book down, swung her feet to the floor, and gritted her teeth as she stood. She got a coffee to work out her stiff leg and to get her brain working, then she sat at the table. She pushed the divorce paperwork to the side as she opened her laptop to work on her *Cat the Great Reads Smut* latest blog post: "Men in Uniform Round-Up." The reviews of her top ten steamy reads featuring smoldering hot firefighters, EMTs, and cops were already written. The next steps were to tighten up the prose, include affiliate links throughout so she would get a small stipend if anyone purchased the books through her links, and get a few pictures for the post and for her social media accounts so she could drive traffic to it.

She also needed to decide if she was going to throw in a book about a dentist or if she would give that one its own stand-alone post. Dentists weren't typically what people thought of when they pictured hot men in uniform, and yet it had been one of her favorite reads of the year so far.

When the author had first approached her about doing a review for her debut novel, *Bite Me*, a steamy enemies-to-lovers psychological thriller featuring an elf dentist and an alpha werewolf, she'd been skeptical. Almost flat-out refused based solely on her horrific experience with B. J. Queene's novel during her drive out.

But something in the blurb spoke to her, and she'd agreed to give it a shot. Just two chapters in she'd been hooked. She stayed up late reading, read through her breaks at work, and even took a dinner raincheck with Lexi one night to finish it.

With a few clicks she found herself starting a new post: "*Bite Me* is the Smutty *Animal Farm* We Didn't Know We Needed."

I am fully aware many are coming into this thinking my title is click bait and that I won't be able to deliver—which isn't too far-fetched given my propensity to embellish the literary merits of smutty novels almost as much as the authors embellish the leading lady's ability to come so hard and so fast Every. Damn. Time.

But this blog post is different because this book hits differently. The social commentary subtly, and sometimes not so subtly, hidden beneath the spicy romance of our elf dentist Delianne and his fated werewolf alpha mate Brodure will have you seeing our current political upheaval in a whole new light.

Sam was in a zone as her light pink nails flew over the keys. The quiet and loneliness fell away as she lost herself in her writing.

CHAPTER 10: GRAY

"**D**o *not* take off your swim trunks," Ronan warned Leo as he eased into the hot tub. "You, too," he added as he shot a look at Jon.

"Too late." Jon pointed to his trunks resting on the thin deck surrounding them and shrugged his shoulders. "My boys need to breathe and move around. Been stuck in my ski gear all day."

Gray and Ronan each put extra space between themselves and Jon. In a hot tub big enough to hold twelve, it wasn't difficult to spread out with only the four of them.

"Don't act like I'm the one who's out of line here. It's Ronan's bachelor party. The guys are supposed to lose their pants and end up naked. Not my fault you're the only ones around when it happens. That's on Gray for booking a weekend of skiing instead of a weekend of club hopping and strip clubs. Back me up, Leo."

They were at a four-bedroom, skin-in ski-out chalet on Wisp Mountain that they'd rented to accommodate all the guys for a weekend of skiing, playing pool, soaking in the hot tub, and DoorDashing most of their meals since they were boozing it up whenever they weren't out on the slopes.

It was snowing again and cold enough outside to have their supply of drinks resting on the ledge of the hot tub alongside Jon's discarded trunks. After a full day of skiing and a heavy dinner, they were all too tired to do much of anything beyond drinking and soaking in the hot water out on the deck.

Leo's head was back against the edge of the tub as he stared up into the vaulted porch ceiling. "I'm too old for clubs." He worked his shoulder a little. "Might be too old for skiing, too. Damn am I sore."

Jon looked at Leo, assessing if he was truly done picking up random women at clubs and bars. "Since when?"

He shrugged his shoulders and grabbed a fresh beer from the ledge.

"I'm out, too," Gray said. "Joined one of those dating apps a few days ago. Nothing ever comes from the women we meet at the bars."

He'd met Jessa at a *Schitt's Creek* trivia game at one of the local taverns. Her team, A Little Bit Mutt, and his team, Simply the Best, were head-to-head at the end leading to a sudden death challenge where each team member was lined up at the front of the bar with a two-sided paddle: "David" on one side and "Alexis" on the other. The trivia MC called out a quote and everyone had to hold up their paddle to show who said it. One wrong answer sent them back to their seats.

When it was down to just Gray and Jessa, Gray leaned over and whispered to Jessa an offer: he'd pay for her dinner and drinks that night if she won. But if she lost, she'd go out on a date with him. With a sweet smile, she held out her hand to shake and then got the next quote wrong. While she swore she didn't do it on purpose, Gray never believed her. They'd dated for three years after that, though he couldn't remember how many were good ones.

Jon sat upright in the water, offended by Gray's comment. "Sex. That's what comes from meeting women at bars. Sex. Usually good sex, but sex nonetheless."

"It's only going to get worse, Jon." Ronan smiled as he puffed on his cigar. Mel hated the smell of them. He only did it when he spent the night away from her, which was rare. "Mel's already stopped taking the pill. With any luck, this time next year, she'll be pregnant. We could even be parents by then."

Leo and Gray congratulated Ronan while Jon looked around at each of them. "You're all leaving me." He shook his head in disbelief.

"Come on," Ronan said. "Join us on the dark side: Sunday brunches with girlfriends and wives. Weekends spent antiquing and roaming around the farmers markets."

Jon shook his head. "Never. I'll take my chances with Gray and Leo."

"I just told you I'm done." Gray said.

"You're on a dating app. Those things never work. And Leo…" They all turned to Leo whose head was upright and showing a furrowed brow in anticipation of whatever Jon was about to say. "He'll miss getting laid on the regular. You'll both be back at the Honi with me by summer. Just in time for the tourists and bachelorette parties. Enjoy your solo brunches and farmers market trips, Ronan."

It was Ronan's turn to shake his head. "Not solo. I'll be with Mel. And eventually with little Ronan."

Jon looked around at each of them. "And this… This is what you guys want, too?" he asked Leo and Gray as he gestured toward Ronan. The bite was missing from his question though. It came out almost as a plea for them to disagree. To tell him that marriage and kids were not suddenly on their minds. That Ronan's current condition wasn't contagious and potentially spreading to all of them.

"Wife, yes," Leo said without hesitation. "Kids... I don't know about all that. I'll see how it goes with Ronan first."

"Same," Gray said.

Jon looked at them with pity. "But the monotony..."

"Not necessarily." More puffing on his cigar. "There's something to be said for being with someone who knows what I like, and I know what she likes."

There was a general consensus from the rest of the guys as they nodded in understanding.

"D'you remember..." Leo started to laugh and could barely get the words out. "That time Jon hooked up with that one chick down in Cancun?" There could be no mistake about which "one chick" Leo was referring to.

The fond memory had them all laughing then, even Jon. "I still have nightmares about that one. Janine. Her name was Janine. I'm almost positive."

"It was Janine," Leo confirmed. "I was with some chick whose name I *don't* remember, but I know yours was Janine because she spoke in the third person. Scratch that, she yelled in the third person. I almost couldn't finish. Having to hear your dumb ass screaming about how you're her giant bull and you're going to put a baby in her. And her yelling back, 'Yes, Janine needs your big bad bull seed!'"

Jon held his hands up in defense. "Hold up. Don't put it on me if you can't perform. I was giving the lovely lady what she wanted. She left satisfied."

"With her boyfriend. She left with her boyfriend who showed up pounding on our hotel door."

Jon was shaking his head again even though he was still laughing with the rest of them. "I, uh... I actually didn't tell you guys the whole story with that."

"I knew it!" Ronan said, pointing his beer bottle at Jon. "I told Mel the next morning there was more to it, but she was so pissy about the whole thing I didn't want to bring it up again at breakfast."

"Why was Mel pissed?" Jon asked, his voice showing a bit of genuine concern even though he was still laughing.

"Aside from the irate boyfriend in the middle of the night, Mel's pretty sure the woman stole half her make-up and…" Ronan's face scrunched up as if he was trying to figure out how to continue. "Shit, she'd kill me if I told you guys this."

"I'm not telling mine 'til you tell us yours."

Gray and Leo looked back and forth, waiting for someone to spill it already.

"Come on, who are we going to tell?" Gray asked. He'd gone to bed solo that night. Jessa hadn't been able to get off work for the trip, and he'd happily played the role of the good boyfriend who didn't sleep around. While everyone else was occupied in their rooms with one-night stands or their girlfriends, Gray had been alone in his room. To drown out his misery, he'd had a generous portion of their whiskey supply. A mistake in hindsight since then he'd been too drunk to jack off to help him fall asleep.

"Exactly. It's just us," Leo added.

They could tell he was on the verge of cracking as his eyes went to each of them, likely a ploy to build tension more than any actual hesitation on his end. "Janine stole Mel's vibrator."

The guys first stared at Ronan with their mouths gaping open, then they turned to Jon.

It was Leo who asked what they were all dying to know. "Did she use a vibrator? Did she use *Mel's* vibrator when she was begging you to fill her with your bull come or seed or whatever the fuck she called it?"

Jon's head fell back slightly as he thought back to that infamous night. "No…. I don't think so…"

More laughter and talk about who would steal a stranger's vibrator, and if she smuggled it out of the room inside her when her boyfriend came to rescue her, or if she simply stashed it in her purse along with all the make-up.

"Okay, okay. Since Ronan so graciously told his side of that night and gave us more insight than we ever wanted into his sex life with Mel…"

"She will castrate me if you ever say a word about this to her."

"I'll fill in a few of the details on my end." He took a long swig of his drink. "I already knew she had a boyfriend. Gray, you remember when she came up to us at the bar?"

"I do. I often think back and am thankful that I dodged that bullet. Even more so now that I know she stole Mel's vibrator."

"That so? Well, you missed out on one of the all-time greatest orgasms of my life." Leo and Gray gave Jon a questioning look while Ronan spit out his drink. "Fuck you. You know what I meant. Anyway, Janine came up to me and Gray at Señor Frog's. Gray," he said as he pointed an accusatory finger at him, "the worst wing man in history, nearly blew it for me with conversation about current events."

"She thought Baltimore was the capital of Maryland," Gray said with a tinge of disgust. He wasn't naïve. He understood Jon cared very little about Janine's or anyone else's ability to read a map or articulate an original thought about, well, anything, but that didn't mean he had to settle, too. Gray would argue that Jon was shallow and had low standards. Jon would argue that Gray's high standards cost Gray a shit-ton of ass. They agreed to disagree on that front.

"She was from… I don't remember, but it wasn't Maryland. And lots of people from other states think Baltimore is the capital."

"Get to it," Leo said as he made a hurry up motion with his hand.

"Gray tuned out as soon as she proved herself to be geographically illiterate. That means he missed the whole part where she pointed out her boyfriend watching us from across the bar."

"No, no, no," Ronan said.

"Why not? What do I care if she has a boyfriend? That chick Leo slept with had a boyfriend she was cheating on. At least my chick's boyfriend knew—he was excited even that I was going to bone her."

"Then why was he banging on the door and screaming at three in the morning?"

Jon shrugged again. "They like the drama."

Ronan sacrificed his cigar as he plunged it into the water to splash Jon. "Not cool, dickhead."

"What?" Jon looked around at each of his friends. "Like you all wouldn't have done the same."

More splashes of steaming hot water and various versions of "fuck no" from everyone who hadn't boned some dude's girlfriend at his request, or at the very least hadn't boned some chick who turned out to be a klepto with no boundaries.

They'd reminisced about the good ol' days for hours until only Gray and Ronan were left in the living room.

"How's online dating going?" Ronan asked as they did a bit of spot cleaning before calling it a night themselves.

"Not good." Not that Gray would admit that to Jon or even Leo. "The first day I got a handful of messages. A few local, and some just outside of here."

"That's good."

"I thought so, too. But I could only hold a conversation with one of them."

Ronan threw a can into the recycling bin and then paused his cleaning efforts. "Are we talking incapable of having an adult conversation or incapable of having a sophisticated, high-brow Gray conversation?"

Gray stopped cleaning as well. "Come on. I'm not that bad."

Ronan was silent.

"Am I?"

He shrugged. "Yeah. You are. With judging people based on first impressions, you're the worst. Not that *you* give off a great first impression yourself. A bit of the pot and the kettle situation happening if you ask me."

Gray didn't argue back because he had asked him, and he valued Ronan's opinion. Ronan was slowly approaching the life Gray had always wanted for himself. Any words of wisdom (even drunk words of wisdom) were held in the highest esteem equal only to Bea and his father.

"Yeah, okay. I'll try to work on it."

"No." Ronan shook his head. "My point is that you're not going to meet anyone with those online dating apps or over drinks at the Honi because it's too easy for them to make a terrible first impression. And I know you'll make a bad first impression, too. You're a touch unlikable at first glance if I'm honest."

Gray shot a nasty look back at him.

"You need to hear it, man. Why do you think I was so hard set on getting you and Lexi together? It's *you*." Ronan pointed at him. "You can't meet someone and start dating them. You need a friend that evolves into it. If she can already stand you, your first and biggest dating hurdle is already behind you."

Gray looked for any sign that it was all just another

instance of Ronan ragging on him—a trademark move for everyone in their group whenever they teetered on the edge of having conversations that had the potential to evoke actual emotions.

No luck. Ronan, as drunk as he was, was dead serious and remarkably coherent.

"How else am I gonna meet someone then? I'm not a hermit; I'm already out there and doing things. I have a book club."

"Are you freaking kidding me?! You started a book club to meet women?"

Gray smirked at that one. He liked books; that was why he started the book club. Still, a girlfriend who liked books as much as he did was a bonus he'd hoped for when he'd first approached Marcy about it.

"Not exactly, but would that be so wrong?"

"Yes! You don't want to be that creepy guy at book club. You meet people through friends of friends. That's how Mel and I met. That's why I'm trying to push Sam on you now. Despite the cluster fuck of a first impression where you ticketed her, I saw the way she looked at you at poker—even with Jon's hands all over her."

Gray walked over to the table and dumped a plate full of food that was left out too long into the trash can he was carting around the spacious kitchen. "Yeah, I thought so, too."

"I know, I know. You slept in her bed and nothing happened. But she's still fresh off a divorce from her high school boyfriend if what Mel's telling me is right. That's a decent amount of baggage to work through."

Gray collapsed on the couch. "I didn't even tell you what I saw at her apartment."

Ronan gave up on the cleaning as well. The empty beer cans, red Solo cups, and general party detritus could wait.

They'd do it in the morning with Leo and Jon's help. He sat down next to Gray, picked up a half empty beer bottle, gave it a quick taste, deemed it drinkable, then finished it.

"Okay, let's hear it," Ronan said.

'You're disgusting."

"There's another one here. You want it?"

Gray shooed away the lukewarm beer Ronan proffered. "I saw some of Sam's paperwork when I got up in the middle of the night to get a drink."

"Snooping around her apartment? That doesn't sound like by-the-book Gray."

"I thought it was her notes about the book club book."

"Yeah. That sounds more like you."

"Just listen for a minute."

Ronan's hands went up in surrender.

"There was a to-do list where she's looking for work, getting her address changed and getting a new license." Ronan nodded along as Gray spoke. "And one of her to-do items is to have epic sex. With everyone."

Ronan's face contorted to show something between pain and pity and laughter. He went to take a drink from the empty bottle before chucking it into the trash can.

"I know what you're thinking," Gray said.

"You don't."

"She says she wants to sleep with everyone, but I'm literally in bed with her, practically naked, and nothing happened."

He tilted his head from side to side as if considering. "Well, yeah. I guess you did know what I was thinking."

"The woman who wants to sleep with everyone, doesn't want to sleep with me." He shook his head. "I shouldn't have let Jessa—"

"No, no, no, no, no!" shouted Ronan as he stood up. "You have to get Jessa out of your mind. You guys had maybe,

maybe, a few good months in the beginning. After that?" What happened after that remained unsaid and they both sat in silence for a beat.

"Going back to Jessa is settling. It's crumbs of what you deserve. And despite your initial, high unlikability rating, you are, overall, a good person."

Not even a hint of sarcasm. Not surprising since Gray was set as Ronan's best man, but touching all the same. "Thanks, man."

"It's true. Women just can't seem to get beyond that first-impression asshole vibe you give off."

"Nice."

"It had to be said." Ronan sipped from another left-over beer. Probably Jon's. He had a habit of losing his drinks throughout the night. "Maybe you can get on Sam's good side by warning her about Mitsy."

"What about Mitsy?"

"You didn't see her selected topic for the next community meeting?"

Gray stared back blankly.

"She's going to rant about book porn. I'm pretty sure that's aimed at Sam and maybe Marcy by proxy since she has Sam giving book chats or whatever she's doing." Still no reaction from Gray aside from sinking further down into the couch. "Does that mean you're not going to say anything to her?"

"No way. She can hold her own. Coming from me she'll assume I agree with Mitsy. There's no way a conversation like that will get me on Sam's good side."

"Alright. You know her better than I do..." He trailed off waiting for Gray to say something else in response to it but thinking about Mitsy killed his buzz. He was ready to crash.

Gray looked around at the mess that still remained. "This place is trashed."

"Yep." Instead of cleaning, Ronan sat back down. "Speaking of trashed, Darla's concerned the wedding pictures will all look similar given my choice in groomsmen and my own drinking habits."

Darla was Mel's mother and the matriarch of everything to do with the wedding. Gray could already tell where the conversation was going given Darla's perfectionist personality.

"Does she want a dry wedding?"

Ronan shook his head. "Fuck no. She loves wine. But she's asking us all to have flasks and to use them discreetly. She wants to cut down on beer bottles littering the tables and becoming, as she put it, focal points in the pictures."

Gray winced. "You hate hard liquor."

"If it's going to keep Darla off my back, I'll do it. I might just suck it up and down a few shots at the beginning."

"Or you could not drink."

"No way. You have no idea how many ways I could potentially fuck this thing up. I need at least a little something to calm the nerves."

CHAPTER 11: SAM

"Here, Daisy. Come here, pretty girl." Sam could finally kneel with only the tiniest bit of discomfort to her knee. She took Daisy, hands down her favorite pup at Bark Sniff Wag, into her arms and gave her a good scratch behind the ears and on the top of her butt. Her generosity was rewarded with over-eager kisses that knocked her on her ass.

"Smith, get up off the floor," Gil said as he stepped over her to get to the front counter.

"Lighten up, Gil. It's a doggie day care. I'm supposed to be playing with the dogs. It's literally my job." She gave a final scratch to Daisy before joining him at the counter.

Gil was a self-proclaimed fat-and-happy married man somewhere in his late thirties. He wore khaki shorts that rested at a point well above his belly button and a short-sleeved polo to work each day regardless of the season. To complete the walking-stereotype look, he hiked his socks up to right below his knees and played only clean, soft rock music whether they were open or not.

He smiled and gave an amused look at Sam as she leaned forward to swipe dog hair off the far end of the counter. "Might be a bit early in your career here for you to be telling me to lighten up." A nervous tick, his hands reached up and touched the sunglasses held around his neck via a strap—what he called his "lens leash." According to workplace lore, he'd lost his favorite pair sometime back in the late nineties and never fully recovered from the incident.

"It's almost been a month already. You're practically a second father to me, Gil."

Gil tried to hide his giggle, but his jiggling belly gave him away. "Low blow. I'm five years older than you."

"Exactly. It was a joke. Hence my suggestion you lighten up."

He gave some sort of *humph* and said, "We'll see how light you are when you're running your own business."

He typed a few entries into the computer as Sam reviewed her schedule for the day. While most of the new hires were eased into some of the more intricate tasks of grooming and helping with first aid, Sam's experience allowed Gil to throw her right into the mix. Her schedule for the day had her spending the morning in the play area, doing a few doggie pedicures after lunch, then finishing the day back at the play area. It didn't pay nearly what her vet job did, but she really did love going to work.

Another *humph*. "Garrett just called out." Gil tapped out a message on his phone. "Can you stay a few more hours for evening checkouts? I'd do it, but I have a meeting across town."

"Yeah, sure."

"Great. Thanks." More typing on his phone, then over to the computer again where he pulled up his calendar. "Did you get your welding certification yet?"

"Not yet—"

"Don't bother. I'm hiring a third party for it. Joan had a fit when I told her I wanted you to do some welding for me here and there."

Joan oversaw finances, human resources, and event planning. A bit of a jack of all trades which was what Gil looked for in his employees apparently.

"She said with the liability alone it wasn't worth it."

Sam's heart sank a little. Not that she was eager to get back behind her welder's helmet again, but she had assumed it was part of the reason Gil had given her a generous salary. At the time she figured he'd offered the pay with the assumption that she'd be bringing more to the table than the average general doggie day care staff member. Hopefully her vet background alone would suffice.

"Had your heart set on welding A-frames for the next few weeks?" Gil asked, reading her slumped posture.

"No, it's not that…"

His attention moved from his electronics to her as he studied her reaction. "You're not thinking of quitting already, are you?" His hands went back to his sunglasses to confirm they were still dangling from his neck. "Because if you are, just tell me now. I know Garrett's on the verge of—"

"No! Not at all. I love it here." She reached out and placed a hand on his forearm to reassure him about how gloriously happy she was to be working there. His cocked eyebrow in response reminded her that Gil was not her actual second father. Boundaries. Right. She took her hand back and busied it instead with straightening the brochures on the counter.

He let out a sigh. "Well, that's a relief. I can't afford to lose multiple employees right before our busiest season. And I just had Joan do your employee profile on our website. She added you to the home page and the employee page." A few clicks on the computer and there was Sam, front and center on the website, having a sweet and candid moment with Daisy. Beneath the picture was a quick blurb about Sam's experience as a vet and how she'd bring her in-depth knowledge of animals to Bark Sniff Wag.

"Wow… That's something," Sam managed. Daisy was lunging to lick her face, and the camera caught her leaning back in surprise. Her eyes were half open and unfocused, though pointed in the camera's direction. For whatever reason, her own tongue looked like it was hanging out the side of her mouth, almost mirroring Daisy's. She'd never seen a worse picture of herself, and yet there it was, the very first image on her new job's webpage.

"Thanks. Took it myself one of your first days here." He marveled at his work a beat before he said, "Anywho, I'd better get back and check on our inventory with Joan. You gonna be okay? You seem off, not quite yourself."

She shook her head as if to brush off the not quite herself version so she could get back to regular old Sam. "I'm fine. Really."

"Knee's not giving you too much trouble? I can keep you on the desk today if it is."

"No, really. I'm good. Go. Count all the things."

Another tap on the sunglasses. He wasn't convinced. "Yeah, okay. I'll be around if you need anything."

During peak summer months, Bark Sniff Wag would have multiple employees in the play area, but during the winter, even with the influx of tourists for skiing and snowboarding, there was usually just one employee hanging out with the pooches.

While some hated working solo, Sam thrived on it. She needed some solid alone time to think things through without the frosty, isolated feeling she got from being in her apartment alone. She couldn't find a better place for deep thoughts than in the play area with a bunch of sweet, non-judgmental, furry animals.

It had been good for her those first few weeks. She got her shit together mentally as she analyzed the last decade of her life with Jeremy, trying to pinpoint where it all went wrong. Depending on her mood and the day, she would say it was March of their third year of marriage or the summer of their seventh year.

The second and third week, while she played with the sweet pups in the back, she'd strategized about how she would run her book recommendations table at Paging All Bibliophiles. After seeing Sam successfully make a recommendation that first day, Marcy had offered official space in her store for Sam to make recommendations and spread the word about her blog. It wasn't a paying gig, and that was fine with Sam. Recommending romance books was one her favorite things to do, and Paging All Bibliophiles was one of her favorite places in Deep Creek Lake.

As with most bookstores, extra space was scarce, with all floor real estate being used to maximum capacity to display as many books as possible. Marcy rearranged an old storage closet to be Sam's new headquarters. It was a tiny space; Sam would need to get creative in how she wanted to set everything up.

Because the first few visits were key in establishing trust and credibility, customers, like the one she'd recommended books to on her second day in town, would be wary of outright saying what they were looking for in a romance novel. Not everyone was comfortable listing off the specifics about what they so desperately wanted to read. She needed a plan of attack for how she'd build trust, which would hopefully lead to an increase in loyal blog readers as well.

Aside from loving the idea of being a personal book shopper of sorts for all things steamy romances, Sam knew incorporating what she was doing at Paging All Bibliophiles into her website and social media presence had huge potential depending on how well she executed it.

Once she'd exhausted everything she could think of in terms of her failed marriage and her upcoming book-recommendation nook, she relented and allowed herself to obsess over Gray, too. Because despite all the play the leading ladies in her novels were getting, she was in a dry spell that could rival the Sahara.

When she'd first started working at Bark Sniff Wag, she'd been sure that as a bonus on top of working with dogs all day, it would also be an ideal place to "bump into" sexy, animal-loving, available guys in the area. She knew it was in poor taste to pick up customers at the front desk. Tacky, really. It wasn't like she was going to slip her number to anyone as they signed in their pooch for the day, but surely she'd be able to engage in some witty banter at the desk and then possibly bump into them again somewhere around town. Small towns were made for that sort of thing. It was part of the reason she'd left Milton. Too much potential for continued run-ins with Jeremy.

Her hopes of finding love at work hadn't panned out as she'd planned. Instead, Sam noticed that just about every guy she had an inkling of attraction to had a wedding ring around his finger or came in with a wife, fiancé, girlfriend, boyfriend, etc. in tow. All but one...

"I was wondering when I'd run into you here," Gray said as he strolled up to the counter for evening pick up. He was in his uniform again. Except this time, she wasn't being pulled over or in a terrible mood, and he had that half-smile thing going on that sent a shiver through her body.

"You know, for a stalker, you're doing a terrible job." *Keep.*

A. Straight. Face. Sam demanded of herself. But what was worse? Some sort of pursed lips move to suppress a smile, or for him to possibly know she was mildly pleased to see him? Ugly pursed lips with the sides curled up for the win... Or rather a loss in this case as she watched his smile falter ever so slightly.

"I see you're still struggling with the definition of a stalker. I've been bringing Dee here for the past seven months. How long have *you* been working here?"

Sam's lady organs seized at the name Dee. She'd heard a few of her coworkers use the nickname Dee for Daisy. Daisy was Gray's dog. Dog-owner and dog-lover had always been on her list of men-to-do. She hadn't even written it down because it was that much of a given along with being alive, of age, and a non-smoker. Jeremy was allergic to dogs, and allergy medicine left him as capable as a drunk toddler. Loving dogs was a non-negotiable for all future hook-ups, lovers, dates, or whatever it was people called it.

She sat a little straighter on her stool as she pulled up the release screen for Daisy's pickup. "Almost a month now," she admitted sheepishly. She swiveled the digital signature pad around for Gray to sign. Even his signature was sexy. What was *that* all about? She desperately needed a shag, immediately, if she was gauging future mate potential by the scribble of their name. And yet, she found his intriguing. She'd expected nothing but quick and indecipherable hard lines and angles, but what she saw were legible and graceful curves. Watching his fingers deftly work the electronic pen led to thoughts of those same fingers running over her body.

Belatedly, because he definitely caught her staring, she turned and went to get Daisy, fanning herself along the way in case she was blushing.

Daisy was already at the door, having heard Gray's car pull up a few minutes prior. "Such a good girl," she said as she opened the door. "You ready to go see Dad?" She absolutely was based on the extensive tail wagging and tiny jumps at Sam's legs.

Sam imagined Gray on his couch, shirtless (because why not) and reading a book while Daisy's head rested in his lap. His hand gently petting and lulling her to sleep while he expertly turned the page with just one hand so as not to disturb his number one gal. Yeah, she could understand how the pup would be eager to get home to that.

Back in the front reception area, Gray kneeled to greet Daisy and whisper to her about what a good girl she was and how much he missed her. Sam felt an ache in her heart thinking about how Jeremy had done the same with her when she'd gotten home from work at the beginning of their marriage. In human form, of course, with a hug and kiss at the door, having dinner cooked and ready for them, and questions about how her day had been.

Maybe it wouldn't be so bad if... her thoughts almost made it there, but then reality kicked through the door as dramatic as the Kool-Aid man's entrance, and it listed off the many reasons sex with Gray, aside from the actual act itself which she knew would be fabulous, would be a terrible idea.

1. Gray was Lexi's close friend and having a one-night stand with your close friend's close friend was a no-go.
2. According to Lexi, Gray didn't do that anyway and was looking for commitment—the exact opposite of her.
3. Gray... He...

Huh... That was odd. She was sure there had been a three, four, and five the last time she'd fallen down the "Can't I just sleep with Gray once and get it over with already?" rabbit hole.

Gil came out from the back and Sam was brought back to the present when he said, "I'm headed out, Sam, but Joan and Larry will be here with you until lock up."

"Sounds good, boss."

He shot her an annoyed look at the boss comment, which had been the point of her saying it, then he said, "Thanks again for staying late today."

"No problem." And it wasn't. She rarely was on the desk but check ins and check outs were easy. Between people coming and going, she even got in a bit of reading or drafted out some ideas for social media and blog posts.

"Officer Hoffman," Gil said to Gray as he offered his hand for him to shake. Gil didn't like the formalities of his own title at work, but he insisted on it with customers—no, scratch that —clients. It was always doctor, miss, mister, father, whatever. It wasn't hard to imagine him running for office someday. She'd vote for him.

"Gil." Gray stood and shook his hand. "How's the arm?"

In a dramatic movement, Gil did a large circular motion with his right shoulder as if he didn't know how his arm was, but since Gray asked, he was suddenly just as eager to find out as well.

"It's getting there. Should be out on the greens just fine come spring." Remembering Sam behind him, Gil added, "Have you met our newest member, Sam? She's something, I tell you."

Sam tensed briefly, thinking Gray's grin at her held some mischief in it. For the briefest of seconds, she wondered if he would dare reveal to Gil the specific details of their meeting. Ever the professional, Officer Hoffman simply said, "I have, yes."

"Good, good. Officer Hoffman here has been a local client

on and off for years now. Though I would venture to guess you're gonna end up keeping this one."

Gray rubbed a hand behind his neck and shook his head. "I wish I could. Daisy's only with me for another month or so. Then her family will be back in their house and able to take care of her again." That did it. She almost, *almost*, hurtled over the desk to scoop the downtrodden man into her arms and perhaps even offer a pity fuck. Luckily for everyone involved, she resisted the urge.

Gil nodded in somber understanding. "Well, that's good news for Daisy, I suppose, but she sure will be missed by everyone here."

At a few minutes till, the club members began trickling in —Lexi and Sam, included.

The last time he saw Sam was that one time at Bark Sniff Wag. Each time he'd stopped in to see Lexi, Sam hadn't been around, and she was never working the desk whenever he'd picked up or dropped off Daisy. Maybe she was right, and he *was* showing some major stalking tendencies. Though in fairness he had already been doing all those things long before he'd ever met her.

Unlike with his poker game, Sam and Lexi weren't dressed like they were on the prowl. Lexi was in her usual jeans, sneakers, and sweater, while Sam was rocking—and yes, that was the correct word to use given her cocky swagger into the room—a long red cardigan over a snug-fitting white tee. Her black pants were fitted and ended above her ankles revealing black heels beneath. It was the perfect combination of business and casual. She topped off the look with a copy of the novel, cluttered with sticky notes sticking out here and there.

Even though she arrived looking like she was ready for a hostile takeover of the meeting, she didn't make any comments until close to the end.

"I have something I'd like to add," Sam said, her hand raised in the air as if they were in school. He knew it was coming. Had watched her throughout the meeting and noted how she bit her tongue and was careful not to dominate since she was one of the newest members.

"Sure. Let's hear it, Sam." He smiled back at her.

"I noticed the book doesn't pass the Bechdel Test."

Marcy and Lexi nodded in agreement, but the rest of the club looked as confused as Gray.

"What's the Bechdel Test?" asked Glenn, a fifty-something biology teacher at the local high school.

"It's used to determine if the media, in this case a book,

includes women to meet diversity quotas and further the male's character arc, or if the women exist in their own right as we do in reality."

Glenn's eyebrows perked up in interest as he considered the idea. "Do you have the list of questions?"

"It's not really a list. Books, movies, whatever, they only need to meet three criteria: two women, who are named, need to discuss something other than men."

It wasn't accusatory in tone, but Gray picked up on Sam's eagerness to point out the sexism in his selection. The nerve. Who went into a book club with the sole purpose of throwing shit in the fan? People in his book club, apparently. At least the wanna-be social-media influencer wasn't there to see it.

The members busied themselves thumbing through the pages of the book looking for any example of two named women discussing anything other than men. They made side comments to their neighbors and the words, "I'm sure I saw…" and "Where's that one part where…" were heard in different variations throughout the group.

Gray distinctly remembered a conversation Valerie had with that one character about architecture. She said she liked the building and the other woman mentioned who the architect was and why it was groundbreaking at the time that it had been built.

"Here," he said triumphantly, "on page 213. They're talking about the building."

Everyone flipped to 213 and breathed a sigh of relief that the book they'd all gushed about for the past hour was not low-level patriarchy propaganda.

"Yup, there it is. Valerie and Meryl, talking architecture. The architect was a woman, too, if I remember correctly, which I think I do," Glenn said.

Damn. Hearing it worded that way drove home the fact that his book barely passed the test.

"Her name's not Meryl," Marcy pointed out. "The narrator says Valerie thinks the bank teller looks like Meryl Streep and calls her that in her mind."

"Right," Sam said. "Like Curley's wife in *Of Mice and Men*; she's in multiple scenes and yet no one bothers to use her name. Though I give Steinbeck credit, he had a purpose in keeping her unnamed. I doubt," Sam paused as she checked the cover of the book for the author's name, "Laurens is making a similar statement."

Fuck. It didn't pass the impossibly simple test. He did a quick mental inventory of their past reads, and he wasn't entirely sure they'd pass either. He couldn't believe that it hadn't come up in their discussions before or that he'd never noticed it himself.

After the meeting, when everyone else had gone home, Gray took his time cleaning up as he replayed the meeting in his mind and wondered why he couldn't get it right. He only paused licking his wounds at the sound of Marcy's footsteps on the stairs.

"I told you I have it, Marcy. You and Buck head home. You've already done too much."

When he turned, he found Sam standing at the top of the steps. Her previous attitude was gone, replaced by something that looked entirely foreign to Sam's personality. It almost looked like regret.

"Hey."

"Hey?" His greeting came out as a question. "I locked the doors. How did you get in here?"

"Marcy gave me a key. I've been coming and going at odd hours setting up my closet area."

"Sure. Your own key. You've already been in town a month. It was time."

She wound a bit of hair around one of her fingers and he was shocked to see she appeared somewhat nervous. "I stand by what I said about the test and how your book failed it miserably."

Ah, all was right with the world again as Sam let her true self shine through once more. Gray continued with his cleaning efforts as he reorganized the chairs and tables back to their original spots.

Sam helped him with the chairs. "I probably could have handled it better rather than ambushing you at your own meeting."

He paused again. If he wasn't mistaken, there was some sort of genuine guilt or remorse in the way her eyes met his and the way the corners of her mouth turned down ever so slightly.

"Yeah, well. It's nothing I can't handle. And like you said, you were right."

"Maybe… but I didn't handle it the right way. I apologize."

Gray went back to his chairs. He didn't want to talk about it anymore, and he didn't want what felt like pity. He felt sorry enough for himself with a book club he couldn't get right, a foster pup who'd become family but was about to leave him, and the recent news that Jessa—a mere few months out of her relationship with him—was engaged to the guy she started dating right after him. Things were shitty enough without Sam, of all people, pitying him.

"Right. I'll leave you to it," she said as she set down the chair she was holding and turned to walk back down the steps.

"Wait." He glanced out the large picture windows at the pitch-black night. Tiny town or not, he didn't want her walking alone in the alley and parking lot. He'd seen too many things in his line of work. Not that he thought Sam was an easy target. He pitied anyone who would dare attempt to lay a finger on Sam. No doubt she would fuck them up, but there were bad people in the world, and it was easier to avoid the situation altogether. "I'm almost finished here. I'll walk you out."

She gave him a quizzical look. He could almost see the wheels in her brain turning as she analyzed if she should be offended by his offer.

"Sure. Thanks." Then she turned and busied herself with straightening a few display stacks while he tidied up the last bit of mess from the meeting.

"All set?" he asked.

She was working through some strategic book place-ments at the end of one of the aisles.

"Let me place these last few books."

"Does Marcy know you're rearranging her book displays?"

She set the last book on the holder and stepped back to get a better look at it. "It's my display." She pointed to a sign at the top of the display that read "Cat the Great Recommends…"

She'd found a handful of books that all had complemen-tary colors and images, though they weren't part of the same series or even sub-genre. He found his eyes naturally moving from one book to the next, and he could tell each one had been placed with the utmost thought. He could see why Marcy took such a quick liking to her.

"It looks good," he said with a nod.

"I know. Come on. We should go before I get started on something else."

He was glad he'd offered to walk her out, because when they got to her car, they found yet another flat tire.

"Have you met Smitty?"

Sam was already punching in a few messages on her phone. She sighed. "You already asked me this. No, I don't know who that is."

"Okay." Except that he couldn't let it go. It would only happen again in the future and odds were he wouldn't be there to help her out.

"Have you spoken with anyone about soap operas?"

Her fingers paused, and she looked up at him. "A guy at one of my book recs was asking for books similar to soap operas."

"Flannel shirt?"

"No, weird-ass kangaroo tee with a hairy middle finger."

"That's Smitty."

Another quick message on the phone, then it went back into her purse. "Are you telling me I have a stalker? And it's not you?"

"Smitty's not a stalker. I mean, he sort of is, since he obviously knows your car. But not like you're thinking. He just let the air out because you said something negative about his stories."

"His *stories*? Are you kidding me right now?"

Gray shrugged his shoulders. The tiny town had come to terms with Smitty's erratic tire flattening behavior. He was a war vet who experienced extreme head trauma overseas. Hadn't been the same since. It didn't make what he'd been doing right, but Gray also couldn't bring himself to arrest or formally charge Smitty with anything. No one else in town expected him to either. He went to counseling, and for the most part, seemed to be doing better.

"Come on. I'll give you a ride home, and I'll fill you in on Smitty."

The only way Gray could think to describe their drive was to say that it felt like home. He told her stories about Smitty and some of the other more notable townspeople, and he told her about his family and time as an EMT. She told him about growing up with her vet dad and taking on the family business and leaving it, and she told him about the end of her marriage and the random Christmas lights decoration documentary she and her friend Jackie were part of back in Milton last year.

Since it was a short drive home, most of the conversation happened in the driveway with the car idling. She had taken her seatbelt off and turned towards him. Gray, hyper-aware that his seatbelt was still on, didn't know how to nonchalantly unbuckle it at that point. They'd been parked for at least thirty minutes, and it still wasn't long enough for him. He feared any change or sudden movement from him would break the moment and send her running up the stairs to her apartment. To prevent that from happening, the car stayed on, his belt stayed buckled, and the radio stayed at a volume just above a whisper.

"Jackie told me the documentary is going to stream this summer. A whole Christmas in July thing due to some sort of scheduling issue. I don't know the details." Sam's eyes fixated on something beyond Gray—or perhaps they fixated on nothing at all as her mind wandered to the events that would be unfolding that summer.

"I was only there helping to make some of Jackie's Christmas displays. She randomly inherited a house whose entire street is part of a huge annual lights display, kind of like 34th Street in Baltimore, and the first year she moved in they happened to be filming it. She really felt the whole go-big-or-go-home pressure, so it was all hands on deck with family and friends to present something spectacular and never before seen. We dug up the front lawn to put in a temporary beach, created a temporary aquarium that took up her entire bay window, set up thousands of lights... The works.

"Anyway, it's mostly about Jackie and all her neighbors setting up their displays and doing the big reveal when the event officially begins the day after Thanksgiving. I doubt I even have that much screen time, but it's a fleeting glimpse into the end of my previous life, from an outside view."

The chic hanging lantern from Lexi's front porch shone in through the windshield, providing just enough light for him to make out the deep-rooted sadness in her eyes. He shifted slightly in his seat, unsure of how to comfort her or if she even wanted to be comforted at all. His sister, Bea, had always yelled at him for trying to fix her problems when all she wanted was someone to vent to.

He thought of his previous conversations with Bea, and instead of suggesting she not watch it, he asked, "Are you going to watch it?"

Her soft blue eyes left whatever object behind him they'd been fixated on and found his eyes again as she considered his question. "Absolutely. Mostly to support Jackie—she's so excited and she worked her ass off for it. She's always wanted her own design show on TV. This is probably as close as she'll get unless the documentary takes off. Not that she's that naïve to think that's a likely outcome. She's too practical to put all her eggs in that dodgy of a basket." A smile formed at the thought of her friend on TV in all her glory.

"Although to be fair, I worked my ass off for it, too, creating all of the larger outside metal displays for her underwater beach theme." She noticed his eyebrows arch upwards in surprise and added, "A while back I took on welding as a bit of a side hobby. It's not a big deal."

"That's not something most people randomly take on as a side hobby. It's impressive. Really."

Even in the dim lighting he could see her cheeks redden. It was cute.

"Our crowning achievement was a giant animatronic

Santa Claws crab to go out front of her house. It tipped its Santa hat and everything."

Her smile faded again when she continued. "Lots of good memories, for sure, but that's just the surface stuff. I'm also going to watch it because I have to see it for myself... Jeremy and me, together. This outside vantage point of us interacting."

Gray wanted so badly to reach out and cup her jaw, to run a reassuring thumb over her cheek. A tear ran down and he was a heartbeat away from reaching out for it. Sam beat him to it as she hastily ran the back of her hand across her face. The movement was enough to break the spell, just as he'd known it would.

She shook her head. "Ugh, I'm such a mess. Don't mind me and my fucked-up life." Her hands waved in front of her to emphasize her desire for him to forget it all.

He cleared his throat. "I, um, could come in... If you want. We can—" He wanted to suggest he go in with her, so they could finish their conversation.

Sam turned forward in her seat and ran another hand over her face as she regained her composure. "No, no," she said before he could finish what he was going to say. "I've got Lexi and Jackie's coming to visit this weekend. Besides, you've already done more than enough with the ride home and the book club, too."

He cocked an eyebrow at her. She was crying in his car, and yet she was throwing pity comments to *him*?

"No, I mean it. I was so set on calling out the lack of well-rounded females, I lost sight of everything else. I loved everything you had to say about Max. It was spot on with what I thought, too. And your question about Max's and Valerie's limited morality and the ethical implications of their decisions... You did good, Gray."

Had she still been turned and facing him, he was certain

they would have kissed. Her mood had done a complete turnaround from crying to looking at him with something akin to reverie. Instead, she leaned over the center console a few inches, decided against whatever it was she was going to do, and simply said, "Thanks for everything," before she climbed out of his car, hurried up the steep stairs, and disappeared into her apartment. She didn't look back.

CHAPTER 13: SAM

"Jackie!" Sam screamed as she put a vice-like grip on her oldest friend. She and Lexi had gotten close, but there was something to be said about oldest friends knowing her best.

"You look good. Really good, Sam," she said as pulled back to take a good look at her. They were on the tiny platform at the top of the steep stairway leading up to the apartment above the garage.

"Thanks! I love it out here. Come in, come in. I have wine and all the snacks. I want to hear about everything happening back home. Work, Scott, Babs, all of it." Sam grabbed Jackie's bags and led her into the kitchen area to uncork a bottle of red wine.

"The apartment looks great." Jackie hadn't been up there since they'd shared the room as kids and teens on vacation, and a lot had changed since then. The place had been mostly unfinished. Nothing but plywood floors and studs around the walls. As teens they'd painted the floors using whatever was leftover in old cans in the garage, and they'd created their own furniture with wood and cinder blocks. The current laminate flooring, actual walls, and store-bought furniture were quite the upgrade.

"Thanks. It was a disaster for a few weeks after I first moved in. Took more than a couple of late nights, but I think I'm finally settled. So... How's Scott?" Sam asked as they took their wine and bowls of snacks over to the couch.

"He's great. No regrets about switching over to photography. Working with Tim and doing real estate photos is a challenge sometimes, but in his spare time, he's building a portfolio to do portraits and other photographer-for-hire type work."

"And Babs?"

"My mom misses you so much. Actually, I have mail and a few items for you from her." Jackie reached into her overnight bag and pulled out an envelope.

"Really?" Sam asked when she saw the ornate lettering on the envelope and opened it up to find sturdy card stock with gold lettering.

"Really," Jackie confirmed.

"Holy shit. Babs is marrying Mort. Good for her." She pulled out her phone to put in the details in her calendar.

"I know. I never thought I'd see the day."

"Are you okay with it?"

Jackie's father, Tom, passed away their freshman year of college. For the longest time Babs eased her grief believing Tom had been reincarnated as a cat. She hadn't show any interest in dating for years afterwards.

"Yeah. Mort's a good guy."

Jackie watched Sam fill out the invite and place it back into the return envelope for Babs.

"No plus one?"

"No plus one."

"It's still a ways off. Maybe plus one now and by then—"

"Yeah, I don't think so." Sam was going to leave it at that, and Jackie would have let her, but if she couldn't tell her closest friends about her rejections, who could she tell?

"I had that thing with the hot cop." She'd already told Jackie a few stories about Gray.

"Where you both slept chastely in the same bed?"

"That's the one."

"That doesn't count because you were too injured for any boom-boom anyway, and *you* rejected *him* first."

Sam took a sip of wine. "Still, there was that rejection." Jackie rolled her eyes, but she didn't bother trying to correct her. "Then there was the manager at the barbecue place…"

"I don't think you told me about that one yet."

"It's too tragic. This one can only be told in person and with booze."

"Check, check there," Jackie said as she pointed to herself and raised her wine glass. "Besides, it can't be worse than that time my blind date stole from me, and I went out with him again hoping it was just a misunderstanding and he stole from me, again."

"It might be worse."

Jackie's eyes widened. "Now I have to know. Spill it." She topped off Sam's glass to take the edge off.

"Okay. I'm not even going to ask you not to laugh because I know that's not possible."

Jackie put a hand to her heart. "Thank you for that. You know me well." She took a sip. "Now let's hear it."

Sam took a breath, feigning that she was bracing herself to relive the trauma as she told the tale to Jackie. "I was at Dick's for lunch the other day. I was in a hurry, so I hit up their to-go wall for a sandwich and cornbread. At the counter some kid was getting trained on the register, so the manager was there with him."

Jackie nodded and nibbled on a hunk of cheese.

"I'm at the counter and the manager and I are making

eyes at each other. He's cuteish. Not someone I would notice at first, but he was flirting with me, and he had my attention. While the kid is hunting down the right buttons on the register, the manager asks, 'Do you wanna grab a drink?' and I play it cool; I'm like, 'Sure. Sounds good.' And then we're just staring at each other. Even the kid stops his hunting and pecking of keys to look at me expectantly. I start to panic because I've never done anything like this before. But I power through it, and I say, 'Do you want my number?' Again, trying to play it cool, I grab a napkin and the credit card signature pen off the counter and write out my number for him.

"The manager makes no move to take the number, and it's just hanging limply from my hand. Then he says, 'I meant a soda for the combo meal: sandwich, cornbread, and a drink for $5.99.'"

Jackie made zero effort to hide her shock, horror, and amusement at the tragic scene Sam had laid out for her. "What did you do with the number?" The question was hesitant—she was afraid to hear how the train wreck ended, and yet she needed to know.

"I was still trying to make the connection that he wasn't asking me out and was actually helping me to get a good deal on my order, when the kid at the register reached out and snatched up my number napkin."

Jackie raised a glass to the kid at the register. "A bold move. You sure you want to rule out the register trainee?"

"I don't even think he's legal." Sam put her hands over her face and sank back into the couch, willing it to swallow her up whole and save her from her newfound spinster, celibate life.

Jackie poked Sam and said, "So you haven't…"

"Nothing." She peeked through a crack between her

fingers to properly accuse Jackie. "You should have warned me how hard dating as an adult is."

"I bitched about it all the time! You watched it play out with Scott. We're happy ever after now, but that was years in the making. Years."

Sam groaned. "I can't go that long without sex."

"Not if you spend every night getting all hot and bothered reading spicy romance novels, you can't." Jackie motioned to the stack of Amazon Prime boxes by the door. "More books?"

Accepting that the couch would not be consuming her that night, she sat back up. "I can't help what I like to read. And I'm not even buying them anymore. Mostly, it's authors and publishers sending me their books."

Jackie looked around the apartment at the small piles of books scattered across the counters and tables, and at the overflowing bookshelves.

"Sam, that's amazing! Tell me all about it! I'll top us off." Jackie went to refill their glasses while Sam pulled up her website on her laptop. Her book review work had become a lifesaver of sorts for her, helping her through the shittiest of times as she buried herself in her reading and review writing, or even just checked her numbers. Her blog hits and comments served as cheers from an unseen audience:

"You're fabulous!"

"We love you and your giant, sexy brain!"

"Do more! Do more! What would we ever do without you?!"

Okay, so none of the comments had ever come close to that, but the effect was still the same, and she wasn't sure where she'd be without her blog to fall back on.

"Here," Sam said to Jackie as she pointed to the lowest mark on the graph, "is when I did my first post. It says five hits, but that's just me. I visited it five times that day. And then here." She pointed to a small spike not far off from the first point. "That's where I first posted on Instagram, and a few people clicked my website link in my profile."

Sam changed the timeline to show the entirety of her blog life. The first two points were non-existent in the larger graph since her blog hits went to just under a thousand hits each day.

Jackie checked her phone. "It's not even four and 578 people have already visited your blog today?"

Even though *Cat the Great Reads Smut* had already been successfully climbing the search engine ranks for a few months, Sam shared in Jackie's excitement and amazement. It still surprised her as well since it started as a hobby. Something she did more for herself than for anyone else. To be getting comments from around the world about her posts and reviews was mind blowing.

"And…" Sam continued as she pulled up another page on her site that showed her new table display and nook at the bookstore, "I'm a bit of a personal book shopper, if you will, for romance novels."

"You're working at Paging All Bibliophiles?" As kids, they'd both fantasized about running a bookstore together in some exotic location. Holding book chats one hour a week at a bookstore owned by someone else in Western Maryland didn't exactly fit the bill, but at this point in their lives, it was obviously as close as either would get to that dream.

Sam tilted her head right and left as she considered Jackie's question. "Not exactly working. I don't get a paycheck or anything. But I get to talk to people about books, which I love to do, and it's good business for the blog. I can post pictures of myself at the store on my blog page and on my social media accounts which is a huge benefit for me."

"Fuck guys. You're doing just fine on your own." Jackie raised her glass in a toast.

Sam raised hers to clink glasses. "True. I'm crushing it on

my own, but that doesn't mean I don't want a nice shag every now and then."

"Babs thought you might need a little help in that department." Jackie pulled a large purple satin pouch from her overnight bag and handed it to Sam.

"Babs thought I might need help getting laid?"

"Yes, when I told her I was visiting, she gave me this bag and said, 'It's to help her get laid.'" Sam narrowed her eyes trying to determine if she was serious, so Jackie added, "No, obviously she didn't say anything like that. She said starting over is difficult and you may need a little boost."

Sam took the pouch and pulled out a white candle.

"Chakra candle?" Sam asked. It was one of Babs's go-to gift ideas.

"A navel chakra candle. To help stoke the fires of your inner confidence."

She took a whiff of the sandalwood and myrrh scent—fitting for her current location in the wooded lake area of Deep Creek.

"Babs rocks," she said as she replaced the candle lid. "I'll light it tomorrow and send her a thank-you text and picture."

"And she sent this, too." Jackie pulled out a large paper bag with "Samantha" written in colorful flowing letters across the front.

"Aw, pretty." She took the bag from Jackie and went to open it, but it was stapled shut.

"You're supposed to burn it."

Sam tried to peek inside with no luck. "What's in it?"

"Didn't ask. Didn't want to know."

Tentatively, she sniffed at the top. Babs was into tarot readings, auras, and the like. But every now and then, she'd take it further than that, and she wondered if this was one of those occasions. Best not to find out.

"It's not too cold out tonight. Not too windy either. We can use the fire pit out back; I haven't seen a bear in weeks."

"Perfect! I'll grab the wine." Jackie, making herself completely at home as Sam knew she would, grabbed a few plastic tumblers and some bottles of wine.

"Grab one for Lexi, too, please. I'll text her now to let her know we're heading outside."

The women were bundled up in coats, gloves, and hats as they sat around the fire. Music played from a portable speaker, and they'd banished all phones from the area. The Babs bag had been successfully burned with zero casualties (that they were aware of since no one dared to open the bag before tossing it into the flames) and Lexi and Sam had moved on to chucking their granny panty underwear into the fire while Jackie egged them on.

"What are you doing?" Gray's deep voice boomed from behind them, followed by the sounds of Daisy's excited barks.

"Nothing," Sam said. Like a child who'd just been caught stealing, she hastily threw her last pair into the flames. It was the ones with the bleach spots and the holes that showed the elastic beneath. No way did she want Officer Gray, looking hotter than sin in his rustic outdoor wear, to catch her red-handed with a pair of those.

"Come here, Daisy!" Lexi laughed as the pup licked at her face. "We're torching all our gross old underwear. It's part of an official cleansing ritual."

"Lex," Sam hissed. Damn. She really didn't have even an inkling of a crush on the man if she could divulge all of that to him.

"Makes sense," he deadpanned. "At the end of my shift I got a noise complaint. No surprise that you're part of it,

Sam." But his tone and expression didn't match his words. From the smirk on his face, and the look of intrigue as he walked towards the fire, he was nothing but amused by their antics.

While Lexi quizzed Gray on who made the complaint—most of the houses on the street were empty rentals or full of vacationers who were often louder than the women were that night—Jackie whispered to Sam, "Is this hot cop?"

She nudged Jackie to keep her voice down. Drunk Jackie's whispers were a bullhorn over the water. She was sure the Duhnman family across the cove had just heard her.

"Yes, and don't you dare say anything," Sam threatened in what she hoped was a hushed tone.

"It was Mitsy," Lexi announced to Sam and Jackie. Then she killed the music because clearly it was traveling down the water to Mitsy's house.

"Ugh… I should have known." By then, Sam had had the pleasure of meeting Mitsy in person when Mitsy had stopped by their house to drop off a neighborhood community watch newsletter. Along with tips on how to accurately set up porch cameras and adequate property lighting, it also included a police sketch of Sam dressed like a prostitute. The words, "Don't let Lake Shore become the next Red-Light District," shouted from above the image in large, aggressive, red block lettering. Lexi insisted she hang it on her fridge. Mitsy had looked right at Sam, who had been in her work clothes and had her hair back in a ponytail, and had given her a long lecture about how the neighborhood hadn't always been like that, but it was up to all of them to get help get it back to its former prostitute-free glory.

"Who's Mitsy?" Jackie practically shouted.

Lexi gave a brief but succinct rundown of who Mitsy was before turning her attention to Gray. "But, more important-ly…. Gray, this is Sam's friend from Milton, Jackie. Jackie, this is Gray. He's been my closest friend and confidant for the past year."

Jackie shook Gray's offered hand. "Gray, the jackass cop who gave Sam a speeding ticket her first day in town. So nice to put a face to the name."

"That's me." He gave Sam a wink and a devilish-looking grin. It should have annoyed her, so she gave the appropriate sneer in response, but inside she was lighting up hotter than the fire pit at that self-assured wink and smirk.

"Right. The one who runs the male-dominated book club," Jackie pushed. She was treating the visit to see Sam as a bit of a vacation, so she was drinking like a vacationer as well.

"Still me," he said, unaffected by the comment. "Been talking about me much, Sam?" Jackie would have kept shaking his hand all night if Gray hadn't released it.

"No," Sam said at the same time Jackie said, "She sure has."

Sam narrowed her eyes at Jackie who shrugged and mouthed back, *He's hot.*

"You should stay. Join us," Lexi offered as she passed Gray a beer. Before Sam could even begin to process the change in the night's itinerary, Lexi added, "Leo's on his way over, too."

Gray and Sam locked eyes, each searching to see if the other knew anything about why Leo was showing up.

Jackie, the newest member of the crew, asked, "Who's Leo?"

Lexi gave yet another rundown for Jackie while Gray tentatively took a drink and looked at Sam for some sort of confirmation about the status of Leo and Lexi's friendship. He wouldn't get anything from her; she was still trying to catch up herself. She and Lexi hadn't been spending as much time together lately with their increasingly busy schedules, so it was possible she and Leo had become chummy without Sam noticing.

"You and Leo are friends now?" Gray asked when Lexi finished talking.

Sam couldn't tell if his reaction was fueled by hurt or confusion—maybe a mixture of both. Either way, she couldn't help but feel a touch of jealousy thinking Gray didn't want Lexi dating Leo because maybe Gray wanted to date Lexi all along.

"Yeah. We are."

"When did that happen? *How* did that happen?" he asked.

Instead of answering him, she looked at Sam and said, "I didn't mention it earlier, but Leo showed up at the grief support meeting the second time I went."

Sam had gone to the first meeting, but afterwards Lexi assured her she was okay to fly solo from then on.

"Leo was at grief counseling?" Gray asked at the same time Sam said, "And now you guys are... together?"

She hadn't thought their interactions during poker had been promising, but maybe Lexi saw something in him that the others had overlooked.

Gray shook his head. "Together? Where is all of this coming from? Leo doesn't need grief counseling, and he doesn't do relationships."

Lexi finally turned back to Gray and loudly asked, "How are you even friends with him when you think he's such a jerk?" It was the first time Sam had ever heard Lexi raise her voice.

Gray didn't flinch, but Jackie did. "I'm going to run in and get some things. Anyone need anything? No?" She barely gave them time to answer, and no one did, before she disappeared into the house, snagging a bottle of wine on her way in. Given the light dinner Jackie had eaten that night and the excess of booze, Sam had a feeling that was the last they'd see of her until morning. She'd likely pass out on the couch within the next half hour, mid-conversation with her boyfriend Scott via text message.

"I don't think he's a jerk. He's a great guy, but he's probably slept with every woman in the area between the ages of 18 and 40. I've never seen him *date* any of them." He grimaced and then turned to Sam. "Not that there's anything wrong with that, if that's what you want to do."

Sam and Lexi exchanged questioning looks. Did Gray think Sam slept around?

Before she could call him out for his hasty judgments towards her sex life, he turned back to Lexi and added, "You're better than some guy who can't commit." After a few beats of silence he said, "I don't want to see you get hurt."

"*He's* hurt," Lexi shot back. "It's not my place to give specifics, but we got to know each other in grief counseling. There's a reason he's struggled with commitment before. And we *both* have massive baggage, but he's willing to take a chance with me, and I'm willing to give him a chance."

"Hey, guys," Leo called from the yard as he made his way over to the fire. They all turned to see him, and she was sure every one of them was thinking the exact same thing: *Leo just heard everything we said.*

CHAPTER 14: GRAY

D aisy was nestled in Sam's lap as she sat in one of the
Adirondack chairs around the fire. "Keep an eye on
Dee for me?" Gray asked her. Without waiting for a response
from her, he turned and walked over to where Leo was, a few
yards from the fire pit. Behind him he heard Sam say to Lexi,
"Tell me everything. I had no idea…"

"Leo," Gray said. They were a few yards from the fire pit
and out of earshot of the women.

Since he couldn't articulate anything beyond Leo's name,
Leo filled in the gaps for him. "Looks like Lex told you all.
This wasn't exactly how we planned on doing that."

"I'm not mad about Lexi," Gray offered. He wanted to get
that out of the way so he could ask him about all the other
stuff. He was supposed to be one of Leo's closest friends, and
he had no idea that he was in grief counseling or what he
could be going to meetings for. He'd given Leo plenty of shit
for being a womanizer. Leo had only laughed about afterwards, but clearly there had been so much more to it that
they'd all missed.

"Very generous of you." Leo started to walk past Gray to get to Lexi, but Gray stopped him.

"Wait. Just talk to me for a minute. Please."

Leo looked down at Gray's hand, holding a beer pressed against Leo's chest. After relieving Gray of his beer, Leo took a sip and took a step back to hear him out.

"I didn't know... I'm sorry." Without the beer to occupy his hands, they felt useless. He stuffed them into his pockets and forced himself not to look down to the ground, no matter how badly he wanted to.

"It's fine. It was a while ago." He started to walk again, and Gray stopped him. He couldn't remember the last time he'd had a conversation with Leo with actual substance. They'd spoken briefly at the bachelor party about various ideas: marriage, kids, politics, careers. But in the end, the comments were a light form of sparring as they toed around the heavy stuff. Everyone abided by the unwritten rule that the trip was a fun vacation from their everyday life, and a celebration of Ronan's impending nuptials. Deep conversations that could have hindered their buzz were not expected nor were they welcomed.

"Just wait. Don't you want to talk about it?"

Leo gave a jaded laugh. "Do I want to talk about my grandmother dying five years ago and my crappy childhood? No. I don't, Gray."

There it was. He remembered going to her funeral, but he didn't remember Leo being all that affected by it. At least nothing beyond what any of them experienced or showed when one of their grandparents had died. Gray also knew very little about a crappy childhood. He'd met Leo's distant father, but Leo never talked about his mother and the guys never asked.

Leo turned to walk away, and he let him. It was unfair of Gray to corner him on his visit to see Lexi. Unfair of him to try to repair years of damage and misunderstandings in a quick conversation off to the side. He'd eventually get a chance to talk to him when Leo was ready. In the meantime, he needed to get used to the idea of him and Lexi together.

Gray followed him to the fire pit. Lexi hopped up from the chair, and she and Leo embraced like the lovers they apparently were. It still sat uneasy with Gray, even after he knew a bit of their backstory. He looked to Sam for mutual support on the "Save Lexi's Heart" bandwagon, but he found none. Her expression was like Bea's when she was watching the end of a Hallmark movie.

When Lexi broke away, she turned to Gray who had taken a chair next to Sam. "Now that you all know about us, I wanted to tell you I asked Leo to take me as his date to the wedding."

"I told her she didn't have to ditch you. I don't mind if you still take her," Leo said as his gloved fingers interlaced with Lexi's, and they snuggled up on the bench on the other side of the fire.

"No," Gray said. "She should go with her boyfriend—you. She should go with you." There was no way Gray was going to take another man's girlfriend to a wedding, especially when that other man was a friend who was going to be there as well.

"You can take Sam!" Lexi called out, as if she had the winning answer to a trivia game.

"Oh, God no," Sam said with a laugh.

"Why not?" Leo asked. "You know all the guys already, and Lexi." Leo squeezed Lexi's hand and then brought it up to his lips to kiss the knitting of her glove.

"Gray and I don't…." Sam flicked her wrist as if the wave of her hand conveyed everything she left unsaid. Her legs up on the edge of the pit, she finished her beer and looked into the flames beyond her feet.

"It's fine. I don't mind going solo," Gray said. He certainly wasn't going to beg her or anyone else to go with him. He wasn't *that* hard-up to find a date that he'd need to resort to pleading or quid pro quos. When he looked up, he found Lexi's face was full of pity.

"Really," he insisted. "I was only taking you to help you get out and meet new people. I don't need a date." He got up to get himself a beer from the open cooler on the back patio. The snow had melted but the night temperatures were still cold enough to keep their drinks at the perfect temperature without ice.

"You need a date," Lexi insisted. "No date means an empty seat at your table and a meal that won't be eaten." She was the master of wedding planning among them, having been the only one to plan one of her own, so he didn't question it.

"And you marked plus one, Leo?" Gray asked. It was hard to believe someone like Leo would show up to a wedding attached. He could have sworn that when Ronan had first announced his engagement, Leo and Jon had made some bawdy comments about looking forward to the bridesmaids.

"No." He turned to face Lexi, his hand falling on the top of her thigh and gently rubbing like he needed to touch her and would settle for whatever he could take. "But then Lexi and I got coffee after our meeting, and I just knew. I called Ronan that night to see if it was too late to change it. I wouldn't say why, though. Too afraid to jinx it, I guess." They gazed into each other's eyes, oblivious to the others around the fire.

As if remembering he was mid-conversation, Leo looked back to them and said, "I did tell them a few days later though. Mel was all over rearranging everything. Said she couldn't wait to double date again with some of Ronan's friends instead of just hers all the time."

A dull ache formed in Gray's gut, and it refused to budge,

regardless of how much numbing booze he ingested. He and Jessa had done dinners, wine tastings, concerts, axe throwing, and road trips with Mel and Ronan. Hearing Leo mention his plans gave Gray an unexpected realization: The old Foo Fighters t-shirt he'd stumbled across in the closet, the one that pissed him off enough that he'd ticketed Sam, his anger hadn't at all been about Jessa. It was that they'd gone to the concert together as one of their first double-dates. The feeling associated with the shirt wasn't his lingering, undying love for Jessa, but a remembrance of the excitement he'd felt seeing how well Mel and Jessa had gotten along. It was a reminder of the broken promise of all the outings and fun times that he had thought they had in their future.

"Speaking of…" Lexi said as she gave a sweet nudge to Leo's side. "We should probably call it a night soon if we're going to get up early tomorrow and hike to the falls with them."

Leo casually reached across to check her watch. "Oh, shit. You're right. I didn't realize how late I was getting here."

"Don't worry about it. A few more weeks—months tops— and you'll be out of there."

And then they actually nuzzled noses before kissing. It was too much, too soon. Right? He once again turned to Sam for support in his concern, and once again he was met with a face that melted in their romance.

"You're leaving Poradma?" he asked when he finally registered what Lexi and Leo were talking about. It truly was a night of surprises. Gray knew Leo didn't love his IT job or his current boss, but he hadn't realized he was on the verge of quitting.

Leo pulled away from Lexi to answer. "I put out a few feelers to see what's out there. Turns out there's plenty if you have the home office set-up I do. A lot of places will let me work from home with minimal traveling—sometimes only a week or two a year of travel time. I have a handful of Zoom interviews lined up for next week." He stood and reached for Lexi's hand. "Alright, we'd better head in. You guys need anything out here?"

Gray was about to stand to head out himself when Sam asked, "Can you throw two more logs on before you go?" Maybe he wasn't leaving after all.

Leo placed two logs on the fire and set two more next to the pit for them for later. Daisy's head perked up at the sound of the sliding door and she leaped from Sam's lap to follow Leo and Lexi into the warm house, leaving Gray and Sam alone with the rejuvenated fire.

CHAPTER 15: SAM

W hile Gray and Leo had had their heart-to-heart by the house on the wrap around porch, Lexi and Sam had done the same at the fire. Lexi told her everything once Sam promised to keep it to herself, as if Lexi had even needed to remind Sam of that.

Their first night out after the grief counseling meeting, they'd gone for coffee. Leo had already shared a large portion of his history during the meeting, but he'd wanted her to have the full picture of what he'd been through.

As they sipped their coffees, Leo detailed out his childhood: mainly a mother who walked out when he was a little kid and a father addicted to painkillers. When it became obvious he wasn't fit to raise Leo and his two younger brothers, Leo's grandmother took them in. The memories were sometimes fuzzy for him, but he was with his grandmother for a large chunk of time when he was in elementary school.

By the time he and his brothers finally got back under their dad's roof, his dad had turned into a different person. No longer on painkillers, which was good, but still mostly absent emotionally from their lives. Lexi had explained to Sam how there was much more to it, but that was the gist of why Leo had spent so many years not getting too close to anything resembling a relationship with anyone outside of his small group of close friends.

After Lexi and Leo went inside for the night, Gray asked what she and Lexi had discussed while he'd been talking with Leo. Sam knew the question was coming. It was the main reason she'd asked for more wood after everyone else had called it a night. She wanted to give him a chance to talk to someone if that was what he needed.

She took another long swig of her wine. She'd felt mildly drunk when he'd first shown up and she'd been throwing undergarments into the fire with Lexi, but she'd slowed down since then so her head wasn't too cloudy for serious conversations.

"Just some background," she said. "Some context for… everything." She turned back to the fire, mesmerized by the flickering flames.

He continued to stare her down. "You're not going to tell me?"

"It's between them."

"It's not if Lexi told you about it."

"She confided in me as a friend, and she knew I would worry about her if I didn't know. You should ask her, or Leo." She knew that one would sting slightly, but she was serious about letting Gray, Leo, and Lexi sort it out between themselves. It wasn't her place.

"I did. He didn't want to talk about it."

"No. Not here, he won't. Take him out for coffee, like Lexi did."

"Funny."

"I'm serious. Have you ever gone out for a coffee or something with Leo, or Ronan, or Jon?"

She could almost see the montage of scenes with his

friends playing out in his mind as he skimmed everything, looking for an instance where they were getting coffee only for the sole purpose of talking or shooting the shit.

"No. We go to the batting cages and driving ranges, or we go camping and hiking. We talk there."

He turned in the oversized chair and Sam noted how that slight gesture, not even something out of the ordinary really, made her uneasy at the idea that all his attention was on her. Not uneasy in a negative way, but more that she hoped she lived up to whatever expectations he had for the conversation, and that he would deem her worthy of his attention in the future.

She and Jeremy had used similar communication strategies throughout their marriage. When a rift had grown between them, they filled their schedules with joint activities, just the two of them, to reconnect and get their conversations going again. But the activities only served as distractions from all the meaningful conversations they should have been having. It sounded a lot like had happened between Gray and his friends.

"There's too much noise at those places," she said. "You end up talking about what's happening around you or talking about your hits and drives."

He rubbed his five-o'clock shadow. "And to avoid that, you think I should call Leo up to see if he wants to get coffee with me?"

"Yeah, I do. It doesn't have to be coffee, but no sports or any other activity that requires thinking."

There was silence as they both looked back to the fire. Then he gave a noncommittal, "Yeah, maybe."

Gray glanced down at his beer and thought about getting another. At least that's what she assumed he was doing, since she was doing the same. He'd had two drinks, and she knew from their poker night he wouldn't drive home that night if he had another.

"I'm going to top off my wine. You want a beer?" Was that light and airy? Probably not given the awkward hand gestures that followed. There was comfort in having her hands in her pockets, but she had gloves on. Undeterred, she tried to shove them into her pockets anyway, gloves and all. It didn't work out. She looked like she was rubbing her belly as her gloves slipped over the pocket openings each time she tried. Finally, she gave up and crossed her arms before remembering that it made her look closed off, and she dropped them again before picking up her empty wine glass.

She'll never know if he was originally going to get that third drink or not when she first stood up, but there was something about her awkwardness that disarmed him. One corner of his mouth eased up into a smile and he said, "Sure. I might as well. Daisy is probably already passed out inside after a full day of doggie day care."

Sam got them each a fresh drink and sat back down in her seat. She turned once again to face Gray as the fire no longer interested her nearly as much as he did. She couldn't tell if she'd changed, or he did, or maybe she'd just misread him all along. Either way, there was very little about Gray that annoyed her anymore. The urge to lift a middle finger in his direction had completely dissipated.

Gray cleared his throat and shifted in his seat, the sudden movement pulling Sam back to reality. "What's your plan here, Sam?"

"I'm not sure. I guess finish this drink while the fire dies down again. Maybe call it a night after that?"

He chuckled at her response. "I mean, how long are you staying in town? How long will you be living with Lexi?"

"Oh, right. Long-term plans... huh..." She picked at a loose thread on her gloves, choosing her next words carefully. "I was running away from everything, obviously." Her eyes darted up to his to see if there was any accusation in his expression. She found nothing but interest and undivided attention as his dark eyes, practically black in the night, focused on hers.

"I thought I'd find some crappy job to take my mind off things and regroup. Head home a few months later once I had everything sorted out."

"But now you're staying longer?"

Did he want her to stay? If she allowed herself to indulge in fantasies—and she often did as perhaps a side effect of reading so many romance novels—she could hear the tiniest ask in his voice. It wasn't an ask about if she was staying; it was an ask to see if she would stay for him. Okay, so that was a stretch even for her, but they were alone, at night, by a fire and sharing a drink. Without the stereo playing, they could hear the music from the woods and lake surrounding them, and they could clearly see the stars above them with the lack of light pollution. How could her mind not jump to that romantic conclusion?

"Now," she continued, "things are different. I love my job and living with Lex. Aside from some residents, Mitsy and Smitty, to name a few, I adore this town even more than when I visited as a kid. And I love working with Marcy at the store."

He gave a slight nod of confirmation. "Then you should come with me to the wedding. Ronan and Mel were both born and raised here, and Mel's a sort of local celebrity. Half the town'll be there. It'll be a good opportunity for you to meet more locals."

Crimson spread across her cheeks. She could have sworn she'd blown it when she responded so rudely to Lexi's initial suggestion that she join him at the wedding. It was a defense mechanism to reject him before he'd had a chance to reject her. Even so, she weighed her response so as not to look too eager. He was being polite and doing it as a favor to her. It was not a date.

"Are you sure?" *Stupid, stupid, stupid...*

"It's hardly a hardship, and I think it would be good for you, and you know… your goal."

"My goal?"

"Yes, your goal…. The have-epic-sex-with-everyone goal. I saw your list on the table the other night." He took a sip and clearly wanted to disappear into his beer.

She felt her jaw slacken as her mouth slid open in abject horror at the idea of Gray thinking she literally wanted to shag everyone.

"That was a joke… To make Lexi blush…"

Despite the cold, he was the one whose face was burning red. "Well, yeah, I figured. But still, I'm sure you want to get out and meet people."

"It's because of the books I read, right?"

He held up his hands. "Look, I'm not judging-"

"You are! And you did that first day when you pulled me over."

He tilted his head towards her, giving her the are-you-freaking-kidding-me look. "You were speeding because you were too distracted listening to… I don't even know what I'd call that. Word porn, I suppose, though in truth I think the porn I watched as a teen was much more realistic—and that's saying something."

Sam threw her head back as she let out a roar of laughter. "I was only listening to it as a favor to an author who wanted a review. One I knew I couldn't give once I listened to the book."

He let out a laugh that rivaled hers in tone and in the way it came from deep down within him. "I thought… it was so bad… and that's not even how it all works…" He managed to get out between his fits of laughter.

"I know that! I know how everything works! I really do!"

When they collected themselves again, Sam said, "I still need you to admit that you were judging me without properly getting to know me first."

If she'd expected him to bow down to her and beg for forgiveness, she was quite mistaken about whom she was dealing with. "What about you? The next morning, I had the door slammed in my face, and you flipped me off. You were the judgmental one."

Sheepishly, she swirled her wine glass. "You're right. I wasn't in a good place those first few weeks, and I'm sorry that I treated you that way." It wasn't difficult for her to say the words. She'd had a gnawing feeling in her gut that she'd been in the wrong, and it was a relief to say as much to him.

"Forgive me?" She tilted her head down slightly so her eyes were batting up towards him, and she said it with the faintest hint of huskiness in her voice. The first part had been a genuine apology. But somewhere along the way, when the relief of admitting her past errors lifted the weight off her chest, she took it ten steps further and slid right into flirting. At least she hoped it counted as flirting. It had been far too long to know for sure.

To her relief, his right eyebrow, the one right above the hot-as-fuck crescent scar she was certain he'd gotten in some uber sexy and manly way, twitched ever so slightly as he picked up what she was throwing down.

He took the last sip of his beer as he considered his options. "Unfortunately, it's not that simple."

Sam was shocked. Was straight and narrow Gray Hoffman really about to proposition her with something sexual as part of some sort of retribution for her past wrong doings?

"It's not?" she asked coyly, playing along with his banter to see where he was going with it all.

"Your words, and in all fairness, I would say drunken words based on what I've seen of your behavior tonight, sound empty and insincere."

Her jaw dropped. "You don't accept my apology? What satisfaction can you have tonight?"

He paused and shot her a look. "Did you really just quote *Romeo and Juliet?*"

"Did *you* really pick out that one line as a quote from *Romeo and Juliet?*"

"I have a younger sister who was obsessed with Leonardo DiCaprio."

"Fair enough," she conceded. No need to tell him she and Jackie had also been "fans" of Leo and could quote the entire movie verbatim, as well as sing every song from the soundtrack.

"So… what kind of satisfaction then, if not an apology?" Fuck. That half smile rose, and she melted into her chair. She really hoped he wasn't being sleazy. It didn't seem his style, but then she had to admit that she still didn't know him all that well.

"A book."

The word released a dam of wetness down below. Not sex. He wanted literature. He wanted literature that she recommended. Regency was her most loathed romance sub-genre, but at that moment she understood the whole swooning thing, because had she not been seated, she would have done it herself. The sexy, tattooed, dog-loving cop wanted a book.

Still not believing she was hearing him correctly, she cocked an eyebrow at him. "A book?"

He lifted one shoulder to suggest how nonchalant he was about the whole thing. "Marcy's been non-stop telling me about your smutty book-whispering skills. Figured I should see for myself, especially now that I know you weren't enjoying that audiobook I caught you listening to." Gray produced one of her business cards from his wallet. "You have your own business cards, right? You must be good."

"That is me. Yes. Alter ego Cat on the off chance my parents ever stumbled upon my site."

Gray carefully placed the card back in his wallet as Sam chewed her bottom lip. She hadn't been ready that night after poker, but that didn't mean she was clear of all regrets. Many a night since then, she'd laid in bed playing out in her mind the hot sex she could have had if she hadn't been so hell bent on seeing him as nothing more than a jackass disguised as a hot guy.

Her lady parts would never forgive her if she let another opportunity pass with nothing to show for it. First impressions of Gray and his crew left her assuming they were life-long players of the game—always on the prowl for the next beautiful woman. From what she'd seen of Leo and Lexi, she'd been dead wrong about him. And given Gray's hands-off approach (hands off her, that is, since he'd been all over himself in her bed) she could tell he was too nice of a guy to make a move on her when she'd already denied him once before. Especially when he knew she'd been drinking all night. She would have to make the first and probably second, third, and fourth move if she wanted anything to happen.

"Alright," Sam said as she stood up and doused the fire with the bucket of water. "Let's head upstairs, and we'll get you matched up with the perfect smutty romance."

CHAPTER 16: GRAY

He looked around the apartment and was surprised to find that beneath the chaos he'd witnessed before, lurked a clean and seemingly well-organized living area. Yet another thing he'd misjudged about her.

If there was any question about how long they were going to be perusing her book collection, she put it to bed by taking off her coat and offering to hang his up as well. It was warm up there, so he gladly gave it up and rolled up his sleeve. He didn't miss her eyes finding the bit of tattoo that crept out from beneath his sleeve.

She was all business as she led him over to the social-media famed bookshelf. Though there wasn't a definitive organizational strategy from what he could see, it appeared she kept most series together, and there was a certain aesthetic appeal to the way she'd grouped similar and complementary colors throughout.

"Alright, Gray," she said as she jokingly cracked her knuckles and stretched her neck in anticipation of some heavy lifting on her part. "I'll be giving you the noobie treatment tonight. And while I know it's not your first time, and we won't be popping your smutty-book cherry, so to speak, I still promise to be gentle." She reached out and gave his forearm a brief, reassuring squeeze. "Are you ready?"

Her hand fell back to her side, but the feeling of her skin on his remained. "I *was* ready..."

"That's the spirit." She gave him a wink and Gray wondered at which point they'd switched positions so that he was the timid and unsure party while she took on the opposite role, coming off as cocky and yet irresistibly charming.

"Are you interested in something—"

"I want the book that made you melt." He needed to even the playing field. They may have been in her apartment and discussing her favorite pastime, but he wasn't used to being passive with women he was interested in. Sure, he was polite and respectful of boundaries (hence his actions the last time he was there) but it was part of his natural instincts to go after what he wanted.

While she was at a loss for words, he continued. "Don't ease me into this, and don't play coy. Let's not pretend I didn't wake up jerking off in your bed last time I was here, mumbling about Mercury from *Fire Down Below*."

Sam was cute when she was caught off guard, but if she felt at all uncomfortable with what he was saying, she didn't show it. Instead, he felt her eyeing him up as if assessing whether he could in fact handle whatever book she was considering loaning to him.

"On one condition," she countered.

"Name it." *Please be that we act out every filthy scene in the book*, his dick pleaded as his brain waited for her terms.

"You pose with it for me. Shirtless. I'll use it on social media and maybe on my blog, but I'll make sure I don't include your face or your name."

She held out her hand and Gray took it, appreciating the

soft, smooth feeling of her skin. He hoped whatever she had in mind for her picture, it didn't involve him losing his jeans. The thick denim was the only thing keeping his growing excitement from being detected.

"Deal."

"Deal," she agreed. She pulled a tattered copy of *Autumn Fell* from one of the far corners of the bookcase.

"How many times have you read this?" He took the book and flipped through the pages, noticing scribbled notes here and there in the margins. Just like he did with his book club books.

"I couldn't say for sure. Dozens, maybe? I reread it at least once every fall. It speaks to me."

"And you're trusting me with it?"

"No offense, but you're the squarest guy I know. I'm picturing coasters regardless of condensation, turned down bed unless you're in it, weekly dusting of the top of the fridge... Am I right?"

Still fully clothed, Gray felt remarkably seen and naked. It was all eerily on point. "Do you know how much dust accumulates up there? I can see yours from all the way over here."

"No, you can't. Point is, I know it's safe in your care. Now, let me swap that one out for a prettier copy for the picture. And ditch the shirt while I get everything set up."

Within no time, Sam set up a ring light in front of the bookcase with her phone docked in the center. With the spotlight on him and Sam's critical eye behind the phone lens, Gray was mildly self-conscious of his pale winter skin and little handfuls of love handles, which age, along with his love of doughnuts, fed and maintained regardless of the hours he clocked at the gym.

Sam popped her head out from behind the phone. "Okay, shake your arms out, then go back to holding the book with both hands, one on the top corner and then one on the opposite bottom corner."

While he shook it out, she tapped a few times on her phone, and the loft filled with the vengeful lyrics of Taylor Swift.

"Really?"

"Yes, really. One, Taylor's exceptional. And B, it'll help you relax." She dropped her head behind the phone again, and Gray got back into position while she snapped more pictures.

"Okay, let's try something else..." Sam stepped around the light so she was right in front of Gray. With her eyes locked on his, she reached up and pushed a section of hair away from his forehead. When she felt the soft brush of her fingers along his hairline, his body begged to lean into them. To feel her fingers raking through his hair, tugging and pulling as their rendezvous heated up.

"I thought my face wouldn't be in it." There was zero accusation in his voice. In fact, it came out as practically a whisper.

"It's not." He was certain her eyes glanced down to his mouth. Her hands moved to his torso and began to ease his arms this way and that before moving on to the pristine copy of her beloved novel.

While she focused on tilting the book ever so slightly to the right and then back to the left, Gray noticed her tongue peeking out, an adorable testament to her level of commitment and concentration. Unfortunately, it was combined with the light grazing of her nails on his bare chest. Accepting defeat, he surrendered and stopped trying to fight the raging erection straining against his pants.

He cleared his throat and finally asked what he'd been dying to know since he first logged on to her website. "Who was your last model?"

"Scott. Jackie's boyfriend."

"Really? She didn't mind?" As if sensing the mood of the room and accommodating accordingly, Ed Sheeran came on and crooned about a gorgeous soulmate he would passionately love forever.

Sam chuckled. "No, she didn't mind. Jackie had the night of her life after that photo shoot. I had her doing all the adjustments and yes, I could almost see the electricity and sparks. By the time we finished, she practically dragged him away caveman style to have her way with him."

His voice turned rough when he said, "Lucky guy."

Her mouth drooped almost imperceptibly. "Sure is. Jackie's amazing."

Gray wanted to slap a hand to his forehead. He'd meant it in reference to how badly he wanted Sam to do the same with him.

Unaffected by his comment, she took a step back. Her brow furrowed as she tried to work out what wasn't working for the photo.

Believing he could salvage both the picture and his chances of taking things to the next level with her, he dropped his perfectly placed arms. "You don't like it because it's too similar to the picture with Scott."

He should know. He stared a little too long at that photo, trying to somehow discern from Scott's abs or pecs what kind of relationship he'd had with Sam.

Her eyes moved from his chest to his face as she considered his observation. "Yeah, I think you're right. The bookshelf is an easy go-to and I've been overdoing it."

She didn't ask for suggestions. After a few beats, he stopped waiting and offered his thoughts whether she wanted them or not.

"Let's use the bed."

They both looked at the bed as they considered their next

moves. Well, she considered her next move. From the moment he said it, Gray was all in. He walked over to the bed and got to work messing it up as if it had just been well used. He slipped off his jeans and made his way to the center in only his boxer briefs. Thanks to Sam's gentle caresses, he had an obvious hard-on which he tried to somewhat tuck at the top of his waistband. It didn't embarrass him in any way, but he wasn't sure how keen Sam would be on having *that* in her photo.

"Okay. Yeah, sure." Sam followed him over to the bed with her lighting equipment. Once she had it in place, he expected her to step back to get some shots from either side of the bed—perhaps even from the foot of the bed depending on her creative whims. Just as he'd caught her off-guard, suggesting and then occupying her bed, she did the same as she kicked her shoes off, climbed up on the bed, and planted a foot down on each side of his hips.

It did nothing to alleviate the strain of his length against the thin bit of fabric separating him from the gorgeous woman straddling him.

CHAPTER 17: SAM

"Alright…" Sam said, all business even though she was hovering over a half-naked, sexy as sin cop laying in her bed reading her favorite smutty romance novel. "Put your right hand behind your head. Yup, just like that. And then hold the book open with your left hand and hold it up and out towards me a little."

The book moved between them so she could no longer see his face. Perfect since she needed to move her shot up to his head to cut out his hard-on. No way could she miss that. In fact, she was painfully aware of its presence right beneath her as she tried to focus on getting the right shot. Her blog needed the extra boost, and shirtless men with smutty books always did it for her.

The book covered his face, but she could still see the edge of his forehead, his dark hair, and the slight hint of stubble on his chin below the book.

"Almost there. Hold it just a minute longer." She adjusted her position and tilted the phone forward then backward, working to find just the right angle and shadows for her shot.

She felt his hips shake, and even though she couldn't see his face she was certain he was trying to stifle a laugh.

"What?" She could think of a million things he may be laughing at given their current situation, but she wanted to hear him say it.

"I'm so weak… My arms are about to start shaking and it's a fucking disgrace."

He was cute when he was vulnerable.

"Scott struggled a bit, too. Modeling is not for the weak." She looked at the shot she'd just taken and tried to figure out what was missing. It was the hair. It needed to be mussed up like he'd just had a woman's hands clutch it as she rode out the best orgasm of her life. Lucky woman, as Gray would say.

"Hang tight." She kneeled so her knees were on the bed, and she was sitting on his waist. *Thank you, alcohol, for the blurred boundaries*, she thought as she felt him pressed up against her begging—nay pleading—nether regions.

"I need to fix your hair again." She set the phone down on his chest, lowered the book he was holding, and got to work running her fingers through his silky locks. She could see why the hypothetical woman in her mind had had the orgasm of her life; combing her hands through his hair and sitting on his hard cock was doing wonders for Sam's own pleasure.

That was when disaster struck.

Having finished her work, she took a quick glance below his hairline and found his dark, piercing eyes hooded and staring straight back into hers. Which was fine, just so long as she didn't look down at… *Fuck!* she screamed in her mind. Why did her eyes flicker down to his soft, inviting lips?

Except… Maybe it wasn't the disaster she imagined. Because for all the reasons she'd once had to loathe Gray, she couldn't remember a single one. Before she could talk herself out of it or even untangle her fingers from his hair, she dipped her head down to meet his slightly parted lips with hers.

As much as she'd worried about having her first, first kiss since she was a teenager, it really was like riding a bike. Her lips opened on instinct as his tongue found hers and began a soft caress and exploration. Like a dance, she followed his lead before she could no longer hold back. Her lips and tongue miraculously knew what to do, a lifesaver since her brain was mush and offering no help beyond repeated variations of *want more* and *fuck, yes*.

The book was... She had no idea where the book had landed. Somewhere since both of Gray's rugged hands were groping her ass while she dry humped him like there were a couple of horny teenagers sneaking in a clothed quickie while the parents were out at dinner.

She pulled away long enough to lift her shirt over her head, and Gray eagerly freed her from her bra. "Perfect," he said as he took in her breasts. Then his hands were reaching for her. Pulling her back down flush against him as his mouth found hers, not remotely satisfied with the previous brief encounter.

"Wait," she said as she sat back up again, his cock grinding just the right spot between her legs that she almost forgot why she'd sat up.

As if a cop had said the word, Gray's hands flew up in the air, evidence that he was innocent and unarmed—though they both knew that wasn't entirely true.

"You're right. We shouldn't," he said as he started to get up from under her.

She set her hands on his shoulders and shoved him back down onto the bed. "Oh no, we definitely should. But first I need to make sure we're on the same page."

Relief flooded his face and his eyebrows raised up and down playfully. He nudged his hips to grind up against her again and his hands went to her hips, guiding her over him. "Feels like the same page to me."

"But it's just sex, right?"

He stilled beneath her for half a beat before recovering so quickly and flawlessly she wasn't completely sure she'd seen it at all. "Is that what you want it to be?" His finger dipped under the waistband of her jeans but then he pulled it out again. Probably unsure of how far he should take it when she was giving off vibes of having second thoughts about the whole thing.

"That's where I'm at right now in my life." She'd tucked a binder full of her divorce paperwork in a cabinet in the kitchen. But now and then she could hear it thumping like a heart, reminding her it was there and that it wasn't going away anytime soon.

"If I say yes, do I get to take off your pants?" he teased as he slid his finger back under her waistband and tugged.

"I mean it, Gray. You're by the book; I don't even know if you're capable of a one-night stand." How she was getting herself to say the words—words that may very well end whatever it was they were doing—while he was shirtless below her, ready to go, and sporting mussed-up, just-been-fucked hair, was beyond her.

"I don't do it often, but I *am* capable of having no-strings-attached sex."

"A one-night-stand."

"No-strings-attached sex."

"Just this one time. One night."

"Yup. No strings."

"Gray, I'm not taking off my pants until you admit it's only going to happen this one night."

Like a typical man, throughout their conversation, his eyes had darted back and forth between her eyes and her tits.

She leaned forward and cupped his jaw as she held his gaze with hers.

"Say it," she demanded.

"It's a one-night-stand."

She gave a quick peck on the lips as a reward for his good behavior. "Perfect. Let's fuck."

CHAPTER 18: GRAY

That was all Gray needed to hear. He grabbed her by the hips and rolled so that she was on her back, and he was nestled between her legs. Legs that were still covered with a snug-fitting pair of jeans. He'd enjoyed the view of her ass in them earlier that day each time it peeked out from under her coat, but it was time for them to come off.

Feeling brutish, he tugged at the button with his teeth then quickly shimmied off her jeans, along with the lacy black panties underneath, and discarded them to the floor somewhere. He took a moment to admire her naked body and found her sitting upright and doing the same as he kneeled in his boxer briefs between her legs.

He knew that with a recent divorce it may have been a while since she'd been properly seduced. As much as he wanted to pounce like the feral animal he was at that moment, he resisted. Instead, he lifted one of her legs and planted a wet kiss just above her ankle. Then another a little higher, and another.

Sensing what was to come, Sam let her torso fall back onto the bed, and closed her eyes as soft moans escaped her.

Somewhere around her knee, he could feel her impatience when she moved her leg to try to guide him to his final destination.

He might have obliged if it were any other night and any other woman, but it was Sam, and she'd sworn it was a one-time thing. Nothing more. While he couldn't tell for sure how set she was on the one-night stand part of it, he wasn't going to risk fucking it up by skipping any of the foreplay. He had one chance to make Sam beg him for more. Just one opportunity to thoroughly worship the perfection of her body.

"Your body is too perfect to rush," he said between kisses. "Relax, I'm setting the pace tonight."

"Who said you were in charge?" Her breath hitched at the end as he moved closer to her center. The impatience in her voice added fuel to his fire, knowing that she was desperate for him—all of him—had him straining to hold himself back.

Again, Sam's magical playlist changed songs and began "Lose Yourself." As if he needed Eminem driving home the point that he had only one shot.

After kissing up each flawless leg, Gray finally gave in and ran his tongue over the drenched area between. He assumed she'd be wet given the bit of foreplay during the photo shoot and the kissing on the bed, but he hadn't been prepared for just how thoroughly soaked she was.

"You're so wet for me. Have you been thinking about this? Been having dirty dreams about my tongue on your pussy and slipping inside?"

"Maybe a few."

Gray looked up to make some sort of smart-ass remark but he forgot how to make words when he saw her hands on her tits, teasing and twisting her nipples while he was working below the belt.

After a few beats she her hands stilled and she opened her

eyes to look down at him.

"Don't stop," she pleaded. He'd been so mesmerized watching her take care of herself that he'd left her hanging. Rather than wait for him to rectify the situation, her hand went to the back of his head and pushed him back down between her legs.

Fuck, she was going to be the death of him. He loved that he didn't have to guess with her. Sam's hands in his hair and her moans and whimpers told him everything he needed to know about which spot she wanted him to hit and with how much intensity. While he'd worried about it before, he was only mildly intimidated and distracted by how much sex she'd read about in her books and whether he'd be able to live up to any of it.

With his left arm looped around her thigh, holding her tight, he moved his right hand to dip a finger into her soaking wet pussy.

"Yes, yes," she said as her hands tightened their grip on his locks, so he slid another finger in. As he gently moved in and out, he made a "come here" motion deep inside of her, and he made sweeping circles with his thumb as his tongue continued to explore every inch of her.

Just when he felt like she was about to come, she pulled his head back from her and said, "Get up here."

Before he could question if she was one of those women who didn't like to kiss after he went down on them, she was pulling him towards her and crushing her mouth against his. He hovered over her, his arms straddling to keep his full weight from her. His cock had sprung free at some point, and she raised her hips so it rubbed up against her as she nipped at his lower lip.

"Condoms," he managed between kisses.

"On the bookcase."

Gray slid off the bed and she watched as he took off what

little clothing remained.

Sam killed the music, then she went to retrieve the only thing standing in the way of him finally feeling that perfect pussy wrapped around his dick. She pulled a copy of *Moby Dick* from one of the shelves of her bookcase. But when she opened it, in lieu of pages, there was a hidden compartment with a handful of condoms in it.

"*Moby Dick?*"

She shrugged. "Amazon impulse buy once I decided to start dating again. Seemed fitting with the whole white whale thing. Having "Dick" in the title didn't hurt either."

Sex is her white whale? If he'd been anyone else, the thought might have killed his hard-on and sent him running for the door from performance anxiety. But her assessment of him being a cocky bastard was spot-on, and he knew he would leave Sam more than satisfied.

"Come here," he said. Then he eye-fucked her as she walked back over to the bed, hips swaying like she was on a runway. Sam crawled over to Gray, but when he went to reach for the condom in her hand, she held it out of his reach.

"Not yet... I haven't tasted you. It's my turn." That adorable pink tongue peeked out of her mouth again, and he watched in anticipation as she lowered it down to him. If he hadn't been so hell-bent on seeing it all, he was sure his eyes would have rolled back into his head at the pure ecstasy of Sam's tongue slowly working its way around the tip, licking up every bit of precome, before dragging down his length.

"Fuck," he moaned. Her hair was a mess, and she had patches of beard burn starting to show on her jawline. To him, she'd never looked hotter as she eagerly, yet slowly, swirled her tongue while maintaining eye contact with him.

When she took him into her mouth and eased her way down, he could still catch glimpses here and there of her tongue slipping out from her mouth and curling around him. Aside from the sorcery she was performing with her mouth, Gray was also acutely aware of the feeling of her nipples dragging over his legs as she worked. With considerable effort, he held back the orgasm that threatened to overtake him with every passing second. She wanted fiery hot sex, and he was going to give it to her.

From what he could tell, she was enjoying the blow job as well. So for many reasons, but mainly that one, he didn't want to cut that short until she was ready to move on.

A good call since she pulled a Mercury and did that thing with her tongue. After she gave a final swirl around the tip, Sam curled her tongue around his shaft as she dragged it down to his balls.

Knowing he was heading over to Lexi's house and would likely see Sam, he'd made the executive decision to shower and change out of his uniform before leaving work. He was able to relax while Sam licked and teased and flicked and gently sucked around and on his balls. Gray couldn't take it anymore. He closed his eyes and focused on not coming before they actually had sex. He felt her hand cup and lift his balls, then her tongue trailed down and made a confident swipe around his asshole.

"Oh, fuck… You're going to make me come," he grunted. Mercifully, she gave one last hard lick up his shaft before she sat up and relinquished the condom.

Gray kneeled on the bed as he slipped it on. Unable to wait the few seconds for him to finish, Sam got to her knees as well. Her hands raked through his hair again as she pulled him towards her and softly licked the sensitive area of his neck under his ear. As her nails dragged over his skin, her teeth gently nipped at his ear and tugged.

"Hurry up," she teased, knowing full well she was the distraction holding him up.

Once he'd rolled the condom down, he tried to ease her back onto the bed. She stopped him by planting her hands on his shoulders.

"I like to be on top," she said.

"Sounds good to me." And it did. Anything involving him and her having sex sounded fucking amazing to him. He eagerly laid back on the bed and she wasted no time straddling him and slipping him into her with ease. Sam leaned forward to put her hands on the headboard behind him, which placed her tits within reach of his mouth.

Her moans intensified as he flicked her nipples with his tongue before taking them into his mouth and lightly pinching between his lips. He could tell she was close to the edge as she sat upright and pushed him even deeper. He himself was hanging on for dear life.

"Smack my ass," she demanded.

"Yeah? You like it rough?" He gave a satisfying *smack* to her left ass cheek.

"Yes, I love it rough," she said as she worked his cock.

Gray's hand moved from her ass around to where their bodies met as he worked his thumb over her slick, wet skin. His other hand went up to her collar, his thumb grazing over the section of skin between her chest and her neck. He was curious to see how rough she wanted it.

In response, Sam tilted her head back slightly to give him easier access and nodded. "Yes, please," she said, her eyes already closing in anticipation.

He slid his hand over her neck and curved his fingers and thumb to follow the natural shape of her. It didn't take any pressure aside from the feel of his hand against her neck. That did it. Sam's orgasm had her spasming around his cock, sending him over the edge with her.

While he was still riding out the final jolts of pleasure coursing through his veins, Sam collapsed on top of him. She bit his ear and whispered, "That was amazing," before cupping his jaw and giving him one final sensual kiss.

He disposed of the condom while she headed off to the bathroom. It was late, and he was exhausted. He crawled back into the bed, taking in the hit of Sam's scent when his head hit the pillow. Even though his body was incapacitated with fatigue, his mind was as alert as ever. He grabbed the worn copy of *Autumn Fell* to read in bed.

"That's it! Don't move a muscle."

He didn't. With his head buried in the book, he couldn't see what she was doing, but he heard the rustling of the sheets, the rearranging of the lighting, and the sound of her steps around the bed as she worked.

"Okay, sit up just far enough that I can slip this pillow behind you." A little tricky to do without using his arms, but he managed. "Good. And then this arm," she said as she moved his right arm, "will go up here by your head to make your pecs pop with this lighting."

As he held the book, she guided his hand higher and lower until she found the sweet spot.

"That's it. Right there."

After a few minutes of semi-silence while she snapped pictures from different angles, it was over, and she flopped back onto the bed with him. She made herself comfortable using his upper stomach and chest for a pillow.

"Here," she said after a few more taps on the phone. She held it up so he could see the black-and-white photo of him holding her favorite book in her bed. His hair was sticking out around the edges of the book since it had been thoroughly messed up from the sex they'd just had.

"Damn, I look good."

Sam turned so he could clearly see her rolling her eyes at his comment.

Dropping his teasing tone, he added, "It looks better with

the worn copy."

"Yeah. I think so, too."

When she swiped again at the photo to bring up her camera roll, he noticed a large erect penis in the photo right next to his picture. His eyes darted over the screen and found a few more tucked here and there among the everyday photos of her, her friends, and even Daisy at Bark Sniff Wag.

Feeling his eyes on her phone, she lowered her hand to place it firmly against her stomach and out of his view.

"Was that…"

"We should probably call it a night."

"Why is 15% of your camera roll filled with dick pics?"

"Fifteen? That sounds excessive—"

"Agreed. That's a lot. What are you doing with all of those? Did you take them all?"

Sam shrugged. "Guys assume that if I like dirty books, I must want pictures of their crotches in my DMs. Unsolicited. I don't, of course, but I get much enjoyment from saving them and sending random dick pics back as responses."

She treated the topic as something minor and inconsequential, but her expression showed that it hurt the way people judged and made assumptions about her based on her blog. He reached out his hand to offer her some sort of comfort.

She moved out of his reach. "Jackie gets up ridiculously early in the morning, even when she's hungover. I better crash now so I can keep up with her tomorrow."

"Yeah. I'm beat, too."

Sam turned off the lights, and they both made themselves comfortable on their respective sides of the bed. No touching. It didn't feel right, but she'd set the tone pulling away from his hand. Besides, she wasn't making any effort to touch him. She even rolled away from him and faced the opposite wall.

CHAPTER 19: SAM

The next morning, Sam woke up spooning Daisy, the absolute sweetest dog that ever lived. Poor Gray. She couldn't imagine how badly it was going to hurt him to give her up in a few weeks. She herself was struggling, and she barely had half the bond she knew Gray had with her.

A note from Jackie on her nightstand explained how Daisy had gotten into her apartment.

Brought the dog up. Didn't want to wake you. Will be back with coffee and doughnuts.
J

Daisy, along with Jackie's impending return, meant no additional morning quickie with Gray. It was just as well. Last night was not the beginning of something.

As Sam stirred, so did Daisy. She stepped over Sam to get to Gray, her one true love. Sam wasn't offended. She'd considered doing the same when she saw how adorable he was just waking up. She hadn't had the chance to really take it in last time with him trying to rub one off in her bed and muttering dirty things about Mercury.

Gray was facing away from her, but she could see him rubbing his nose groggily and giving Daisy a nice pet and scratch. Then he gave his own ass cheek a good scratch. No doubt he'd be mortified once he took in his surroundings and realized where he was. Or maybe not. Men were a different breed.

"What time is it?" he turned and asked with a stretch that pulled the covers down to reveal his bare torso. She could barely make it two minutes without thinking about sleeping with him again. Her plans to walk away from him after their one night together didn't feel as achievable in the light of day.

"Early. Sorry. Jackie brought Daisy up so she could run out and get breakfast."

He gave a conciliatory pet to her, unwilling to put any sort of blame on the animal. "No, it's fine. I don't like to sleep too late."

"You staying for coffee and doughnuts?"

"I have to get to the gym with Ronan."

She furrowed her eyes at him. "He's hiking with Leo. Their double date this morning? Remember?"

Gray's muscles tensed at the realization. She could practically see his mind racing with a new lie to tell so he could get the hell out of there.

"I'm messing with you, Gray. We're not dating; you don't need to tell me where you're going or feel obligated to stay for breakfast."

He stood and got dressed, slowly and without any reservations. "Ronan and I usually hit the gym on Saturday mornings. I forgot he had plans."

As he worked the buckle on his belt, Sam bit her bottom

lip and glanced at the clock, still debating if they could get in a quickie before breakfast. What was it about men and belt buckles that led her mind to dirty, wicked thoughts? Oh, right. Stevin from *It Only Takes One Night*. His creative belt use in the bedroom had rewired her brain Pavlovian style to equate belts with mind-blowing sex.

Gray walked over to Sam's side of the bed and leaned in. "I wasn't trying to come up with an excuse to leave." He gave her the softest kiss, their lips briefly brushing against each other before adding, "I was hoping we might extend our one-night stand to the morning." Again, he gave a quick, chaste kiss before moving to her jaw, under her ear, and down her neck.

Sam closed her eyes and let herself get lost in the feeling of his mouth easing its way down the sensitive skin on her neck, and she took in the smell of him mixed with the lingering scent of sex that clung to his skin. Right before his tongue could move from her neck to her achingly needy tits, Daisy jumped onto the bed and trotted over to them.

Gray sighed and pulled away so he could finish getting dressed while Daisy made herself comfortable with her head in Sam's lap.

"Doesn't look like she's going to allow it. I should get going anyway. I'm still planning to hit the gym and you have company." As if on cue, Jackie gave a complimentary knock before easing the door open just as he pulled his shirt on. Why was the universe so against her having morning sex?

Jackie's mom, Babs, would have said it was a sign for Sam to stay the course with the whole one-night-stand idea. The night was over and so was their time together. Besides, she'd only just started dating again. She may run into her next date later that day. Someone even more amazing than Gray had been the night before? Well, one could dream, though she didn't dare expect to find such a rare gem so quickly.

"Morning, Gray," Jackie greeted. It was obvious he and Sam had slept together, and Jackie was no longer smashed, so she was much kinder to him than she'd been the night before. "Staying for breakfast? I have coffees and a dozen assorted doughnuts. Three have some sort of strawberry flavoring for Lexi, but I think they already left for their hike since her car is gone."

"Thanks, Jackie, but I was about to head out, too." Gray leaned down to meet Sam who was still in bed, propped up by a few pillows with the cover pulled up over her chest. One of his hands cupped her jaw as he went in for one last kiss. No tongue—whew, morning breath's gross—but it wasn't a brush of his lips either. When he pulled back, he pulled her lower lip with him, as if the thought of them separating was too miserable to bear so he'd tried to take a small part of her with him.

"I'll see you around," he whispered in her ear before planting a quick kiss on her cheek. Gray patted his leg. "Come on, Daisy, let's get you home for some breakfast. See ya, Jackie."

"See ya, Gray."

"Wait, don't forget your book." Sam snagged the book from the nightstand and tossed it to him.

Gray caught the book, thanked her, and gave Sam a wink. Then he grabbed his coat and was gone.

Jackie's mouth dropped. "Holy shit. I caught a glimpse of that man-chest before he got his shirt on. Well played, Sam." She set the box on the table and helped herself to a chocolate frosted, chocolate sprinkled doughnut. "You guys did have sex this time, right?"

"Yes, we did. And, check this out…" She climbed out of bed, threw on a shirt, and grabbed her phone as she made her way to the table. After a few taps, she found the picture of

172

Gray reading her favorite edition of *Autumn Fell* in the bed where they'd just had epic sex.

Jackie took the phone to get a better look while Sam refueled with doughnuts and caffeine. The new start to her life had been rocky, to say the least, but at that moment, she felt like she'd finally found a bit of what she'd been missing for so many years.

"Are you zooming in?"

"I wanna see more of that tat on his arm. I'd love for Scott to get one, but he has this thing about needles."

Sam chuckled at a memory of Jackie and Scott donating blood together. He may have been the one with a fear of needles, but Jackie had been the one to pass out afterwards— into Scott's lap, naturally.

She took the phone back from Jackie and admired her own handiwork. Though to be fair, Gray had done most of the heavy lifting, spending countless hours at the gym. All she'd done was mess with the lights and pose his arms.

"Are you posting that today?"

"If I get around to it."

"I can head out soon if you have work to do here. I don't want to impose."

"You're hopelessly addicted to work, Jackie. Anyone ever tell you that?"

"Scott does. All the time. He said it again when I tried to bring some of my work with me here."

"And?"

Jackie looked down in shame. "I may have three tomes in my bag. A biography on the Chesapeake Bay, a how-to book for social media, and *The Joy of Cooking*."

"Cooking?" She cocked an eyebrow at Jackie.

"Now that Scott and I have some free time, we've started cooking more. He's been schooling me, so I wanted to surprise him by secretly learning to cook on the side."

There was no way in hell Scott thought any less of Jackie for having subpar culinary skills, but it wasn't surprising she wanted to learn regardless and that she probably wanted to be the absolute best—beginner status or not.

"Enough about me and my neurotic tendencies. I'd rather discuss yours instead." Jackie pointed her doughnut at Sam to drive home her accusation.

"What neurotic tendencies?" Between the two of them, Jackie was notorious for being the neurotic one. The one most likely to lie in bed at night stressing about some off-hand comment she'd made to a semi-stranger three years prior.

"I know you're over-analyzing whatever is happening with hot cop." Jackie paused for a rebuttal and gave a smug smile when none came. "You practically caressed the phone just now, and I just witnessed a very sweet and affectionate goodbye kiss.

"But—"

"There's no but! I gave you a list of reasons Scott and I wouldn't work, and you shat on all of them before shoving us together regardless."

"Excuse me? I *shat*?"

"Stop deflecting."

No more deflecting? Sam took a giant bite of doughnut as a plan b stall tactic, which did not go unnoticed by Jackie.

"Nice. You eat like that in front of Gray?"

When she finished chewing, she answered, "Yes, I do. Because it doesn't matter. He and I were just a fling."

"Were? He just left with your most prized smutty book."

"It was only a one-night stand."

Jackie looked thoroughly vexed at the concept even though Sam knew she'd had at least a few in her lifetime, too.

"I'm not even officially divorced yet. I'm in no place to take on anything beyond meaningless sex."

They sipped their coffees, each lost in their own thoughts.

"Didn't look meaningless to me…"

"You witnessed all of five minutes of us together. I promise you now that we've scratched whatever sex itch was between us, we'll go back to being acquaintances who are mildly annoyed with each other at least 90% of the time."

Jackie shrugged. "If you say so."

"I do. Now, enough about Gray. I need to introduce you to Marcy."

After swinging by Bark Sniff Wag to show Jackie how fabulous her new job was, they went over to Paging All Bibliophiles.

"Hi, Marcy!" Sam called as she walked into the store. "One of my oldest friends is in town for the weekend and I wanted to bring her by to meet you. She used to come here with me when we were kids."

Marcy's smile was tense and forced. "It's a pleasure," she said to Jackie as she shook her hand. Jackie started to say some sort of salutation in response, but Marcy had already turned back to Sam. "Did you get my message?"

She fished her phone out of her purse and found a smattering of missed calls and text messages. She and Jackie had both agreed to silence and stow away their cell phones for what little quality time they had together.

"No, it's been on silent. What's going on? Is everything okay?"

Marcy pressed her lips together then said, "'Fraid not, Sam."

Sam scrolled Marcy's original messages and found a picture she'd sent. It was a shot of the front sidewalk, but someone had written all over it in chalk: "Stop Spreading Smut. Save Our Children." It was detailed and used similar colors and a similar style to her business card and website. It was directed at her. She handed Jackie her phone so she could see as well.

"That was this morning?" Jackie asked as she looked back to where they'd just walked in.

"We found it when we opened at nine. It was only sidewalk chalk, so a quick spritz of water was all it took to wash it away, but not before other people snapped pictures and posted them all over their social media accounts."

"Oh, shit…"

"Sam, I appreciate everything you've done for us here linking your blog sales to our store…"

But it wasn't enough, Sam thought with a mixture of personal regret and bitterness towards Marcy and Buck—though she wasn't sure if her bitter feelings were valid or not, all things considered. She'd increased sales in the store with her Tuesday evening recommendations, but more importantly, she'd restructured her webpage links, so all paperback and hardback purchases went through Paging All Bibliophiles rather than a certain online retailer that enjoyed global domination in most sales categories.

That didn't matter in the end, though. Paging All Bibliophiles was Marcy and Buck's entire world. It kept them financially stable and, she assumed, emotionally stable as well. They had to look out for their business, and she couldn't fault them for that.

Sam couldn't find the right words to respond. She was afraid that even opening her mouth would cause her to cry from frustration or anger. Instead, she nodded, hoping that would be enough.

"We simply aren't in a position…"

Sam held up her hand. Marcy felt horrible enough without having to say the words aloud. Besides, Sam wasn't sure she could hear them at the moment. Jeremy had always said this would happen. He'd always worried her father would have a similar reaction if her blog ever took off and her identity was discovered by anyone in their small town.

"Can I get some of my things?" she asked Marcy, motioning to her little converted closet towards the back at the store. Jackie put a supportive hand on her shoulder and gave a squeeze.

"Oh, no, Sam. It's not forever…" Marcy said. "Just until everything blows over. People will find something or someone else to attack in a few weeks. Maybe sooner."

"Right," Sam said, relieved she didn't have to pack up her things straight away. "I'll leave it here. For now." There was nothing but sympathy and support coming from Marcy's demeanor, but Sam felt ashamed and embarrassed all the same. "We should get going."

"I'm sorry; I didn't—"

"No, Marcy. Don't apologize; this isn't your fault. I do need some time to process it all though, so we really should get going."

"Okay, I understand. But I hope you'll come back and see me sometime this week so we can talk more."

"Absolutely. I'll see you soon."

"It was nice meeting you, Marcy." Jackie said as she and Sam turned to leave the store.

"Yes, you, too!" Marcy called after them.

Outside, Sam pulled out her phone again and checked the Bark Sniff Wag website. The photo of her and Daisy was no longer on the main page. In her mind she could see someone at work showing Gil the online posts and comments, and see his hand go to his sunglasses for reassurance before deciding to put distance between Bark Sniff Wag and Sam's offensive side hustle by taking down her front-page photo.

Jackie was fiercely supportive on the way home, offering to create a fake profile on the neighborhood site to attack

Mitsy's credibility. Luckily, by the time they arrived back at Sam and Lexi's, they had both calmed down enough not to create bogus profiles for an online ambush. Instead, they decided to have some lunch and regroup to come up with a strategic and more logical solution to the problem at hand.

That had been the plan until they got to the house and found Sam's soon-to-be ex-husband standing at the front porch of the house.

CHAPTER 20: GRAY

When he and Daisy left Sam's, he checked his phone and found a plea from Yasmine to cover her shift that day, meaning he would need to be at work in an hour.

Back in October, he'd come down with the flu. It had hit him hard and fast. Yasmine took his shift with even less notice than she'd given him. He texted back that he'd cover for her and rushed Daisy home for breakfast before dropping her off at Bark Sniff Wag.

His reward for helping was a particularly draining workday that included too much time with Smitty. The station had gotten three more calls about flat tires in the area, and those were the only ones people were reporting. There were probably more.

And yet Smitty had been even more defiant than usual when Gray confronted him. He'd showed up at his house since he wasn't working at the store that day, and Smitty refused to fess up to any of them. Despite the therapy and what had looked like a positive turn regarding his mental health, something must have happened to set him off course again. Gray had gotten nowhere with him earlier in the day and may have even damaged the frail relationship he had with him. The years he'd spent building up trust were obliterated by the shouting match that ended their conversation.

The only good thing to happen that day was that Ronan missed his morning workout, too. That evening they fit in a quick trip to the gym.

"You look like shit," Ronan said when Gray arrived at the treadmills.

"Yeah, I was up late last night." He stepped up and put in his usual settings. Then he turned to see if Ronan had his headphones.

"Dropped them in the john this morning." Ronan said, reading Gray's mind. "I'll get some more, eventually, but I have some things I want to talk to you about anyway."

"Yeah? What's up?"

"Mel and I finally found a place, a Victorian fixer-upper in Mt. Lake Park. We put in an offer yesterday, so now we're just waiting to hear back from them."

"Congratulations! That's great news. You'll have to send me the Zillow listing so I can check it out."

"Thanks; I will." Ronan paused for a moment and then said, "If they accept the offer, I could be moving out of the apartment in a month or so. Are you going to be okay with that? Do you have anything lined up yet?"

Financially, he was fine, but his apartment was about to get that much lonelier with both Daisy and Ronan heading out. Ronan had been his only roommate since he'd moved out of his parents' house, and he wasn't sure how he felt about finding someone else.

"Yeah, I'm good. You're getting married in a week; I knew this was coming."

They ran in silence for less than a lap before Ronan piped

up again. "Have you seen Leo with Lexi? We all went hiking and had lunch together today. He's like a new man."

"Yeah. I think Lexi and grief counseling have really been good for him."

They fell silent again as the treadmills whirled beneath them.

"Did you know? About all the family stuff?"

Gray shook his head. "You?"

"He told me and Mel earlier this week. You should talk to him."

Gray nodded.

Understanding there was nothing more to say about it, Ronan changed the subject. "Leo said you're thinking about bringing Sam to the wedding."

"Yeah, she's coming with me." He was feeling confident that even though he'd spun it as the perfect opportunity to meet *other* people, it would also be the perfect opportunity for him to lay on the charm. He looked damn good in a tux, and he excelled at working a room. Potentially another perk of his time as a police officer since he needed to adapt his personality and conversation skills based on the situation, and he'd gotten to know a large chunk of the community through his interactions at work: speaking at school assemblies, taking Scouts on tours of the station, and volunteering at various fundraisers and rec activities on top of the general duties of his position.

"And you crashed at her place last night? Again?"

"Sounds like you already know the answer to that one."

"But I like to hear you say it. Besides, you know that's not what I'm *really* asking."

Gray glanced over at Ronan and gave a subtle nod. "Yes."

"Alright. That's what I'm talking about. Now we just need to get Jon on board with pairing off and we can be done with the whole singles bar scene."

"Sam and I aren't together. And Jon's not settling down. Did you hear about the new app he's using? It helps him find couples to have threesome with. He's probably out with one tonight. He's never coming back from that."

"A threesome app? You know he and I had a threesome once. It was okay, but now that you mention it, I remember he was really into it."

Gray almost tripped over his feet; he grabbed onto the handles to steady himself again.

"Get your shit together, Gray. People are watching."

"You were in a threesome with Jon?!"

"Yes," he hissed. "Not so loud. Mel knows, but I don't want to be next in line for Mitsy's crusade against immorality."

Gray looked around the gym. No one was paying attention to them.

"When did it happen?"

Ronan shrugged as if they were discussing the date of his last dentist appointment. "I don't know. Before Mel, obviously. Doesn't matter. Let's get back to you. What's going on with you and Sam that you're *not* together? Does she hate labels?"

"She's still married."

Gray could tell the comment hit close since Ronan was about to get married.

"Right," Ronan said. "Forgot about that. Did she say what happened between them?" Ronan steadied his gaze on the machine's simple screen in front of him, watching the little dots slowly fill in the intervals around each lap. He already knew Sam was the one to leave the marriage and the one to move across the state for a fresh start. It wasn't anything like Ronan and Mel's situation, but he could see Ronan putting himself in Jeremy's place, regardless.

"Not to me. It's known but left unsaid. That night after

182

the poker game, I saw some notes and email printouts left out on the table. There's animosity. Doesn't look like there's a chance for a reconciliation."

Ronan nodded. "Lexi hasn't said anything about it when you stopped by?"

He shook his head. Gray had every intention of leaving it there, but Ronan kept his eyes on him, waiting for an explanation.

"Lexi's canceled on me the last few weeks. I assumed it was because she was busy with Sam, but now I'm thinking it's because she's been busy with Leo."

Later that night, Ronan left him yet again for Mel's apartment. Unfortunately, he'd also gotten word that Daisy's family was ready to get her back and would arrange for a pickup later that week. His loneliness was suddenly exacerbated by the impending loss of the only friend who hadn't yet left him.

It wasn't the first time Gray had fostered a dog. He had HART for Animals, the local animal shelter, in his contacts on his phone and he used it frequently. At work he'd sometimes have a misplaced animal in his charge that he would need to take to a shelter or watch for a few hours until the owners or a responsible party could care for them. HART did amazing for the animals in their care, but Gray still struggled to walk in with an animal and walk out without them. His heart broke a little as their sad eyes watched him leave them behind. To help relieve some of the guilt he felt, he'd started fostering through them.

Daisy differed from the other dogs he'd watched over. It was hitting harder that she wouldn't be around after a few days, and that he'd likely never see her again since the family was about to move to another state for their own fresh start.

Sitting on the couch that evening, he decided the only thing that would cheer him up was reading *Autumn Fell* as Daisy's head rested on his legs. He read for hours, occasionally reading aloud to Daisy the passages Sam had underlined and the notes she'd scribbled in the margins. The handwriting and style of the notes varied. As if throughout the years, as she grew older, her penmanship matured while her point of view and understanding of the novel had changed and grown, too.

CHAPTER 21: SAM

"You should sit and talk with him," Jackie said as Sam pulled into the driveway and Jeremy gave a nervous wave from the front porch. "Babs has a list of you-can-only-get-them-in-Deep-Creek items she wants me to bring back. I have at least an hour of errands to run. Longer if you need it."

"No way! He doesn't get to show up unannounced and have everyone drop their plans for the day." She slammed the car into park and went to open the door to give him a piece of her mind, face-to-face. Something she should have done a long time ago.

"Wait!" Jackie had a death-grip on her arm. "*You* left. *You* called him a man-whore on Christmas Eve." Oh… right. Sam's mind often blocked out that wine-fueled incident back in Milton when she'd spotted him at a bar with another woman. Even though she had left him, effectively declaring their relationship and marriage over, the sight of him with someone else triggered her enough to throw a snowball at the front bar window as she shouted, "Man-whore!" It was not a good look for her. Not only was she physically not fit to be seen in public, but the other woman turned out to be his cousin. It had been bad. Very, very bad.

"He's making an effort, Sam. I know he's been a dick about assets and everything... but maybe you set that tone." When Sam didn't respond, she added, "Besides, look at him. I don't think he's here to fight."

She looked back at the porch. His shoulders were slumped, hands shoved into his pockets, and he was shifting his weight back and forth on the balls of his feet. If she hadn't known any better, she would assume it was a sort of fight-or-flight reaction leaning dangerously close to flight mode. But she did know him better than that. She was the one who fled situations, not him.

"Did you tell him to come up here?" Sam asked.

"What? No. Give me some credit, Sam."

She took a deep breath and shook her head slightly. "I know, I know. I'm sorry. It's just so weird he's here the same weekend you are."

"Agreed. But it also makes everything that much easier. You'd have called and said he showed up out of nowhere, and I would have dropped everything to drive out here to make sure you were okay. It's kinda nice I'm already here. I'm not a good driver under pressure."

"Yeah. That's true. And it has already been a shit morning. Might as well take whatever hits are coming while I'm already down."

"Love the optimism."

"I try." She looked down at her hands in her lap before looking back up at Jackie. "You'll be okay?"

"Babs's list is downright overwhelming. I have plenty to keep me busy." They both glanced at Jeremy again. "Are you going to be okay? This on top of everything at the bookstore..."

"Oddly enough, it's still better than where I was a few

months ago. I'm good. Want to meet back here for an early dinner before you head out?"

"Sounds good." Jackie squeezed her shoulder. "You've got this. Call me if you need anything."

After the most awkward small talk Sam had ever endured, she and her husband were up in her apartment at the kitchen table with glasses of water.

"So... Why did you come out here?" she asked once they'd covered the weather, her new job, and his promotion at work.

He leaned back in his chair and turned his glass in his hands before looking up at her. "Really? No guesses as to why I'm here?"

"Why are you here *unannounced*?"

He pulled out his phone and held it up for her to see. It was nothing new. She'd seen their text messages—had been the other half of them.

"This isn't working."

The most recent messages read:

Jeremy: I need that signed contract

Cat the Great: Waiting on Grant

Jeremy: ...?

Cat the Great: He's on vacation.

Grant was her lawyer. She did eventually have him review and edit the contract which resulted in more aggressive texting.

. . .

Jeremy: Why are you fighting every fucking line of the contract?

Jeremy: So that's it?

Jeremy: Sam?

"Separating via text messages and lawyers isn't working for us," he said.

No, it wasn't. There was too much to read into everything. When he didn't immediately respond to her texts, even though she was almost positive he wasn't at work, she assumed he was doing so out of spite. That it was all part of his plan to make her as miserable as he'd been since she left.

She couldn't tell him how a month after she'd left, when his initial anger abated and they'd moved on to civil conversations about the mortgage and other joint possessions, she couldn't handle it. Their familiar and comforting interactions contrasted with her then current status of unemployed homeless squatter who'd been sleeping on Jackie's couch with zero direction in her life.

Her text messages with Jeremy were part of the reason she'd left her hometown to begin with. She'd needed to get as far away from anything she could glean any comfort from, or else she'd run back to it—without regard to what was best for her or Jeremy in the long run.

When she'd left town, his first messages bordered on frigid, and she responded in kind with icy, usually one-word messages of her own. Once he'd started to be a dick (ish, since when she looked at it objectively, she knew deep down most would consider him a saint when compared to what she'd done) she was reassured of her decision to leave. She'd been able to sit with Lexi and make a pact to start dating again, which she had followed through with Gray.

Jeremy lowered his phone and waited for her to respond,

but she couldn't. In her mind, she understood what had happened, and yet saying it out loud, to him, felt like an insurmountable obstacle.

He shook his head. "I didn't plan on coming here like this, and I didn't mean to run Jackie off."

"She has Babs errands."

He smiled at that. He'd always had a soft spot for Jackie's mom. It was one of the many things Sam had loved about him when they'd first started out.

They sat in silence until Sam couldn't take it anymore. "I don't know where to start…"

He smiled again, but it was shallow and perfunctory. "I can start. I've been running this conversation in my mind on the drive over."

Sam returned his smile, but it was fleeting.

"I was angry when you left, and I was angry before you left. I understand that's probably what pushed you away to begin with."

Sam gave a light nod. Hindsight had allowed her to see it more clearly as well. Last fall she hadn't been able to pin-point what had come between them. Couldn't even adequately explain it to Jackie, why she was one foot out of the house she'd once blissfully shared with him. The fact that he changed his mind and seemed to want kids was a large part of it, but there was so much more on her end, too.

"I don't want to fight anymore." He put his hands up for emphasis. "And I'm done being angry. You were right; it wasn't working. We're better apart."

"It wasn't right to walk out like that, or to be jealous when I thought you were with another woman."

Jeremy gave a sad chuckle. "No, she still hates you for that one."

"Understandable," she said with a weak smile in return. "I don't know what happened, Jeremy." Except to some extent, she did. "I remember one day, after a particularly heart-breaking surgery, I needed to get milk on the way home, and I was furious with you since you drank the last of it that morning. You probably would have done it yourself if I'd asked—I know that now—but at the time it sent me into a red rage. I lost it. I was in my car with the milk on the passenger seat, and I was crying and slamming my fists on the steering wheel, shouting every obscenity I could think of."

His expression was blank. She couldn't tell if he wanted to hear it or not. But she needed to say it. She needed to feel the cathartic release of everything she'd held in for so long.

"Then I put my head on the steering wheel and let it all out. Gut wrenching sobs for everything I'd lost: the sweet dog who'd flatlined on my table, our perfect marriage… my happiness.

"When I picked my head up, I noticed a store employee staring at me from the parking lot. Her hand was poised over her walkie-talkie as if debating if she should call for back-up."

Jeremy leaned forward, resting his arms on the table as he furrowed his brow. Recognizing it was her turn to lay it all out, he remained silent.

"She didn't, or no one responded. Maybe I left before they came out. It doesn't matter. The whole thing shook me up. It put this idea into my mind that I was walking a thin line being that out and open with my emotions. It felt like I needed to lock it down and ride it out. I thought better times would come if I could tread through the misery first.

"I now know that was more to do with me than you. And while you say your anger pushed me away, I know my shutting down and my attempts to merely exist without acknowledging my own anger and sadness or attempting to make it better are part of what led to your anger.

"I'm sorry it took me leaving the way that I did for me to realize that."

Jeremy reached across the table and took one of her hands in his. It was nice. Comforting, just like she'd known it would be all those times she'd imagined it since she'd left.

"I get it. I wasn't open with you, either. About wanting kids…" he said. It was amazing how she'd been ninety-nine percent sure he'd felt that way, regardless that he'd denied it at the time, and it still was a punch to the gut to hear him say it. She pulled her hands away from his and he didn't stop her.

"Yeah, I figured," she said with a sad nod. "Why… What happened?"

"I guess it's like with you. I don't know when it changed or what caused it. But I think the first time I really felt it was at Easter dinner at my parents' house. I was playing with all the nieces and nephews—wrestling and whatever random games they came up with—and I had this need to have my own. And it's the same way I feel about breathing. Almost like instinct."

Sam felt a tear form as she remembered what she was sure was the Easter he was referring to. It had been a great day and it had led to a night of passionate sex. Had he thought or even hoped she'd somehow get pregnant, even though she was on the pill? Hoped they'd be the statistic, the one in a million or whatever the odds were of getting pregnant while on birth control?

"I didn't push it because I thought if I changed my mind once I was older and was around kids more often, you probably would, too. Eventually."

"No." She shook her head, hoping the movement wouldn't send her lone tear down her cheek.

"I know." His hands were still on the table, but she didn't want them in hers. They were a false sense of comfort; a memory of what solace had once felt like when she and Jeremy made sense together.

Accepting that, Jeremy pulled his hands back to his glass. "But I want you to know that I don't have regrets, Sam. Some of the happiest times of my life were with you by my side."

"Me, too."

It wasn't immediate, but eventually Sam pulled the divorce binder out and they pored over it together, without lawyers. As the mature adults they'd become, they covered all the major parts of their impending divorce, their biggest decision being to sell the house and split the sale fifty fifty. Relief washed over her for more reasons than she could even name. But mostly it had to do with the dropped battle about housing. It wasn't just the money aspect, either. She struggled to imagine Jeremy and another woman in her house and in her bed. Not that she allowed herself to burden him with those unfair feelings.

"We can use Tim for our realtor. You like him, right?"

She gave a genuine smile. Tim had led the crazy neighborhood Christmas lights event she and Jackie had been a part of.

"Yeah, I like Tim. He's intense, but thorough. We should get a decent price with him taking the lead. And Scott's working as his photographer now."

"Davis?"

Sam nodded. "Can you handle being nice to him when he shows up to take the pictures?" she teased. When Jackie and Scott had been just starting out together, Jeremy was constantly on Jackie about how Scott suffered from wanderlust and would never settle down with anyone in a tiny town like Milton. It had resulted in more than a few arguments.

"Yes… I've seen him around town. I'm always nice. Turns out he and Jackie are good together."

"They are."

They sat in limbo as the conversation died down. It wasn't comfortable, but it wasn't uncomfortable either. They merely existed at the same time around the table.

"With the house and taxes settled," she said, "it feels like we can probably do everything else through email and mail from here." By everything else, she meant all the other minor and major details that came along with dissolving over a decade of matrimony. While Jeremy's visit had brought a certain amount of relief, they still weren't friends by any means, and that was what she needed to surround herself with at the moment.

"Yeah. That should be okay." He checked the time on his phone. "I should get going." Then he did that thing with his hands that always made him seem like a bit of a dad at heart. He played the drums with his pointer fingers on the table to make a *bah dump dump bah* sound. The official we're-wrapping-it-up soundtrack he'd carefully crafted over the years. Except this time, it announced the official wrapping-up of their marriage.

"But before I go…" His lips formed a thin line as he chose his next words. "Chastity's friend's sister-in-law lives out here, and she sent Chastity, who forwarded it to me, a link to an op-ed on you. It's basically how you're single-handedly leading the crusades to spread depravity throughout Deep Creek Lake."

She was speechless. She'd never single-handedly led anything in her life.

"It's by some woman named Misty or something like that, but I'm sure you've already seen it."

"Mitsy. Yeah, I've seen it." She wasn't sure why she felt the need to lie to her soon-to-be ex-husband; perhaps it was that saying about old habits dying hard. They did, indeed. Another habit creeping in was the powerful desire to blame Jeremy, even though he was only the messenger, and he didn't have anything to do with Mitsy or her new life in Western Maryland.

He nodded. "You okay? I know we're not… With the way things are now, I wasn't even going to bring it up, but it was damning enough that I still felt like I should check on you. You know, make sure everything was okay." His eyes softened, a final release of the residual anger they'd had towards each other. "I should have known Jackie would beat me to it."

She gave him the saddest smile that had ever existed, and he reciprocated. They weren't the perfect match anymore, but he really was a nice guy. She nodded and said, "Jackie and I are on it."

"I figured. With the two of you together, I'm sure you'll get it sorted."

Just like when they'd first greeted each other, they didn't hug, but she did walk him down to his car, thanked him for coming out, and wished him a safe drive home.

Once he was around the corner and out of sight, she pulled her phone out to check for the op-ed he'd mentioned. There was Mitsy's stupid smiling face next to that damn artistic rendering of the time Sam pretended to hook on Lake Shore Drive.

Her thin thread of hope that things would blow over went up in flames. Just like Jeremy had said, it was damning. Even worse, the comments below were entirely in support of Mitsy.

CHAPTER 22: GRAY

He'd spent the week trying to have a conversation with Sam, but she thwarted his attempts: his texts got one-word responses, and she was always in the back or off the last days he picked up or dropped off Daisy at Bark Sniff Wag. He even showed up at Paging All Bibliophiles for her romance recommendations session only to find that her services were on hiatus for the indefinite future.

He understood the reality that their one-night stand was likely just that—a one-time thing—but he thought they would still be friends. He could have used her support when Daisy's family came to take her back. Jon was almost useless in that department; Leo and Ronan were decent enough to listen to him about it for a minute or two during their poker game. But Sam, the former vet and current employee at a puppy day care center, she'd get it.

He knew she was going through her own shit, too, with Mitsy on a warpath and gunning for her, and Marcy pulling the plug on her book whispering services. He couldn't legally do much of anything to help her since Mitsy was entitled to her opinion, and her low-level bullying tactics weren't illegal, regardless of how immoral he and most people found them to be.

Luckily, even though she'd had one hell of a week, and she'd dodged him for the entirety of it, she hadn't backed out on being his date to the wedding.

Lexi and Sam pulled up to the church in Sam's clunker of a vehicle, and Gray met them at the door.

"Lexi's car is in the shop. Ironically, my car is the most reliable," Sam said as they got out of the car and took in the confused look on Gray's face.

"It was a hot, but lovely ride. Thank you, Sam." Lexi said as she got out and pulled bag after bag from the car's trunk.

"Do you need help with that?" He moved towards her to help, but by the time he reached them, Lexi was already strapped down like a pack-mule.

"No, I've got it. Mel texted me an hour ago in a panic. Her hair went all wrong despite the *two* dry runs she'd had. Lisa and I are going to fix it, but we needed a few things to get the job done." She patted the bag strapped across her chest. Then she turned to Sam. "I need to run up and get started. Are you coming up with me or staying with Gray?"

He cocked an eyebrow, daring her to stay with him.

"I'm good here; I wouldn't be much help with hair or makeup."

"Okay, text me if you need anything."

"I'm fine. Off you go."

More spritely than Gray thought possible with the extra emotional and physical weight she carried, Lexi went up some side stairwell, leaving Sam and Gray in the entryway.

"You think she'll be okay with all the wedding stuff?" He almost hadn't asked Lexi to be his date all those weeks ago. Had feared it would bring a flood of bad memories about that time she'd planned a wedding but never got to attend it.

Sam set her purse and keys on the table next to the giant heart centerpiece announcing Ronan and Mel's wedding nuptials. "I thought the same thing. I preemptively stuffed my purse with tissues, but this hair disaster seems to be helping. It's giving her something to focus on. Hopefully Mel has a few more catastrophes up her silky white sleeves."

She checked her vibrating phone. "Right on cue… It's Lex. A bridesmaid left a mini sewing kit in the coatroom down here. She asked me to run it up."

Sam walked over to the spacious coatroom closet off the main entranceway, and Gray trailed close behind her, not entirely unlike an animal stalking its prey. Did she want to be alone with him? He wasn't so sure given the rocky last week, but if her choice of dress was any indication—a gorgeous gold with a plunging neckline and a bottom that fell to the floor with a slit that went well above her knees—she definitely wanted to be alone with someone. He should probably see if that someone was him.

"I'll help you get it," he said.

She looked back over her shoulder with one eyebrow raised impressively high. "It's the size of a deck of cards and Lex told me exactly where it is. I think I can manage." The tinge of sarcasm in her voice reminded him of their banter during the poker game and photo shoot. Since both had ended with them in her bed, he was feeling optimistic.

"It would be my pleasure. I *live* to serve and protect, Samantha." He took his time looking her up and down, letting his eyes roll over every curve as the blood started rushing south. She knew it, too. There was a definite strut to her walk where her ass swayed tantalizingly with each step, begging him to reach out and cup it, to pull it towards him.

When she didn't protest his entry to the closet or what

he'd said, he shut the door and locked it behind them. He had no idea why there would be a lock on a coatroom door, but who was he to question the genius of whoever had put it there.

Unable to hold back any longer, his large hands caught her perfect ass mid-sway and he stepped forward to press his hard length against her so she could feel exactly what she did to him. He lowered his head so his mouth was right at her ear. "You look so..." he whispered before he paused to kiss down one side of her neck, perfectly exposed thanks to whomever styled her hair. Her head fell back to give him more access and to send the signal that whatever he was about to do, she was all in. "Fucking..." he continued, before his lips were on the other side of her neck, trailing down and taking in her quickening pulse beneath his mouth. "Sexy..."

She gasped when he turned her towards him, then he crushed his mouth against hers. His tongue greedily entering and taking in every inch of her. It wasn't enough. He'd been dreaming about those perfect pink lips on his before they trailed down his neck, torso, and beyond.

He nipped at her bottom lip in frustration as she pulled away. The need for release so strong it pained him to feel her pull back.

"We're going to be late with the sewing kit," she said in a breathy voice. She bit her already puffy lower lip and her hooded eyes dropped down to his mouth, ready to retaliate despite what she'd just said.

He pulled his phone out to check the time. "I think they can wait ten minutes."

"Just ten minutes?" She gave him a devilish grin. The same one she'd flashed right before she'd mounted him the week before.

"Maybe less," he conceded. "You are absolutely stunning in that dress." Again, his eyes went up and down her body greedily taking it all in as if he hadn't already seen her naked. He made a move towards her but then stopped with a chuckle. "Do we take the dress off and hang it up? Feels apropos given our location."

He trailed a finger along one of her dress straps and hooked it underneath, tugging playfully and enjoying the quick flash of the top of her breasts.

"Such a gentleman: cornering me in a locked closet and then worrying about my dress. It's downright chivalrous."

"That's me." He rested his hands on her sides, up at her ribcage where the dress revealed her skin. His thumbs slid under the material and over the underside of her breasts. So soft and begging for his attention. "I'm the perfect gentleman."

"Don't be." She gave him a deep kiss and moaned into his mouth as his thumbs grazed over her taut nipples.

Her lip gloss had the faintest hint of lemon, and her mouth tasted of fresh peppermint. Together it created the nostalgic warmth of his favorite childhood summer treat: a peppermint stick stuck in half a lemon. *Fuck me*, he thought. *She tastes like summer.*

"I have an idea," she said, breaking their kiss. He hadn't even realized that as they were kissing, she'd lifted her dress so she held the bulk of the material delicately in one hand. She turned away from him, giving him the perfect view of her almost bare ass—covered only with a bit of thong. With the help of her high heels, that alluringly ample ass nearly lined up with his cock. Just when he thought things couldn't get better, she raised her hands up and tipped forward to gently grip the coat rack rail above her.

"I love this idea," he whispered in her ear, tugging at the soft skin with his teeth. He wanted to continue down her neck with plans to give a gentle bite on her shoulder when he finally entered her, but Mel had already warned him and the rest of the groomsmen not to give any bridesmaids hickeys or to "rough them up" so much that it was obvious in the pictures that they'd found their own happy ending at her wedding. Sam wasn't a bridesmaid, but that rule probably extended to all wedding guests.

It took all his willpower not to bite her shoulder, rip off the ridiculous article of clothing pretending to be underwear, and recklessly grope her through the thin material of the dress. He was relieved he'd already been able to take his time with her. It had clearly paid off as she was just as eager as he was to go another round. More importantly, while the danger of being caught was undoubtedly heightening everything they were feeling, he wouldn't have wanted her first time to be bent over in a coatroom, *in a church*. Call him a hopeless romantic, but it felt better that this was round two for them.

Instead of assaulting her smooth, unblemished skin, he busied his mouth with two of his fingers before hooking his thumb on her underwear and sliding her thong down to her knees. As soon as his fingers grazed the top of her inner thighs and reached their final destination, Sam's head fell back again, and he could see her biting her lip, trying to suppress the moans so desperate to escape her sweet mouth.

Lipstick can be reapplied, right? He put his hand over her mouth to muffle her moans and said, "Shhhh…I'm going to give you what you need, I promise. But you have to promise to be quiet. Can you do that?" He flicked her ear with his tongue and placed a kiss to the spot below it.

She nodded her head yes.

"Good girl. If it gets to be too much, bite down on my hand. I can handle it."

Another nod of understanding.

Still fully clothed, he inched his hips forward to nestle

himself against the groove of her ass, a desperate attempt at some sort of friction and contact.

With his fingers he spread her lips open and gently massaged the wet skin around her clit, enjoying the way her ass grinded against his cock as she rode his fingers. Sam was in no way submissive—quite the opposite under normal circumstances—but the way she was bent over in front of him in the coatroom sent him spiraling into primal mode. He pulled a condom from his pocket and ripped it open with his teeth before unbuckling his pants and sliding it on. It was slightly cumbersome with the excess of clothing he had to wear as a groomsman, but like a person who gets super-strength to save a small child trapped under a car, he made quick work of it and soon his pants were around his ankles, and he was ready to go.

She mumbled into his hand and he moved it to hear what she was saying.

"You brought a condom?" she asked.

"You didn't?" It was part banter and part genuine curiosity. He wanted to know what went through that giant sexy brain of hers.

"There may be one tucked in my purse along with all the tissues."

"Good. We'll save that one for later." Gray's palm made two large circles around one of her asscheeks, admiring its utter perfection, before he slid his cock into her wet pussy. He kept one hand working the bundle of nerves where their bodies connected, while his other hand found its way back under her dress and to her exquisite tits before settling once again over her mouth to smoother her moans.

"And there will be a later. Because despite what you said the other night, there's no going back from this," he whispered into her ear.

Sam moaned into his hand and then bit down on his one

of his fingers as she bucked her ass back into him so he went deeper - deeper than what he'd thought she could handle.

"Are you going to come for me?" He was so close himself but he refused to leave her hanging. Her first or together, but he couldn't allow himself to beat her there no matter how wet and unbelievably sexy she was with her pussy wrapped around his cock.

She bit down again and moaned into his hand and he felt her starting to come around his dick. Unsure he could trust himself to stay quiet as he came undone with her, Gray buried his face into her soft neck, his tongue tasting the salt from the sheen of sweat they'd both worked up.

Slumped over her still, he gave three sweet kisses to her neck and took his hand away from her mouth. "You are perfect, Sam." She turned her head and before she could say anything back his lips were on hers again due to an insatiable need to be kissing or touching her at all times.

"How do I look?" she asked in a tone that said she knew she looked awful.

The smeared lipstick made her look like some demented offspring of The Joker and It. "Gorgeous, like always."

She smiled and said, "Liar. Hopefully I can fix it in here enough to get to a bathroom."

He disposed of the condom using some paper towels he spotted on a janitorial cart, and they both got to work putting themselves back together to be wedding presentable.

"Do you want me to run it up?" Gray offered when he saw her pull out a sewing kit from one of the coat pockets. He'd already buttoned up his pants while she was still working to get her dress and undergarments sorted. As careful as he'd been, it was obvious that she'd just been fucked in a coatroom.

"I know how to sew. Maybe I can help," he offered.

"You sew?"

"I was a boy scout. Besides, everyone should know. It's a basic life skill."

"Very true. You'll have to teach me sometime." She planted a hand on his chest, gave him a quick kiss, and handed over the small box. "Thanks."

When he opened the door, he almost stopped short, finding Ronan standing in the entryway. Not wanting to hear whatever bawdy comments he'd have for him, and to prevent having his personal life spreading like wildfire through the hundreds of guests who'd be arriving shortly, Gray shot Sam a look to hang back, and then he closed the door all but a crack behind him as he walked out.

"Just getting your lovely bride-to-be a sewing kit from one of the bridesmaid's coats," he said, holding up the kit for Ronan to see.

"Thanks. Did you see her? Are you allowed to? She's all over these wedding traditions."

Ronan looked mildly frazzled as he rambled with questions and fidgeted with his tie and collar.

"It was a text request, but I'll make sure I don't look at her unless she says it's okay."

"Good, good."

"You okay?"

"Couldn't be better. I'm getting married."

CHAPTER 23: SAM

Gray had given her a look, eased the door mostly closed, and then started talking to someone in the entryway. She could hear only muffled sounds from within the coatroom, and she wasn't sure if she should stay put or not.

When the conversation ended, she peeked out the sliver of the opening. Ronan was standing by the table, and it didn't look like he'd be leaving anytime soon. If that's who Gray had been talking to, which was likely given the context, he'd know right away what they'd been doing in there since Sam hadn't had access to a mirror to adequately fix herself back up. Not that *she* minded much, but she wasn't sure where Gray landed on the whole thing.

Come on, come on, she thought as Ronan stood and stared at the front door. No, not at the front door. Something beyond the front door. Through the tiny slit, she could see him grab the keys from off the table—her keys. He hefted them in his hand, but not to gauge the literal weight of the keys. There was something symbolic about it. As if he was weighing his options: fight, flight, or freeze.

Still hiding out in the coatroom, which they'd thoroughly heated up with their steamy activities, she could feel cool beads of sweat popping up all over her body as she tried to make sense of what she was seeing. She almost opened the door to talk him down when she noticed him furrow his brow and then set the keys back down.

That was close. She silently and slowly let out a long breath. Just when she thought Ronan had gotten his shit together and would head back upstairs to his groomsmen, he pulled a flask from his jacket.

Lucky bastard. Sam was immensely jealous of his secret booze stash. She could use a shot or three at that point, too, but she'd made the egregious mistake of picking a sexy, yet pocketless, dress with nowhere to store a secret supply of libations. Maybe a garter with a flask next time...

He tilted his head back and took a large swig before leaning a hand on the table to hold himself up. While he'd seemed eager at the time for the drink, it clearly wasn't his favorite based on his reaction. Nonetheless, he repeated the process five times more before he screwed the cap on, tucked it back into his jacket, and made his way upstairs to the rest of the bridal party in their preparatory suites.

An hour later, Sam sat next to Lexi and set her eyes firmly on Ronan at the altar. She'd witnessed him almost flee his own wedding and then down enough liquid courage that he could probably perform party tricks later with the candles around the room and his booze-filled breath. As far as she could tell, Ronan was either experiencing a touch of cold feet, or he was suffering from an unrelenting remorse at having proposed in the first place. Or perhaps he fell somewhere between. If only she had one more clue....

Then what? she asked herself. Would she really be one of

those people who stood up in the middle of the ceremony to object to the union of two souls she barely knew? Certainly not. She'd already spied Mitsy sitting a few rows up. So no, not only would she not ruin the wedding, but she also wouldn't give Mitsy any more ammunition to paint her as the epicenter of the immoral blight currently spreading through Deep Creek Lake.

Her mood darkened just thinking about it. She'd taken the week off from blogging and she'd never made it in to see Marcy since she'd shown up with Jackie the weekend before. She was determined to keep a low profile, so any action at the wedding would be a terrible idea. But damn was she curious about what was going on with Ronan—even if nothing would come from it, she was dying to know what had been running through his head.

She also wanted to know because it was affecting her as well. A few hours ago, she probably would have thought Gray sneaking glances her way mid-ceremony was adorable. Lexi sure thought it was cute each time Leo threw her a look or a wink. Sam could hear a faint giggle and see the blush rising on her cheeks. But Sam? She was tainted goods. Knowing the wedding they were witnessing wasn't as sunshine and rainbows as they'd all thought, it gave her anxiety to think Gray had wedding bells or anything beyond a quick shag in the coatroom on his mind.

She knew he eventually wanted a wedding of his own based on what Lexi had told her. While Sam had had mild reservations before, she was quickly on her way to being categorically against becoming a bride ever again. The realization hurt all the worse each time she caught one of the love-struck looks Gray slipped her way every few minutes.

To her surprise, she hadn't caught even a glimpse of Ronan's nerves or any sign of hesitation throughout the entire ceremony. She would know since she never took her eyes off him. She wondered if she'd really seen it at all since he looked nothing short of elated to be Mel's one and only for as long as they both shall live.

Afterwards, they had cocktails off in a side room while the bridal party slipped away for more pictures. Before making his way with the bride, groom, and crew, Gray branched off to chat with Lexi and Sam at one of the high-top tables set up around the cocktail room.

"Having a good time?" he asked as he slipped one arm around her waist. Gray's attention and question hadn't been directed to her as much as they'd been to Lexi, so she tried to relax under his too familiar touch and let Lexi take the lead in answering.

"I'm surprisingly okay," Lexi said as she looked around, confirming that she was indeed at a wedding, and that she was still okay with everything. "Yup, this is… fine. I think the hardest part was the ceremony, but Leo and our counseling group have been helping me work through some things to prepare for all of this."

Lexi was the sweetest and yet most badass of them all. Sam was certain that had she been in Lexi's place, she would have run out of town to avoid all the reminders of her tragic past, and she never would have set foot in a church again or watched anything that wasn't a thriller or murder mystery on the ID channel.

She could see the admiration in Gray's eyes, too. Understandably, he knew more than Sam ever could about what it meant for Lexi to not only attend a wedding, but to be there with a date.

Being the adorable dork that he was, Gray kept one arm around Sam and held his other up to give Lexi a high-five, middle-school style. "I'm proud of you, Lexi." He gave Sam's side a squeeze. "And you? Have you ladies had a chance to mingle yet?" She was hyper aware of his thumb affectionately stroking her side the way a lover would.

"No, not yet."

"Keeping it low key," Lexi added.

"Avoiding Mitsy?" he asked.

"Like the fucking plague," Sam said. She wasn't usually one to hide from her problems, but that did seem to be her MO lately—especially that disaster earlier where she'd literally hid in the closet watching Ronan contemplate the biggest decision of his life.

Gray leaned in and planted a quick cool kiss on her cheek. "Want me to plant some coke on her and take her out in handcuffs?"

"Tempting… Tell me more…"

"No, that's not necessary," Lexi said, cutting in. "Jon's waving at you. You'd better get over there for pictures. Mel will be pissed if you hold them up."

"Offer stands. Think about it." Another chaste kiss on the corner of her mouth, and then he was off.

Lexi raised her eyebrows at Sam, silently asking what was going on between her and Gray. She knew Gray had spent the night after the fire pit and that they'd had sex. She probably also saw the pictures on Sam's social media pages of Gray's bare torso, in her bed, holding one of her books.

She swirled her apple cider martini, the featured cocktail for the wedding, and took a sip before answering. "We were just messing around."

"Does he know you're just messing around?"

She gave a confident nod. "I refused to take off my pants until he agreed it was only a one-night stand. Literally made him repeat the words back to me."

"You had a password to access your vagina, and it was 'one-night stand'?"

Sam sat up straighter. "Yes. And it worked. We didn't have sex again all week."

"This past week when you forced me to help you dodge him?"

"That's not how I remember it…"

Ignoring Sam's feigned poor memory, Lexi said, "And then today while I was helping Mel with her hair and her dress…" she trailed off allowing Sam to fill in the rest.

"That obvious?"

"To the layman, no. But *I* did your hair and makeup this morning. I can tell you've been man-handled a bit."

Gray, having finally made his way through the crowded room, flashed them a quick smile before he walked out of sight.

"And there's that."

"He smiled at you, too," Sam argued.

"He was being polite. That panty-melting love-sick smile was just for you."

"The panty melting, I agree with. But lovesick?"

"Love. Sick. Was today's vagina password, 'I do'?"

Sam put her head down in mock shame. "Nope. No hoops today. I was easy."

"What are you doing, Sam?"

"Well, one-night stand didn't make sense anymore—"

Lex grabbed Sam's drink and set it down on the table. "Are you drunk already or just trying to dodge my question? You know what I'm asking."

No, Sam wasn't drunk. But she'd bet money Ronan was tipsy, if not flat out drunk. While she hadn't planned on sharing that intimate moment with Lexi, she also hadn't planned on Lexi calling her out on her bullshit. Deflecting from the questions she knew were coming but she hadn't yet figured out for herself, Sam laid it all out there and told Lexi everything: the car keys, the shots, and the overall uncertainty of it.

"Noooo…" Lexi said once Sam shared every detail of what she'd witnessed. Based on the large gulp of her drink, Sam could tell that while she was saying no, she was just as concerned as Sam was.

"We just hiked and did lunch with them. They looked… I would never have guessed…" She killed the rest of her drink and then tipped the empty glass, trying to get every last drop. Sam slid hers over, and Lexi gratefully accepted. Sam was the designated driver anyway.

"I know. I had my eyes on him during the entire ceremony and didn't notice anything else. It's bizarre."

Lexi polished off Sam's drink, gave a sigh of relief, and shook her head. "Then it's not how it looks."

"You're saying he *didn't* almost flee—by stealing my car, I might add—and then down a fifth of something strong to numb the pain of going through with his wedding?"

Lexi shrugged. "Must not have since that doesn't fit with anything else we've seen. And whatever you did see was completely out of context. Maybe Ronan needed to run out for something at the last minute and almost took your car but didn't because it looks like it's going to crap out at any moment."

"But I know what I saw."

Lexi put a hand up to stop her. "Why are you pushing this?" There was hurt and concern in her voice and in her demeanor.

It was an excellent question. What kind of monster was she to be actively looking for reasons to believe Ronan and Mel's marriage was doomed? The miserable kind who loved company, it seemed.

Before they could explore it any further, the crowd was shuffled around once again as everyone made their way to the main room for dinner and dancing. Mel's extensive list of bridesmaids, which had led to Ronan finding an extensive list of groomsmen to match, all resulted in there being multiple tables for the bridal party and their guests. Leo, Lexi, Gray, Sam, and Jon were all seated with a groomsman Sam didn't know, along with two single bridesmaids she was meeting for the first time as well.

Following dinner, she allowed her charming date to drag her out to the dance floor. As they walked out, he took a quick sip from a flask in his jacket.

"Bourbon?"

He nodded as he swallowed and held the flask out for her. "Want some?"

"Designated driver."

"Perfect. Because I might need a ride home tonight."

He held her close, and she could feel the heat his body was throwing off. From the dancing? The tux? Her?

"Do you always bring a flask with you to special occasions?" He hadn't seemed like much of a drinker when she'd first met him.

"Never. It's a groomsmen gift."

"From Ronan?"

"From Mel, actually." He casually turned them on the dance floor to face a table near the bride and groom. "See the woman in the red, off the shoulder dress?"

"Yes. She's hard to miss, even in this crowd."

"By design. That's Mel's mom."

Sam's own mother would scold her for the very unlady-like face she made at that realization. "She looks like she's younger than me!"

"She's particular about appearance." Having made his point, he turned her again, and they continued their dance. "They're mother and daughter, but Mel's nothing like her; she's much more low key, low maintenance. Since this isn't

Mel's show, it's her mothers, all the groomsmen were given flasks and asked to use them discreetly."

If it had been a movie, the screen would have flashed to a fuzzy image of Ronan, pulling the flask from his jacket and taking long swigs before making his way back upstairs, back to the photographers getting candid shots of the bridal party as they got ready.

"Ronan and Mel went along with that? And everyone else in the bridal party?"

"Not the women. Darla—the lady in red—thinks women with wine glasses look elegant, while men with beer bottles or any other glass look less so. I think she also hoped it would limit the amount of booze."

Sam glanced over at the easy-to-spot bridesmaids all gathered in a corner. A herd of women dressed in black with white sashes that hung precariously from their shoulders and elbows. Their wine glasses sloshed onto their dresses as they tried to make TikTok videos and capture perfect selfies. Classy indeed. Looking back, Sam was sure her own wedding had been similar since all her bridesmaids had been in their early twenties, too.

"Do you want me to introduce you to her? She runs the local chapter of Women Rising."

"Darla? No, thank you." She already knew the Darlas of the world. Had already successfully avoided them throughout high school and most of her adult life. With a welder for a husband, she'd never had to attend any highbrow functions full of Darlas and Jims—Jims being the equally obnoxious men Darlas tended to marry. And she gave Jeremy the same courtesy by refusing to attend any of the events her father tried to push on her. Maybe her departure from the clinic hadn't been that surprising to her father after all—she'd always had one foot out *that* door as well and had been woefully uninterested in the networking side of it.

"You sure?"

"Positive."

"Don't let the first impression scare you off." They danced while they spoke, and Gray expertly guided her through the crowds of couples. They were headed for Darla. "She's a good person to have in your corner."

Sam was ready to break off their dance if that's what it would take for him to understand she didn't want to meet this random woman, but it was too late. She heard Darla purring Gray's name as Darla caught sight of them heading her way.

CHAPTER 24: GRAY

"Darla, I'd like you to meet Sam Smith; she moved to town earlier this year. Sam, this is Darla; mother of the bride, and the fearless leader of the esteemed local chapter of Women Rise."

He dropped his arms so Sam could properly shake hands and engage with the indomitable Darla Beaufort. He'd told Sam he would introduce her to all the important people at the wedding. He started strong with Darla to show her he'd meant it. That he cared about her, and she meant more to him than their beyond-amazing coat-closet meet-up.

Before the wedding, Sam was relaxed and flirty around him. Then during the ceremony, he'd tried to catch her eye, but she was intensely focused on the bride and groom. Afterwards, she'd felt stiff in his arms, even while they were dancing. He could sense something was off, and that she was maybe pulling away from him. He hoped going straight for Darla with the meet and greets would set them firmly back on pre-wedding-flirty-banter ground.

"Darla," Sam said as she extended her hand. "Pleasure to meet you. It was a lovely ceremony."

"It was, wasn't it? Thank you for coming, Sam," Darla returned with a cocked eyebrow. "Or shall I call you Cat?"

Sam's smile remained, but he saw the slightest twitch of her mouth. "No, please. That's a pen name, really. Nothing I ever…"

Darla looked around to her immediate left and right. The cover band they'd hired was blaring Billy Joel, causing at least a hundred tipsy guests to break into spontaneous song as they belted out the well-loved verses. With no worries of being overheard, Darla said, "Don't let them shame you into silence."

"Oh, no… That's not what I'm doing."

Her perfectly manicured hands reached for Sam's, pulling her towards the empty seat next to her. "Gray, be a dear and get me another glass of wine? It's Spiced Wassail from Boordy. Do you want one, dear? All the drinks are local, just like everything else we're serving. Maryland-made and fabulous."

Sam took a seat. "No, thank you." Then she looked at Gray, her eyes asking if he was going to leave her with Darla.

"Just one glass of red?" he asked. He may have worried if he'd been there with someone else. But Sam? If anyone could hold her own, it was her. "Are you sure? Can I get you anything else?"

"No, thank you." Darla turned back to Sam and Gray heard her say, "A fine specimen of a man. If it hadn't worked out between Mel and Ronan, I'd have taken *him* for a son-in-law in a heartbeat."

Gray let out a slow, low breath. A few good words from Darla couldn't hurt to put him back in Sam's good graces.

Not long after he took a spot in the lengthy bar line he heard, "Gray, so nice to see you again." Mitsy had saddled up behind him in line.

"Mitsy."

"Was that Samantha Thornton I saw you here with?"

As much as he hated playing games, he also didn't dare get confrontational with her at Ronan's wedding.

"Samantha Smith, yes. She's allowed me the honor of her company this evening." He'd tried to pour it on thick, but he forgot what an admirable adversary Mitsy was.

"Smith, yes. She's in the middle of a nasty divorce, isn't she?"

Gray continued to look towards the bar, refusing to fall into whatever entrapment she was laying out for him.

"Though I suppose next to the prostitution allegations and her distribution of pornography, divorce is the least of her vices."

Guests standing in line around them stopped their own conversations to listen intently for whatever juicy gossip they could glean.

"You know none of that is happening or has happened." There was a warning in his tone that he hadn't planned on but also didn't regret.

"Is Captain Moloney aware of the quality of company you've been keeping lately?"

His hands balled at his sides in frustration. Even that subtle action threatened to put them in a bad light as well. Not that he would ever hit someone like Mitsy, but he wouldn't put it past her to claim his balled fists were an aggressive threat to her safety. And yet, for whatever reason, people in town listened to her nonsense.

Gray got his glass of wine and turned to walk away. Unable to allow Mitsy to get away with all the shit she'd said about Sam, he said, "It was a pleasure seeing you again, Mitsy. Please give my regards to Harold. Is that him? Over with the bridesmaids in the corner?" It was, and he enjoyed the look of pure hatred that briefly flashed across her face. Harold and Mitsy deserved each other.

He'd been gone longer than he would have liked due to the long line at the bar and his frequent stops to talk with various guests as he made his way across the room. When he did return, he found Darla with half a glass of wine and Sam finishing off a glass of her own. They were in hysterics over something and leaning in towards one another as if in a deep and private conversation. Just as he'd planned. He knew she and Sam would hit it off.

"Gray! Look, Jackson arranged for me to have my own bottle at the table." She pointed to the half-empty Spiced Wassail bottle that sat between her and Sam. "Do you want that glass? I think we're all set here for the time being."

"I wouldn't dare—"

"Nonsense." She waved her hand at him. "The flask mandate was to keep the wedding from turning into a frat party. For the sake of the photos, really. But then..." She motioned towards the bridesmaids who'd migrated from the corner to the dance floor. Most had a drink in each hand with wine or whatever they were drinking splashing onto the floor as they danced. "Oh, well. Best laid plans and all."

He took in Sam's flushed appearance and decided against having any more alcohol for the night. If she needed someone to drive her home, he preferred that it be him.

"Need a refill?" he said to a bridesmaid as she walked past on her way back to the dance floor. She gratefully accepted.

Rather than interrupt Sam's conversation with Darla, Gray hung back by the dance floor, pretending to watch the revelry in front of him. Luckily, Darla and Sam were just tipsy enough to be shouting at each other regardless of their close proximity.

"Now, tell me, Sam." Gray heard Darla say. "Have you ever considered doing an in-person book club? I can't stand my current one. All we read are books from Reese's and Oprah's book club lists. They were fine for the first few months, but the ladies are growing restless. And by ladies, I mean me. I'm restless."

"I know exactly how you feel!" Sam said, the wine increased her enthusiasm. "I love a critically acclaimed, award-winning book as much as the next person, but you must spice it up now and then. In my personal opinion, it is possible to have both."

"Literary accolades and sex?"

Sam barked out a laugh. "Never. But there *are* books with thought-provoking plot and panty-melting sex. We *can* have it all, dammit. Minus the accolades—as long as there are Mitsys in the world, smut will be synonymous with trash."

"We don't need the praise, just the orgasms. Our next meeting is March 28, about two weeks from now. We're supposed to be discussing *In Lieu of Death*, but it's early enough that we can change it. Everyone waits until the last minute to read it, anyway."

That was the last he heard of their conversation because Ronan, Leo, Jon, and the rest of the groomsmen ushered him out onto the dance floor for their big song and dance routine. The bridesmaids—every one of them an aspiring social media influencer—had insisted on choreographing a dance routine for the bridal party and newlyweds to perform during the reception.

With the extra time he'd recently had living in an empty, dogless apartment and having a girlfriend (of sorts) dodging him, he'd worked hard to perfect his dance moves, so he let himself get lost in the chaos of it all. What had started as a joke turned serious as the groomsmen's competitive tendencies emerged and they all strived to outdo each other.

Afterwards, he spotted Darla sitting with her husband, Jackson. When he didn't spot Sam anywhere, he wandered around looking for her. He found Jessa instead.

CHAPTER 25: SAM

I t was getting late, and she was done. More than done.

While she hadn't wanted to engage with Darla at first, the woman had instantly won her over in the brief conversation they'd had. It was almost as if she'd been gaslighted by Mitsy to think she *was* an immoral person whose poison was seeping into every crack and crevice of the town.

Yes, her friends and loved ones—even Jeremy—had her back and supported her which contradicted everything Mitsy said about her. But sometimes a person needed to hear validation from a complete stranger, and that's what Darla did for her. The woman spoke her mind and knew how to get what she wanted. There was no reason for her to flatter or mislead Sam. When she gushed about how she'd started following her blog and how she loved her recommendations (vanilla erotica was her preference) Sam felt better than she had all week. Felt empowered to move forward again without fear of what Mitsy may do or say.

While Gray was adorably fumbling through the bridal party dance routine, she arranged to team up with Darla to co-host her next book club meeting. The group included more members from Women Rise, as well as some business owners in town. Darla kept company with a fierce group of women, and Sam couldn't wait to meet them.

Once they'd swapped numbers and made tentative plans to make more solid plans later in the week, Jackson had reappeared, and they chatted a bit more before Sam excused herself to use the restroom.

When she re-emerged moments later, she practically ran into Gray as he accepted an awkward hug from an attractive, curvy brunette. He was careful with his hands in where he placed them, safely in the center of her back with his fingers relaxed and barely touching her, while she was all in. There were divots in his coat where her fingers pulled him closer for an intimate embrace. And while he looked wary, with his head held back, she went up onto her tiptoes, even in her high heels, so that she could bury her face in his neck.

Ah, yes, she thought to herself. *Of course single, sexy, and super-confident Gray is catnip for single women everywhere.* Though in that instance, it didn't look like the attention was wanted, nor were the feelings reciprocated. Out of pity, she cleared her throat and said, "Gray?" so the woman would release him.

She picked her head up from where it rested between his neck and chest, and she backed away just enough that Gray could extricate himself from her grasp.

"Sam, I've been looking for you." As if the two women were facing off in a debate, Gray side stepped so that he was behind her, effectively declaring himself team Sam. Safely by her side, he said, "Sam, this is Jessa."

"His ex," Jessa added as the women shook hands.

"Right. And Jessa, this is my girlfriend, Sam."

Both women looked surprised to hear that bit of information.

"Is Shawn here?" Gray asked, looking over Jessa's shoulder back into the reception area.

She gave a bitter laugh. "No, he and I aren't together anymore. Though even if we were, I wouldn't be here with him or anyone else for that matter. I'm working tonight; in the kids' room." She motioned to a door behind them adorned with colorful cutouts of cartoon characters. Then she turned to Sam. "I'm switching careers. Currently teaching fourth grade, but I'm taking night classes to get my degree in social work, and I'm taking on odd childcare jobs here and there to help pay for my classes."

Oh, fuck. This woman, Gray's ex, whose voluptuous curves and gorgeous features made Sam momentarily question her own sexuality, was taking night classes to move from one thankless, though massively important, career to another. Meanwhile, Sam wrote reviews on *others'* artwork and writings—not her own—when she wasn't babysitting dogs all day. In a contest between her and Jessa, she would lose on every front. What possible reason could Gray have for leaving Jessa's loving arms to stand next to bland and banal Samantha Smith. Even her name was unoriginal and boring.

"That's great," she managed after she'd done a quick mental Venn diagram with "Jessa as a Girlfriend" on one side and "Sam as a Girlfriend" on the other. Jessa's side was stacked, Sam's was almost empty, and the only similarity in the middle section was that they both had vaginas.

"And what do you do?" Jessa asked.

Not only did she not want to get into it at the moment, but she was also suddenly aware that *she* may be the only thing standing between Gray and Jessa's happy ending. Jessa wasn't the awkward third wheel in the scenario, she was. She didn't know what had happened between them, but Jessa clearly wanted him back and she was so obviously the better choice with her lack of relationship baggage and clear career goals that involved a job most would consider virtuous.

"Um… Just a few things here and there." She turned to Gray. "I should really get going."

"Okay, I can drive you," Gray said.

"No, you should stay," Sam insisted.

"You can't drive. You and Darla had a case of wine. Let me take you home."

Not taking any sort of social cue that she should step away or look interested in anything but their argument, Jessa watched Sam and Gray's back and forth with open interest.

"Gray, I'm fine. I'll figure out a ride. You should stay and catch up with Jessa." She hadn't set out to hurt him, but in typical Gray fashion he didn't know when to let something go, and the low blow had been her only option. Besides, she meant it. Sam didn't like the idea of him giving up on whatever they'd had on the off chance that Sam might pull her life together and be worthy of his time and attention.

"That'd be great," Jessa said, jumping at the opportunity just as Sam knew she would. "I'm off the clock in ten minutes. It was nice meeting you," she added, formally releasing Sam from the conversation.

"At least let me walk you out." Gray didn't confirm one way or the other if he'd be meeting up with Jessa. Instead, he put his hand on the small of Sam's back as he guided her to the reception area and then to the front door.

His hand helped her navigate through the crowds as she tapped out a text to Lexi about getting a ride home.

"You're not getting a ride home with Lexi; she's drunker than you are," Gray said after reading her text her shoulder. They were in the entryway by then, and she was running out of options.

"Why are you so against me driving you home? What's really going on?" Even though her eyes were glued to her phone, she could feel his eyes on her, waiting for any hint as to what had changed since their previous entryway encounter.

She gave up on Lexi responding and looked up at him. "*Nothing* is going on, Gray. Between us, nothing is going on."

Another jab, another look of pain. "Really? Nothing is happening here?"

"Nothing that can last. Nothing that's in *your* best interest."

"Why don't you let me decide what's in my best interest?"

"And if that's not the pot and the kettle…" When he didn't agree or disagree, she added, "How could you *not* tell I *didn't* want to talk to Darla?"

"You said you wanted me to introduce you to people. I figured you were just nervous. Most people are around Darla. She still intimidates the shit out of me."

"I'm not in a good place right now with everything. People in this town actively hate me. So no, I wasn't in the mood to network tonight."

Gray put his hands in his pockets and took a deep breath. "I didn't realize. I'm sorry I pushed you."

"Thank you."

"But you're so similar. And you hit it off, didn't you? You swapped numbers?"

He'd been so close to redeeming himself. Unfortunately, the whole I'm-sorry-but-also-let-me-remind-you-why-I-was-right speech negated his previous apology. Under normal circumstances, it would have irritated the hell out of her. In that particular circumstance, it was infuriating.

"Listen, and I mean really listen this time. Don't nod your head at what I'm saying and then assume that you know what's best for me regardless of what I've said. I don't need *you* to dictate how I should live my life. I already have Mitsy for that." Another direct hit with her accusation that Gray's actions were akin to Mitsy's. They weren't, but he also didn't seem to understand, and she really needed him to back-the-fuck-off before all the walls closed in on her.

"Saaaammmm," Lexi sang from behind them as she and Leo walked into the entryway. "I got your text message. This sweet guy here's gonna give us a ride home." She gave Leo a sensual kiss that had Sam and Gray looking away briefly.

The kiss broke up when Sam said "Great. Thanks for driving Leo. Are you heading out now?" She expected Gray to protest or to insist on going home with them, but he didn't. It hurt more than she'd expected, and it set her more firmly in the belief that at that moment, all she was capable of was hurting anyone who dared to get too close romantically. She had known what she was doing when she'd made the initial goal of sleeping with everyone rather than dive into anything serious.

"Mini road trip! Let's go!" Lexi flung her arms around Sam and told her how much Sam's friendship meant to her, and how she would never have found the courage to take a chance on Leo without her. Sam very much doubted that, but it wasn't the time to argue it. Unlike Gray, she could read a room and she knew when to let something be.

The men exchanged a few words as Sam helped guide Lexi out the door and into the chilly night. They hadn't brought coats since they'd driven Sam's overheated Corolla to the wedding.

As they power walked to Leo's car, Sam took a quick glance at her own and noticed she had two flat tires. The universe had seen her spirits rise as she'd spoken with Darla, and it was hell bent on putting her back in her place.

It wasn't until they got to the car that Lexi noticed Gray wasn't with them. "Isn't Gray coming?"

"Not this time." She shot a look at Leo and was pleased to

see he had no intentions of chiming in about why he wasn't joining them.

"Why not? I like Gray." She giggled to herself as she climbed into the back seat after Sam. "Did I ever tell you about the dream I once had?"

"Yes!" she accidentally yelled, her voice reverberating off the walls of the compact car. Leo, in the driver's seat by then, caught her eye in the rearview mirror. *How the tables have turned*, she thought. Not long ago, she'd judged him based on his behavior and the stories from his past. She could only imagine what he thought of *her* after hearing her yell at Gray, seeing her leave him at the church without saying goodbye, and then practically yelling at Lexi when she wanted to share an innocent story about a dream she'd had.

Their tense exchange wasn't even a blip on Lexi's radar. She babbled about how important friends were, and about how she would never let anything come between them.

"I love you, too, Lex. Don't worry; nothing will ever come between us."

Lexi had been leaning heavily against her in the back. Sam could feel her tense up.

"You can't promise that. Paul and I were supposed to be together forever..." Her face scrunched up with her monumental effort to hold back the tears, but it didn't do her any good. By the time they'd reached the driveway, Lexi was fully emerged in the whirlpool of emotions she'd suppressed throughout the wedding. Feelings she may have been holding back since the accident.

She suspected Leo had always known the moment would come, because he knew exactly what to do and what to say. Sam did her best to comfort her, but Leo was the one who carried her into the house, and he was the one Lexi could hear.

"It was supposed to be us. I was supposed to marry Paul," she sobbed into Leo's tux.

"I know, sweetheart. I know," he agreed. There was no jealousy in his voice. How could he be jealous of someone who wasn't alive?

"I loved him so much. Too much. I loved him too much."

"And he loved you, too. I know it. What's not to love?"

He didn't tell her not to cry; he didn't tell her Paul wouldn't want her to be sad; he didn't tell her everything would be okay.

Sam, slightly tipsy herself though not nearly as drunk as Lexi, had gone with her first instinct: soothe the savage sorrow before it swallowed her whole. She shushed Lexi's words and tried to still her shaking body. She'd tried to help her push it all back down again, but what good had that ever done anyone?

Sam opened the front door for Leo, and was going to help them get settled, but she wasn't needed. He had it well under control. She doubted he'd had even a sip of alcohol that night, knowing she'd likely need him later when shit finally hit the fan.

Sam quietly closed the door behind her, leaving behind the muffled conversation about what Lexi and Paul's wedding would have looked like, and what they would have been doing in their lives at that moment if Paul hadn't died.

It had been too much for her, so Sam ended up on her comforting couch once more. Her mind was a continuous loop of the events from that evening: the quick but passionate encounter in the closet, Ronan's potentially hot and cold feelings towards the wedding and Mel, Gray's pushy demeanor and her argument with him about it, her pushing him towards Jessa, Darla's encouragement followed by her two flat tires.

Just for fun, her brain sporadically tossed in a few extra

worries about how Lexi was still agonizing over the loss of Paul, how Marcy had had a semi-cold attitude towards her after the Mitsy article posted, and how she'd been permanently assigned the back playroom and was no longer working the front desk at Bark Sniff Wag.

CHAPTER 26: SAM

I t was a rough week after the wedding. Aside from work, where she remained in the back areas and out of the public eye, Sam spent her time holed up in her apartment waiting for a text from Gray while ignoring whatever was on TV. She was unfairly yet thoroughly pissed each day that passed without a call or a text from him. She checked her wi-fi connection, she sent text messages to Jackie and her parents to make sure her phone was working properly, and she checked her phone's notifications volume at least a half dozen times each day.

She didn't realize she'd hit official rock-bottom status until the day Leo popped by the apartment unexpectedly.

"Oh, crap. Sorry, Sam. Didn't mean to interrupt anything." He eyed her up cautiously, slowly taking in her hair, her face, and the rest of her appearance. "We got takeout sushi and forgot we're out of soy sauce."

"No, it's fine. You're not interrupting anything. I have some. Come on in."

He did, but he stayed at the door and cautiously took in the area by the couch where she'd set up camp for most of the past week. Strewn about were a handful of discarded, uber-sexy smut books—the reverse harem ones with at least five dudes half-naked on the cover who are all pawing over an equally scantily clad woman. An assortment of empty snack bags littered the floor around her dirty books. Her need for salty snacks and her lack of motivation to fix anything of substance had caused her to exist on a giant box assorted snack packs for days at a time.

"Are you feeling alright? Can I get you anything?" he asked as she grabbed the sizable container of soy sauce from one of the cabinets.

She put a hand up to her hair to smooth it out and could feel just how out of place everything was. A stretched-out elastic band barely held a small chunk of hair off her left shoulder. The oversized t-shirt she wore, one of Jeremy's old shirts though the fact that he had once owned and worn it held little significance to her, hung limply from her body in a most unflattering manner. To top it off, she'd been reading and notating in her novels like a fiend, leaving her fingers covered in various ink colors. The lengths of her fingers, where only one or two inks had reached, looked rather pretty and resembled a tie-dye shirt. The pads of her fingers and thumbs took the brunt of all the colors and were stained dark brown and black.

She saw his eyes take in the marred skin on her fingers as she handed the bottle to him. "I was writing," she explained.

"And, uh…" He motioned to the other side of her head. Her hand felt around and then landed on a sizable hunk of a puffed, cheese-dust coated snack.

She held out the newly extricated snack and could not form words to explain how an entire serving size of cheese puffs had ended up in her hair without her knowledge.

"Why don't you join us? You know Lexi always orders way more than either of us can eat, and we haven't seen you all week." It sounded like heaven: sushi with friends when she felt like crap. She didn't even have to worry about what to order. It was already there and waiting for her. She just needed to walk over to the house.

"No, thanks." She could tell he was about to insist so she added, "If I'm completely honest with you Leo, and now that you've seen me at quite possibly my worst, I feel like I can be, it's really tempting to go eat and chill with you guys, but standing here with this cheese-puff that was in my hair for who knows how long, I don't think more chill time is what I need right now. I haven't done much of anything today, or even the past few weeks. I don't even think I've looked in the mirror yet today." His mouth opened again to object. "I know. You'd wait for me to do whatever I need to do to be presentable enough to engage with other humans. And that's very kind of both of you, but I need to do something productive with myself."

He nodded. A fair reaction to her lengthy and way too personal speech. "You're sure?"

"Positive. Tell Lexi I'll catch up with her later tonight or tomorrow."

"Okay." He held up the soy sauce. "Thanks. Maybe we'll see you for dinner tonight. Late dinner probably," he said, checking his watch.

"Sure. Maybe." She doubted it. It was a generous offer, and she had already assumed many of her future plans with Lexi would include Leo, but she wasn't yet ready for the permanent third-wheel status that would come with all of that. She had no experience with it given that she'd met and started dating Jeremy in her mid-teens, but to her, being a third wheel sounded like something she'd like to avoid for as long as she could.

.   .   .

It took an hour for Sam to transform into something worthy of the general public. The wrappers were cleaned up off the floor and the discarded books were re-shelved. She gave herself a thorough scrub down and she washed and brushed her hair.

It was a small step in the right direction to take hold of her life again. It had felt safe to back off and lie low. And then it felt cowardly, which quickly turned into something akin to shame. People regarded Sam as someone who didn't back down from a fight. The person in the group who knew what she wanted and charged after it. But with everything that had been happening lately, she wasn't so sure. She worried the trait she'd prided herself on was merely a reflection of how others egregiously viewed her rather than something that was real.

The idea was unthinkable and yet all she could think about as she readied herself. She needed to take action, starting with Paging All Bibliophiles.

"Sam! I was hoping you'd stop by sometime soon." Marcy waved her hand at the other associate working the floor on the busy Sunday. "Glenda, cover the register for me, please. I need to step in the back for a few."

"Hey, Marcy. I'm sorry I didn't stop by sooner…" She'd practiced the speech on the way over, but it was a short drive and she'd gotten nowhere with it. Nowhere but the ugly truth of it. "I've been a bit of a coward."

Marcy waved her off. "Never. You are Cat the Great. Come, step into my back office so we can chat – away from…. all of this." Her conspiratorial tone wasn't lost on Sam, who ducked her head slightly and looked around the store as if it could be full of spies.

"Buck, Sam's here," Marcy called when they made it to the back area.

Sam had met Buck a only handful of times during her brief stint as a smutty book ambassador, so she couldn't imagine him being all that excited at her presence in the store or in the back room. But there he was, jumping up from his computer to greet her. His tall frame towered over her, but she already knew by then what a softy he was. His interest in unsolved mysteries came only from his desire to solve puzzles and help others. Which apparently was why he was so excited to see her.

He grabbed her hand and engulfed it in both of his, giving a slight squeeze. "How you holdin' up?"

"I'm fine." It was a harsh reminder that Mitsy's actions had had that much power over her. The shame rose again. "Really. It's just one, angry person taking all her misery out on me. Well, and on you, too, I guess since it's pouring over and affecting you all as well."

"No, it's not hurting us," Marcy said. "We were worried that first day, but later it was clear to see that it was fully aimed at you, dear." And Sam could see she meant it, too. There was remorse in her tone and in her expression. "We pulled back slightly so we could assess any potential damage and figure out if we were even going to make any long-term moves or changes, but we'd never let something or someone like that completely dictate what we do here. That's why I wanted you to stop back a few days later. Let you get your head straight and let things die down a bit before we plotted out our next course of action."

"Haven't you seen your affiliate link hits lately? Our in-store purchases are up, too. All in romance," Buck said, finally releasing her hand so he could step back to his computer and pull up one of the many, many tabs that lined the top of the screen.

No, she hadn't seen any of the numbers lately for clicks and purchases from Paging All Bibliophiles via her blog. She hadn't even opened her blog since the day Jackie had visited.

It wouldn't have been the first time she'd heard aggressive, angry statements hurled in her direction simply because of what she liked to read. It was part of her daily routine to sort through the positive and negative comments on her blog. She'd leave any of the ones that politely offered an opinion different from her own, and she often left an equally polite comment in response, but she also had her site set so comments were only public once she approved them. Anything rude or downright hateful never made it to the public. Instead, she read them, allowed some of the hate to settle somewhere deep in her bones where she hadn't even realized it had been accumulating, and then deleted them without another thought.

That was before Mitsy's big stunt with the chalked sidewalk and the opinion piece. Then all the previous nasty comments she'd thought she'd brushed off came screaming back at her. Forcing her to take a hiatus from the only thing left that was balancing her currently off-kilter existence. For the past two weeks she couldn't get herself to pull up her big girl pants high enough to dare to check anything on the website.

"See for yourself. Our numbers are up, Sam." Marcy said as she nudged Sam closer to Buck's computer.

"What?" was all Sam could manage. On the way over to the store, she'd imagined all the worst-case scenarios where Marcy would tell Sam how her scandal had ruined their store, and they were on the verge of collapse. She didn't allow herself to even consider the possibility that anything positive could come from it all.

"Look at our sales this week compared to the same week last year," Buck said, pointing a thick finger to the screen where a line graph showed a green line, last year, well below a blue line, that year, for each day after Mitsy's article went live.

"It's like when they try to ban books or tell teenagers not to do something," Marcy said. "It only makes people want to rebel and do it that much more."

Sam let out a breath. She hated that she had been so ready to back down at the first barrier she'd hit.

"That's not even the best part. This is what I really wanted to show you," Buck said as he expertly worked the mouse around the screen until four different boxes pulled up different images of a dark green car. Each square had its own date and time stamp, and each image had its own varying degree of clarity, as security camera stills often did.

"Whose car is that?" Sam asked as she leaned in for a closer look. The license plate was illegible, but the car looked similar in each picture, and in two pictures, she could see a matching scratch on the back left bumper.

"We don't know, but I was in Bait Me the other day and overheard Smitty and Gray having a heated argument about the flat tires again. Smitty was adamant that it wasn't him and it got me thinking that maybe he was telling the truth. Especially since two of your tires were flattened at the wedding. That's just not Smitty's MO. Neither is hitting the same car over and over again. He's a creature of habit—too much to be going off script like that. Unless you've had a recent, particularly ugly encounter with him I'm not aware of." Buck finally paused.

"No, I haven't seen him in weeks. How did you know about my tires at Ronan's wedding?"

"Blue stopped by the other day," Marcy said. "He and I chatted some and I was asking about you, if he'd talked to you or heard from you. He said he hadn't, and that he thought you needed time to sort through some things, and he mentioned the tires. Is everything okay? He seemed awfully concerned about you."

She shook her head slightly. "No, I'm fine. Just a rough few weeks is all." She turned back to the screens. "You think this is the person who's vandalizing my tires? Not Smitty?" Lexi and Leo had helped her with her car the next day, and she'd decided not to pursue charges or anything like that. At least not yet.

"Yes, we think they're vandalizing your tires and some other folks' around town." Buck looked over to the closed door separating them from the rest of the store. "I overheard Gray's conversation with Smitty, and I surreptitiously wrote a few notes about the case." He affectionately patted his breast pocket, out of which Sam could see a mini spiral notebook with a pen tucked into the spirals.

Marcy rolled her eyes at her husband's detective antics. "Columbo here has been greasing the pockets of the local employees to get security footage from the areas where the flat tires have happened. Twice he's found Smitty blatantly driving or walking in front of the security cameras, but the rest of the time, and there have been at least thirteen since your first flat, they all have this vehicle as the only common vehicle."

"Almost all the other times," Buck corrected.

Sam gave him a quizzical look, not believing the efforts Buck had gone through trying to solve the somewhat benign problem of someone letting air out of people's tires.

"You've been watching footage of roads and stores and entryways?" she asked.

"Lots of footage," Buck said. "Hours and hours when Marcy lets me. I can speed up the footage to get through weeks at a time in only a few hours."

"Not that he has Blue's blessing or anything, but Blue's

turning his head on this one on account that he can't devote the hours of time needed to do it himself."

Sam looked from Buck and Marcy back to the screen. She could see how it could draw someone in—all the little bits of evidence sprinkled around the town just waiting for someone patient enough and detail oriented enough to put it all together.

"What's the next step? What can I do?" Sam asked, ready to get back to determining her own fate.

CHAPTER 27: GRAY

A week after the wedding, he finally had that cup of coffee with Leo. Sam had been right. The lack of emotional connection between the guys resulted from many variables, but it had not been due to their incapacity for it as he had once suspected.

Three hours into their sit down, Leo had given Gray a rundown of what his childhood had been like and how he'd finally realized through grief counseling just how much past trauma he still needed to work through.

It had been difficult to hear, especially knowing Leo had been suffering through it silently while they were all oblivious. He knew it wasn't easy for him to talk about it, either, but while his eyes and shoulders showed how much it pained him to relive his past life, on the other end of it there was a lightness revealing another layer of weight had been lifted. One he'd been carrying for so long and without any complaints that Gray hadn't noticed it. He'd walked beside him for years without offering to help share the load.

Then it was Gray's turn. He told him about his argument with Sam, the one Leo and Lexi had walked into at the wedding. About how he hadn't seen Sam or Lexi since then. Sam's absence was self-explanatory given their fight. He hadn't seen Lexi because she was busier since she'd started dating Leo and living with Sam.

He told Leo how miserably alone he'd felt in the apartment without Daisy or Ronan around. He was scarcely there to begin with, but the absence of Ronan's belongings hurt more than he'd expected. For the longest time it had felt almost hypothetical: the wedding, him moving out, Daisy's owners returning for her.

"I'm sorry we haven't invited you out more or over for dinner," Leo said. His hands absently fiddling with a wooden stirrer throughout most of their conversation.

"No, you guys are new and still getting to know each other."

"We can still put aside a few hours to see friends."

Gray nodded. "Thanks."

"What about the apartment? Will you put out an ad for a new roommate?"

"Why, you looking to move?"

Leo shook his head with a sheepish smile. "Not with you."

"What? With Lexi? Really? That soon?"

"Eventually. We haven't said when or anything like that—or even talked about it seriously yet. But I know she's it for me. The next time I ask you to help me carry couches and beds, I guarantee it's going to be to move in with her."

"But Lexi… It hasn't been that long since—"

"I know." He cut him off before Gray could go into detail about all the things Leo already knew. He probably knew more than Gray since they'd attended those grief counseling sessions together and had the intimate conversations people often did while lying in bed together at night, their limbs intertwined and indistinguishable. "And I'm giving her as much time and space as she needs. It looks like I'm the one pushing this, given how often I hounded you about her before, but how serious we are right now is all her."

He could understand that. As much as she fell apart from Paul's death, he could see how much she'd loved and adored him and had loved their life together. Once she'd allowed herself time to accept her new life without him, and to grieve his loss, it made sense that she would want to find it again and dive in. She wasn't replacing Paul; she was determined to get back to happier times in her life.

Gray looked up at the ancient corkboard by the door to the cafe. Each time the door opened ads for missing pets, roommates, and job openings fluttered in the soft breeze before settling again—untouched and unnoticed by the patrons who entered or left. He imagined his own roommate want-ad on the board and was immediately depressed by the thought. It only got worse when a man walked up to peruse what was available and shoved his finger into his nose, up to the *second knuckle*. He dug around for a while before tearing off the various tabs of phone numbers and email addresses.

"No, no more roommates. I had a hard enough time breaking Ronan in. I'm not going through all of that again with a stranger."

Leo caught sight of the green gold digger as well and made a disgusted face. "Fair enough. It's probably only temporary anyway. You and Sam will work it out. You guys were made for each other."

"You barely know her," Gray scoffed.

Leo held up a fist to emphasize the points he was about to make. "She loves animals." He stuck out his pointer finger.

"What monster doesn't like animals?"

Undeterred, Leo continued, extending his middle finger to join his pointer. "She's attractive."

"Are you saying I'm attractive, too?"

"She gets along with just about anyone."

"Which is the antithesis of me according to Ronan."

"No, you're initially unlikable. Once you get to know people, you're like a chameleon blending in with the setting and adapting your personality to match whomever's you're talking to. Who else could handle Smitty or the rest of the unhinged locals the way you do?"

That one wasn't completely accurate given the screaming match he'd engaged in with Smitty the day before.

"Sometimes," he conceded.

"You're both book nerds." Only his thumb remained closed as all four fingers were up.

"*I'm* a book nerd. She reads…" he dismissed the rest of the sentence with a wave of his hand.

"No," Leo said as he shook his head. "Don't do that."

Gray had been leaning forward on the table. He sat back and ran a hand through his hair as he stared down at the table. Then he drummed his fingers on the table and briefly considered ordering another coffee, but he was jumpy enough as it was, so he decided against it.

"You're right. About all of it. She is gorgeous and compassionate and funny and tough and sweet and so freaking smart. But she won't let me get anywhere near her. Each time it feels like we're getting somewhere, she disappears again; completely shuts me off."

Leo nodded, a solemn expression on his face. "You're hurt and it's coming out as anger."

"Don't grief counsel me…"

"You have misplaced anger, and if you take it out on her with comments like the one you just gave to me about her reading, you're going to sabotage any chance you still have with her."

Gray's phone vibrated and he was disappointed yet again to find it wasn't from her.

"It's Buck. He's over at the store and has something he wants me to look at."

"Let me guess. Another scandalous chalk tagging?" Leo grew up in town, but people would never know it by his shocked response to every small-town petty incident. He wouldn't admit it, but Gray knew that was why Leo avoided the town meetings: out of fear he'd publicly lose his mind hearing complaints about grass that was too long, neighbors' dogs who pooped in lawns that weren't their own, and bookstores who recommended too many books about love.

"Maybe. Whatever it is, I should go have a look. I need to get up and get moving anyway."

"Yeah, I should get going, too. We have some yard work to do before dinner. Lexi and I ordered those meal deliveries where they ship out recipes and ingredients, so you only have to prep and cook it."

For a quick moment, Gray really took Leo in. He stood taller, he'd ironed his shirt, his muscles looked more relaxed, and his smiles came easier. It was a good look on him.

"Yeah? What's on the menu tonight?"

"I have no idea. I eat almost anything, so I let her pick."

Gray wondered how long it would take for him to stop feeling guilty about keeping Lexi away from Leo for all those months.

Unable to barge in, even though Buck had asked him to stop by, Gray gave a few quick knocks on the door to the back office at Paging All Bibliophiles.

"Come on back, Gray," he heard Buck bellow from inside.

It wasn't a large area, so it was already almost to capacity with Buck and Marcy around the computer. Add in Sam and Gray, and it was downright snug.

"Hey," she greeted, as if she hadn't called him a pushy jerk and then walked out of his life.

"Hey," he said back, as if he didn't care that she'd called him a pushy jerk and then walked out of his life.

"Come on 'round to this side here, Gray, so you can take a look at this car," Buck said.

His muscles tightened as his mind raced with all the reasons it might not be a good idea to be crime fighting with Buck and the Scooby-Doo gang in the town he lived in. It was one thing when Buck was chasing a lead a few states away and was asking general questions about clues that were readily available through his online group. But this? Buck was scavenging around Deep Creek, uncovering his own evidence, and he'd gone and included Sam in it as well.

Speaking of Sam, she'd accused him of being pushy and uptight. If he remembered correctly, she'd called him the squarest person she'd ever met. The idea repeated in his mind, pushing him until he found himself taking a step forward, a step towards Sam and the computer to see what Buck had found.

Buck's large hands gestured towards the screen, pointing out grainy images of a dark green BMW. Harold Lorrett's dark green BMW. He recognized the scratch on the bumper because it had happened at little league orientation in the parking lot. His unit worked hard to increase community relationships, and one way they did that was to volunteer for the sports rec programs. Ronan and Gray preferred the baseball and softball games since they played back in high school together. After the fender-bender, he distinctly remembered Harold dropping the f-bomb in the parking lot in front of some kids.

Buck gave a quick run-down of where each image had come from and how he was certain the vehicle was involved in most of the tire incidents. He couldn't connect the car to the Bait Me flat tire last week—likely because that incident really had been Smitty. He also couldn't definitively say in regards to the wedding because the green car had been at the church, but so had most of the town.

"Huh," Gray said as he scratched the stubble on his chin for effect. "No plates?"

Buck's head lowered. "No, the surveillance systems some of our local businesses use leave much to be desired."

"That's okay. What you've got is great. It's more than enough to get me started, but now that I'm looking into this beyond Smitty, I'd prefer if you didn't get any more involved than you already are. Any of you." Buck and Marcy nodded; Sam scowled. "I'm serious. Do you understand?" he asked her. She didn't answer and he didn't push it, because he wasn't a pushy guy.

"I think I have an idea of the make and model, so I'll run some reports to get a list of owners. Then I'll start making contacts, but you all are officially off duty."

"Sounds good to me," Buck said. "Sleuthin' Around is counting on me to help figure out the Harding case out in Montana. You heard of that one, Gray?"

He checked his watch. There was a fifty-fifty chance Harold was at his daughter's game at that moment, and he wanted to head over to see if he could ask a few questions before the game ended.

"I haven't, but unfortunately, I need to head out. Fill me in next time I drop by?"

"Absolutely. Bring your lunch with you when you come. It's a doozy of a case."

Marcy reached out to give his arm a quick squeeze. "Thanks for swinging by so quickly, Blue."

"Any time, Marcy."

Sam was still scowling, so he gave a general goodbye to all three before heading out to his car.

"You know whose car it is," Sam accused once they were out of the store.

Gray turned to look at her but didn't confirm or deny the statement. It was a relatively nice, late-March day—perfect weather for a confrontation in front of the store.

"I knew it," she continued. "You say I'm terrible at poker, but I already have all your tells pegged. As soon as you looked at those pictures, you knew exactly who it was."

"I gotta run, Sam, but it was nice seeing you again."

"It's not just my car. I have some sort of stalker, for real this time, who's obviously unstable and whose aggression towards me is escalating." Her scowl was replaced by concern and perhaps fear. It was one thing when she thought her flat tires were the eccentric shenanigans of the town's quirky convenience store owner. It was another thing entirely to have no idea who she was dealing with or what she'd possibly done—if anything—to upset them.

It was a terrible idea. The worst idea he'd ever had. Waves of regret pounded down on him before the words even left his mouth. And yet, he said it anyway. Because it was Sam. "Fine. Come on. There's only a slight chance I even know where he is right now, anyway."

CHAPTER 28: SAM

"Where are we going?" Sam buckled up as she took in the interior of Gray's immaculately clean car. She hoped she didn't have any mud on her shoes, but she also wasn't too concerned because clearly he did frequent thorough scrub downs of the inside and outside of his car. Undoubtedly, he would erase all traces of her presence by the end of the day—the end of the week at the latest.

"To the baseball fields. The guy's daughter plays softball, and they usually have games during the day on Saturdays and Sundays. There's a good chance she might be playing and that he might be there watching her."

He turned and caught a glimpse of her confusion as he put his arm behind her seat to back out of the parking lot.

"It's for work. Ronan and I have a certain number of community volunteer hours we're supposed to put in each year. We like to spend most of them on the fields with the kids."

He wants kids, she thought. Yet another reason she should have continued to keep her distance rather than invite herself to spend one-on-one time with him in the confined space of his ridiculously tidy car.

She tried to conjure up anything she could have done to piss off a softball dad enough that he would repeatedly deflate her tires. She had nothing.

"I know I didn't realize I'd offended Smitty earlier, but this time I'm almost positive I haven't done anything to anyone else. Well, aside from Mitsy, but she'd never dirty her hands with something like this."

Gray shrugged but kept his eyes on the road. "It's not uncommon for people to target the wrong person with this sort of thing, and it's not uncommon for people to have terrible, almost non-existent reasons for doing the things they do."

"You think this is a case of mistaken identity?"

"It could be someone who thought you were someone else, but it could also be a person who's angry about something—anything, really—and taking it out on you. Like the person who kicks the dog as they walk past it, figuratively speaking."

That she could understand. The most hateful comments on her blog were usually made by those types of people. The ones who were mad at the world and vented that rage by taking it out on anyone who upset them in even the slightest way.

Gray pulled into the tiny stone parking lot of a snowball stand. Rocks crunched under his tires as he eased towards the large pieces of timber acting as a barrier between the lot and the lake beyond it. It was too cold for a dessert made of tiny bits of crushed ice covered in sugar flavoring; they were the only car in the lot.

"Okay, time for the ground rules," Gray said.

A dry laugh escaped her; it did not go unnoticed by him. He continued regardless, as she knew he would. He couldn't resist spouting off about rules and ensuring there was order in the world.

"You're staying here," he said. "And while you're in the car, you won't be using your phone to record anything. You will enjoy this picturesque view of the lake. We'll talk when I get back, and I'll tell you everything I can. Okay?"

Sam opened her mouth to argue, but he cut her off before she could even get the first word out.

"I was serious back at the store. I can't have civilians playing cop with me. It's not safe, and it's highly unethical. I won't do it. I'm not on duty right now; that's the only reason you're here with me."

"Okay. I understand. I won't get out of the car." She settled in against the back of the seat and made herself comfortable.

"Good. Thank you."

He got out, crossed the road, and walked towards a collection of baseball fields. Sam turned in her seat to watch him. The dugouts and fields were filled with small children in colorful uniforms.

Jerk. He'd purposefully parked too far away and parked the car facing the lake so that she couldn't see whom he was going to talk to. She opened the center console expecting to find napkins or some sort of paper towel or tissue, hand sanitizer, a first aid kit, loose change that was not actually loose since it was thoroughly secured in some sort of compartment, and binoculars.

There it all was, just as she'd predicted. The only thing she'd been wrong about was a stash of soy sauce packets in a tiny compartment in the console lid. She smiled at his ability to be predictable and yet surprising.

It was a decent day in March, but since they were in Western Maryland, it was still frigid at the fields as strong winds came off from the lake. Through the binoculars she could see the parents bundled up on the bleachers and in their folding chairs. Their coats and hats, on top of the significant distance that separated her from them, made it difficult to make out who anyone was.

Gray must have known the guy fairly well, because he went straight for a man sitting with a woman close to the third base line. Seeing Gray, the man stood and extended his hand while the woman remained seated. Her eyes didn't leave the field. As Gray talked to the man, Sam noticed a bit of hand gesturing, though she hadn't the slightest idea what any of it meant. The man's hands remained in his pockets. Finally, the woman looked at Gray and gave Sam a better view of her face.

It was Mitsy. Even with the hat, coat, and sunglasses she was sure of it.

How had she written off Mitsy so quickly when it was so obviously her? Probably because Mitsy had an air about her that seemed entirely too sophisticated for such things like deflating someone's tires out of spite.

She looked back to Gray and saw he still wasn't speaking to Mitsy. His attention was firmly set on the man, probably her husband. They even walked away from Mitsy as they continued their conversation. Sam kept her eyes on her, wondering if she should take matters into her own hands and approach Mitsy herself. The best way to stand up to a bully was to confront them head-on. Not that she'd ever done that, but that was what she'd heard.

When she got as much information as she could from the back of Mitsy's head, she turned back to Gray. She needed him to be engrossed enough in his conversation with the husband, that she could discreetly get close enough to Mitsy without Gray noticing. When she turned to the left to find him again, all she saw was Gray's larger-than-life crotch (thanks to the binoculars) quickly approaching the car. When she moved them up, she saw his larger-than-life eyes narrowed at her and his head shaking in disgust. Busted. She lowered the binoculars and prepared for the inevitable showdown between them. Because as much as he was annoyed with her, she was sure she was angrier.

"I didn't explicitly state, 'Don't spy on us using the binoculars,' but I felt like it was heavily implied when I laid out the ground rules."

"Someone had to keep an eye on Mitsy—you know, the culpable one."

"I knew it was likely Mitsy—"

"It *is* Mitsy."

He took a deep breath and exhaled through his nose, clearly holding back from whatever he really wanted to say to her.

"When I first saw the car, I had a feeling it was Mitsy." He put a finger up to prevent her from interrupting him again. "I needed to talk to Harold first to confirm my suspicions. Okay? If you just let me talk, you'd have known I was agreeing with you."

Her shoulders slumped in defeat, and she was mildly disappointed their argument had ended so abruptly.

"Right," she said. "Good. Now, where do we go from here?" She put the binoculars back up to her eyes and turned for one last look out the back of the car to study Mitsy. Except this time, Mitsy wasn't facing the game. She was looking right at Sam.

It was reminiscent of *The Exorcist,* with her body facing forward, while her head looked directly behind her. It was so jarring, Sam's first instinct was to hide. Rather than duck her head forward and risk slamming it into the dashboard, she turned and threw her head down into the open, inviting space between Gray's stomach and the steering wheel—right over his crotch.

"Shit," she said, raising her head slightly so that it wasn't directly in his lap. But then her head seemed too high again, and so she lowered it once more. *Great*, she thought sarcastically, *my head is bobbing over his crotch.*

Even with her head down, she felt him turn slightly and noticed he raised one of his arms.

"Are you waving at her?" Sam hissed.

"She's looking right at us. I'm attempting to look natural. You're the one blowing your cover with your head in my lap. Pun intended."

"Do you think she saw me?"

"You better hope not. She already thinks you're a prostitute who loves reading porn, and now you have your head buried in my crotch in broad daylight."

She pinched his side. "This isn't funny."

He squirmed and laughed, knocking her head into the steering wheel.

"Oof. Stop squirming."

"Stop pinching."

"Is she still looking?"

"Yup. Staring right at us. She just mouthed the words, 'dirty whore,' and made an obscene hand gesture."

Sam's head shot up, and she looked out the back of the car. Mitsy's attention was on her daughter's game. Sam scoffed and playfully smacked his arm. "You're a terrible person."

"And as smart as you are, you're incredibly gullible," he said, laughing.

Ah, yes. Back to the flirty banter that would lead to them in bed again, and her running away in the morning. He must have felt it too because he cleared his throat and got out his phone.

"Can you give me a minute? I should call this in to the station. Get everything started."

"Sure, of course." She grabbed the car door handle, ready to get out. "I'm going to hit up the stand for a celebratory snowball. Want one?"

By-the-book Gray had wasted no time and was already connected to the station. "Yeah, thanks. Just pick something for me," he said to her as he momentarily lowered his phone to his lap.

Just pick something? There were over one hundred flavors and ten different toppings to choose from. She didn't even know what *she* wanted. How could she even guess what he wanted? Except she wasn't guessing what *someone* would want, she was guessing what *Gray* would want.

She cringed at the counter, ordering his egg custard snowball. What did egg custard taste like? She couldn't say. All she knew was that it was orange, and it had a disgusting name. but from her experience living in Maryland, people like Gray couldn't get enough of it. Of all the hundred plus flavors the stand boasted, only five, including egg custard, had a jumbo-sized bottle of flavoring located front and center for easy access. Unlike her strawberry cheesecake flavor which was mostly buried by bottles of other strawberry flavors.

Standing by the lake as she waited for her order, Sam breathed easier than she had in weeks. It was almost over. Mitsy was about to be outed for the petty, overbearing, slightly unhinged person she was. Her credibility would tank once word got out, and Sam would be free to get back to smutty book recs at Paging All Bibliophiles, back to the occasional front desk stint at work, and back to blogging without fear of Mitsy's crew descending upon her as if she was a nefarious evildoer cleverly disguised as someone who liked spicy books.

The call must have been easy enough because Gray was already off the phone by the time she got back to the car.

"I can't believe you're letting us eat in your car," Sam said as she got back in and handed him his cup of egg custard.

"Why?"

She motioned around with the hand holding her cup. "How often do you get this thing detailed? Weekly?"

"It's not *that* clean. I transported Daisy and all the other dogs in here. It gets messy."

"I saw your pristine center console."

"I like organization," he said in his defense, the corners of his mouth rising ever so slightly. "So, what flavor did you get me?"

"Egg custard."

He sniffed it. "Huh," he said before taking another sniff.

"You've *never* had egg custard?" An unfair accusation since she hadn't either.

"I don't think so… What did you get?"

"Strawberry cheesecake."

"You got strawberry cheesecake, and you thought I'd enjoy something called egg custard?"

"It's a classic. There's a five-gallon jug of it at the front of the stand."

He took a tentative bite, then another larger one.

"See? I was right. You like it."

Gray rolled his eyes as if it pained him to admit as much. He ran a hand through his hair and turned his body, as much as someone with long legs in the driver's seat can turn their bodies, towards Sam. She considered doing the same. Thought about how easy it would be to casually move her leg as well so that their knees would touch, and she could feel the comforting warmth of him again.

"Why did you walk out on me at the wedding?" he asked, his voice full of curiosity rather than the residual hurt or anger she'd expected.

Sam shifted in her seat, but it wasn't so their legs could

touch. There was no sense in trying to talk her way around it. They lived in a small town, and they had too many mutual friends and contacts. She couldn't avoid him forever.

"Apparently, that's what I do. I walk away when things get ugly or difficult."

"No, you don't." He motioned to the binoculars resting on the center console between them.

She shrugged. "Not always. Just from the big stuff: my marriage and my career—"

"You got yourself out of situations that weren't working for you."

"Gray, I'm a fucking mess. I was trying to put it nicely and your typical self won't allow it, so now I'm spelling it out for you. I am an absolute disaster of a person right now."

"Maybe I am, too."

Sam exaggerated her glance around the squeaky-clean interior of his car. It was sensibly stocked with everything one might need—she would bet money there were more emergency supplies in the trunk—and everything was safely secured in its proper location.

"Oh yes, you're clearly a disaster."

He set his cup in one of the empty cup holders (because Gray didn't fill his with trash, chargers, change, or anything else normal people filled them with) and buckled up.

"I should get you back to your car."

"It's at the house. I was sick of having my tires flattened. When it's not too much of an inconvenience, I ask Lexi for rides if she's already heading out anyway."

"Okay, I'll take you back to the house."

She hated the way his hand went behind her seat as he turned to pull out of the parking spot. It was such a tease to be that close only to have his hand grip the seat, instead of her, before going back to the steering wheel.

CHAPTER 29: GRAY

She was hard to read. On their stakeout, which she'd insisted on joining him for, she flirted with him in the car. It was as if they'd fallen back into their earlier routine of slight jabs and quips along with the underlying sparks and sexual tension that often led to them falling into bed together.

Once he'd brought up their argument at the wedding, she'd gone cold again, giving the impression she was shutting down. It was her way of telling him that their time had ended once more.

Or so he'd thought. In her driveway, she seemed hesitant. There was no urgency as she gathered up her snowball trash and a gum wrapper that had fallen to the floor mat.

Since he wasn't sure when he'd see her again, he figured he'd better get her book back to her. He pulled it out of the glove box and handed it to her. "I meant to get it back to you sooner." He resisted the urge to add that she'd been distancing herself from him making it difficult for him to do so.

She took the book, but she didn't move to get out of the car. "What did you think?" she asked.

Really? After turning ice cold in the snowball stand lot, she was going to try to have an in-depth conversation about a steamy romance in her driveway?

"It was good." His voice sounded flat.

Her eyebrows raised slightly, letting him know he'd failed to meet her expectations with his answer.

Without saying goodbye, she got out and headed up the stairs to her apartment.

Without thinking, he ran after her.

"Wait, I didn't mean—" She'd reached the landing outside her door and was almost inside when he said, "Can we talk about it?" Her hand stilled on the door handle. "Please, don't run off."

He could tell she wasn't fully convinced having a conversation would be beneficial, but it was enough to get his foot in the door, literally, as she held it open for him.

Once inside, his first instinct was to go to her. To remind her how good they fit together when she let her guard down and let him in. Her crossed arms stopped him in his tracks.

"I don't understand what's happening here, Sam," he said.

"Nothing is happening—"

"There's nothing between us? Back in the car we didn't almost kiss? Back at the wedding we didn't have sex in the coat closet?"

"Mistakes."

"You don't strike me as the kind of person who repeats their mistakes."

She shook and lowered her head. "You barely know me, Gray."

"I'd like to know you better, but you're making it really difficult lately."

"Because I'm a wreck." She wasn't screaming yet, but she

was inching her way there. "You're right. I thought I could push past everything at the wedding and give a real relationship with you a chance, but it was a horrible night full of long-term relationship misery."

He thought back to the wedding and couldn't pinpoint anything that would make her think that. He'd been to a few, and Ronan's, by far, had been one of the best.

"After you left the closet, I saw you talking to Ronan. Then I saw him grab my car keys. He was on the verge of leaving Mel at the altar when—"

"What? Why would you think that?"

She held out her hand and pantomimed a scale weighing an object. "He had my keys in his hand like this, debating if he should stay or leave."

Gray thought back to the wedding and his conversation with Ronan beforehand. "Yeah, yeah. I remember he asked Leo to run over to the apartment to pick up a last-minute Amazon wedding delivery. Something for Mel that she'd be superstitious without. He was probably thinking of getting it himself but didn't because of how unreliable and crazy hot your car is."

"But I also saw him miserably take a few shots, like he needed a bit of liquid courage…"

"I already told you about the flasks. Ronan hates the hard stuff; that's why he looked miserable. He did it anyway because he was overly eager to please his new mother-in-law. Swore she wouldn't even see him with the flask."

"Fine," she closed her eyes and shook her head as if to wipe all of that from her mind. Then she opened them and said, "but you can't explain away Lexi's breakdown."

He didn't need her to tell him about it. Leo had already filled him in when they'd had coffee, and Gray had seen it before. Had seen worse that first day when he told her about Paul and then sat with her.

He lowered his voice. He knew Sam was vacillating between wanting him and wanting nothing to do with him, only because she was terrified of it going all wrong again. She feared she wouldn't be able to navigate that awfulness again so soon after she'd just done it with Jeremy.

"No. I can't," he said.

"And it's not even just that. It's you, Gray."

"Me?"

"Yes!"

He made a big to-do about rolling his eyes and letting out a heavy sigh. "Because you think I'm pushy?"

"You *are* pushy: talking to Darla at the wedding, salting my steps, convincing me to let you spend the night after the poker game."

He gave a cocky smile. He'd forgotten about that one.

"And you're cocky," she added.

"You're just as pushy as me: you forced me to say one-night stand before you'd let me into your pants, you forced me to let you ride along with me today, and you've been calling the shots for whatever this is since day one."

When she tried to come up with some sort of comeback, her tongue peeked out from her concentrated effort. The sight was so fucking sweet it sent a panic through him. What if she really did call it off for good, and he wasn't privy to it again?

"*I'm* pushy because I'm trying to get my life back together. I have to be pushy."

"Your life isn't a disaster. Why do you keep saying that?"

She huffed out a laugh. "This looks put together to you?" she asked, her hands gesturing to herself and to her loft. "I'm in my mid-thirties with zero direction for a long-term career or housing."

He didn't immediately answer. She needed to know his response wasn't just words or what he knew she wanted to hear. Gray let his eyes wander from her silky blonde hair down to the fitted black hoodie, snug jeans, and sneakers. Her fingers, with their pink nail polish chipping off, still clutched her favorite book as if it was a lifesaver and she was bobbing helplessly at sea. But she wasn't.

"You left a bad situation to start from scratch on the other side of the state. And you're doing a damn good job, from what I can tell. I've seen you with animals; I know you love it at Bark Sniff Wag, and the apartment looks great. Temporary or not, you're in a good place right now."

She looked around, proof she was hearing and actually listening to what he was saying.

"Your social calendar is going to explode once you start doing book clubs with Darla, you have friends who love you, and your book review blog is… I mean, just look at all that you've done."

She nodded.

He took a tentative step closer, so only a few feet remained between them.

"But all of that doesn't mean I'm in a good place for this."

That stopped him mid-step.

"You think I don't know I've been jerking you around? I do. And I hate myself for it. But I like you too much and it's terrifying me—to the point where I'm actively looking for relationship disasters and then projecting that negativity onto myself and my relationship with you."

"I can handle it; I understand."

"What about Jessa?" she asked, ignoring what he'd said before that.

"What about Jessa?"

"She's who you should be with right now."

"Jessa and I weren't right for each other. You'd be able to see that if you spoke more than a few words with her."

Nothing from Sam.

"I want to be with you," he said carefully, annunciating each word so he was certain she heard it. "I can handle projecting negativity and everything else you throw at me."

"But you shouldn't have to handle it." Her voice was increasing in pitch, and he knew he needed to step back and end their conversation. Pushing her any further or trying to fight it any more would only result in him pushing her away.

"I'm going to go," he said.

As soon as the words left his mouth, her hands were up, gesturing that she knew all along he would leave. That deep down he knew she was right, and the best thing for him was to leave her apartment and to leave her behind.

"No, not because of anything you said. I'm giving you space." He noticed her grip on the book loosen, her muscles relaxed. "I like you. A lot. And I get it that you think I barely know you, but I've stayed up all night reading your favorite book with all your personal notes in the margins that likely span most of your adult life. I've read every word of your blog."

"Just words…"

"And according to you, I've seen you at your absolute worst—a few times." He paused for a moment to let that sink in. To make sure she really heard it. "If you want me to, I'll leave now to give you space. I'm trying to reign back on my *pushiness*," he said, air quoting pushiness since it was her word and not his. It had the desired effect of lifting her sweet lips into the faintest of smiles.

"I don't want kids," she blurted out as he reached for the door.

The tension left his body. He really didn't want to go, and he was relieved to hear she didn't want him to go either.

"Neither do I," he said, turning away from the door to face her. And he meant it. Ever since Ronan had dropped the bomb on them on their ski trip about trying to get pregnant, he'd had a sinking feeling in his own gut whenever he imagined it happening to himself. Her crossed arms dropped to her sides, and he took a step towards her, a step away from the door.

"I may not want to get married again. Ever," she said.

He took another step. One more to go and she'd be in his arms again. "I promise I'll never ask you to. *If* you change your mind, you can ask me."

Sam closed her eyes and took a deep breath. She opened them again and said, "I sometimes get completely lost in books and I'll ignore you. Once I get a house, I want dogs. At least three or four of them. I stress eat, I hate working out, I bite my nails, and I pick at my nail polish, so it always looks like garbage. I'll take the same picture a million times trying to get it just right for my blog, and I'll read tons of smut and have hundreds of book boyfriends…"

"Sam…" He took the last step, and her arms went around his neck, while his found her waist. Right where they should have been all along.

"I need you to know what you're getting into here," she said, her blue eyes looking up at him with such sadness. As if being with her was a life-time sentence to misery that she was trying to warn and protect him from.

"You have no idea how often *you* are at the forefront of all my thoughts. How many nights I've stayed up thinking about you, how many times my mind has wandered because something—a book, a car tire, a playing card, salt, Daisy, fire, whatever—reminded me of you or my time with you."

He brought his hand up to cup her chin and brush his thumb over her lower lip. She bit that same lip when he said, "You don't know how many times I've replayed our time together. Imagined it so vividly I could almost feel your warm, soft skin against mine, smell your shampoo as if my nose was still buried in your hair, and taste the faint tart, but sweet lemon flavor of your lips."

Saying it out loud only increased his need to experience it again. Something he knew he would never tire of doing. Still unsure of where she stood with everything, he gently pressed his lips to hers. The taste, the smell, the feel—it was just as he remembered, that feeling of being home.

After a long, sweet kiss, Sam pulled back with a smile on her face and asked, "You really stayed up all night reading *Autumn Fell*?"

He nodded. His eyes stayed on her lips. They'd just kissed, but he was desperate to do it again, and again, and again.

"What did you think of the scene in the toolshed?" Her voice was breathy, and her hands were in his hair, entangling themselves and tugging gently. All of it sent jolts through his body and forced a light moan from him.

He buried his head in her neck and planted sloppy kisses from her collar up to her ear. Pausing occasionally for a quick response to her questions.

"Very sexy."

He left her neck and went back to her mouth, ending the kiss with a tug on her bottom lip with his teeth. There was something about that sweet, plump bottom lip that he couldn't get enough of it.

"And Foster's decision to leave Autumn so he could find his long-lost brother?" She pulled her face away to see his and properly hear his response.

He let her go and picked up the book on the coffee table next to them. Holding it up so she could see, he flipped through the pages, showing all the sticky notes he'd added. Some he put alongside her margin comments, and some he added where she hadn't written anything, and he'd hoped to add something unique to her already thorough analysis.

Based on her questions and interest in what he'd thought

of the book, he expected her attention to move fully to *Autumn Fell*. Maybe he didn't know her that well, after all. Her hands went behind his neck to pull him back down to her with the urgency of someone starving and full of desperation.

He dropped the book just in time to catch her legs as she jumped up and wrapped them around his waist. She was all in. Really all in this time, and it was clear in their kiss. While one hand stayed firmly in his hair, permanently entwined with her fingernails massaging his scalp, the other was on his cheek. As if it wasn't enough for their mouths and tongues to be one, she needed to cup his face as well. Her thumb placed small strokes under his eye—a stark contrast to the fast pace of everything else. A reminder that there was tenderness and possibly love underneath their animalistic activities.

They continued in bed. Desperately gripping flesh and pumping at a frenzied pace. All the while, their eyes were locked, bringing their souls together as their bodies formed one.

She didn't tell him she was coming. Instead, he saw it in her eyes and felt it in the sweeping of her tongue and gentle moans into his mouth. The love and emotion she showed for him pushed him over the edge. He buried his face in her neck, licking and nipping as he rode out the intense climax.

They spent the rest of the evening in her bed. Gray leaned back against the headboard, and Sam snuggled up against him as they went through all her favorite parts of *Autumn Fell*.

CHAPTER 30: SAM, THREE MONTHS LATER

"Come here, Bruiser," Sam called from the top of the steps to her apartment. When he didn't appear, she followed it up with, "I don't see any bears, buddy. Coast is clear." It was warmer than he liked, but Bruiser dutifully left his doggy bed and joined Sam outside.

"Good boy." She gave him a scratch behind his ears and led him down to the backyard for the barbecue.

"The guest of honor is here," Lexi teased when she saw Sam.

"Nope, that's not what this is. We're just grilling out and having a few people over."

The few people part was a lie. They were expecting Darla's book club, the poker gang with their significant others—even Jon was bringing over a woman he'd started dating exclusively—and everyone from both of her places of employment: Bark Sniff Wag and Paging All Bibliophiles. But they'd planned the barbecue long before there was anything to celebrate.

Leo and Gray took charge of grilling. Leo enjoyed working the grill, while Gray wanted to be there with his meat thermometer to make sure everything was properly cooked. It wasn't that he didn't trust Leo; she'd seen the meat thermometer come out even when it was just the two of them and Gray was cooking.

It was over the top, and she loved him for it. His perfectionist demeanor and abundance of caution were grounding. Not that she'd become fully reliant on him in any way, but it was comforting to know her safety net was beneath her at all times (safely strung up with Palomar Knots and carabiners, naturally).

Still, he wasn't as square and uptight as she'd originally pegged him to be. Especially in the bedroom or when it came to displays of affection towards her. She'd never expected him to be up for acting out some of the racier and more taboo portions of her favorite books—but he was the one who'd suggested it to her.

Similarly, she expected him to be too cautious to jump into a joint dog adoption with her, yet just a few weeks after their Mitsy stakeout, he'd surprised her with a trip to HART, the local animal shelter. Bruiser, a brown terrier who'd immediately won both their hearts that day, had been living his best life with them, mostly at her place.

After the guests had arrived and had a chance to get their fill of food and beverages, Lexi tapped her plastic wine glass with the end of a plastic spoon handle. It didn't have the same effect as metal and glass, but they hated having glass around the water. She placed two fingers in her mouth and whistled to get everyone's attention. Leo turned down the music.

"Thank you all for coming," she said. "Sam insists that this get-together isn't in her honor..." There was a pause for dramatic effect.

She should have known Lexi wasn't one to let this sort of thing slide. While she may have acquiesced earlier at Sam's insistence they not *honor* her, it was clear this had been the plan all along. At least from Lexi's point of view. Leo materialized with a sheet cake large enough to feed all of Deep Creek. It had a picture of a woman reading a book with the title *Sexy Time* written in scribbly icing. At the top of the cake it said, "We love you, Sam." Sam briefly buried her blushing face into Gray's arm before facing everyone again.

"But it's the perfect time for me to make a few over-the-top declarations, so I'm not letting the opportunity go to waste to tell you how much we love and appreciate you."

"How much have you had to drink, Lex?" she teased.

Lexi ignored her question. She was holding Leo's hand and Sam noticed she gave it an extra squeeze before continuing.

"I met Sam over a year ago now. Not in person, though. We were pen-pals of sorts. She didn't even know me when Paul passed, but she heard what happened through her parents, and she reached out to make sure I was okay. Then she continued to write, even though I *know* my first correspondence in return was not so great."

Sam's eyes watered, remembering events from what seemed like a lifetime ago. Her parents had told her about what happened to their tenants, Lexi and Paul, and she had the strongest urge to write to her. Maybe because her life was in shambles, too, and she thought they could ride it out together. Not that she told Lexi anything about what happened with Jeremy, or even held it at the same level of what she'd experienced with Paul, but just knowing she was helping someone else survive their low point had helped her to crawl out of the hole she'd been in.

"And she sent me books," Lexi said.

"The good stuff?" Darla called from her seat at the table.

She had a near-empty bottle of wine in front of her.

"Those came later. We still hadn't met in person or even talked on the phone, but somehow, she just knew the perfect story I needed to hear that month."

That did it. The guys released their girlfriends' hands so Lexi and Sam could share a brief, teary embrace.

When Lexi broke off their hug, she went back to Leo and held onto his hand again. Another strong squeeze. "All the while, Gray was visiting and soothing my aching heart with his company, and with strawberry flavored doughnuts. Thank you, Gray."

She lifted her glass to him, and he did the same with his beer bottle.

"Which leads me to the happiest of conclusions to all of this. Thanks to the two of you, but mostly Sam," Lexi said with a wink towards Gray to show there were no actual hard feelings about him keeping them apart for so long, "Leo and I are moving in together!"

With that, Sam finally understood the kind words and the smuttyish cake in her honor. It was a goodbye of sorts. Another ending. Lexi was leaving to start her own next chapter and the get-together was one final bash as roommates.

After the initial congratulations, celebratory hugs, and details about the move were out of the way, Leo, Lexi, Gray, and Sam had a chance to talk off to the side.

"I don't want to assume anything, but I'll be moving out in two weeks. I made your parents promise not to tell you. Sorry. We wanted to tell everyone together."

"It's fine, Lex. I get it."

A big smile took over Lexi's face as she said, "Once we have all our stuff moved, we'd be happy to help you guys move in. They already said they'd wait to hear from you before finding new tenants"

Sam thought she would have been the one to freeze at the idea of moving in with Gray, but it was the opposite. He was standing behind her with his arms around her waist and his chin resting on the top of her head. As soon as he understood where Lexi was going with her comment, she felt his arms tense around her, and his chest stopped rising against her back as he held his breath.

Since Gray wasn't going to say anything, Sam jumped in about how they'd think about it and that she would get in touch with her mom about it.

Leo gave Lexi's sleeve a quick tug. "We should let them talk. Come on, I'll get you another burger."

Sam turned and tucked a section of her hair behind her ear. She was afraid to look up and see his eyes wide with freight. Like a deer in headlights who was waiting for the vehicle to plow into him.

"Hey," he said, lifting her chin up to look at him.

"Hey." She bit her lower lip as she took him in. His dark hair fell slightly over his forehead, his dark eyes were relaxed and full of concern, and his mouth... That was just as it should be, too. Perfectly poised and put together. That was Gray. He wasn't worried about moving in with her. He'd held his breath and braced his arms because he was worried about her favored choice of flight when faced with relationship fight-or-flight scenarios. Though in her defense, those scenarios had been mostly nonexistent since the night they went through *Autumn Fell* together.

She wore a tank top, and while his one hand cupped her chin, the other gently caressed up and down her bare arm leaving a trail of goosebumps in its wake. How could she not want to wake up and fall asleep next to this man every day?

"Do *you* want to move in with me?" She hated how weak her soft, vulnerable voice sounded. She hated even more that she followed her question up with reasons he shouldn't want to. "Because I don't want you to feel obligated or like if you don't, I'm going to pull away again. I know I'm still anxious sometimes about things and that can't be easy for you to live with. Not to mention how messy I am compared to you—"

"Sam," he said, interrupting her rant against herself. "I want to move in. I really do. But only if you're ready. I don't want to push anything."

She gave a half smile at the "push" comment. He'd been anything but since that final argument.

She nodded her head, afraid she might cry again.

"I've wanted to talk about moving in together for the past few weeks, but I don't ever want to be the first one with all of this. I want you to set the pace. Please don't ever think I'm not interested. I'm only keeping quiet about it so that you're the one calling the shots with how fast or slow we take this."

Holy crap, he's in love with me! Sam's mind screamed. There had been so many times lately where she'd felt like he was on the verge of saying it, but he'd held back. She thought he'd stopped himself out of uncertainty. As if in the moment it was there, and he'd felt it, but once the moment was gone, he was relieved he hadn't let his emotions get the best of him. That wasn't it though. He was only holding back because he was letting her be the first to say it.

"I love you," she said before her head could catch up to what was happening.

There was only a slight, yet torturous, moment before Gray's mouth was on hers for a long kiss. He did his signature move of tugging her bottom lip as he pulled away. "I love you, too." More kissing and sweet whispers into her ear about all the things he loved about her.

"Now," he said when he finally pulled away. "How long do we have to wait till we can sneak back up to the loft?" His cocky half-smile almost had her pulling him away that very second.

WANT MORE? OF COURSE YOU DO!

Scan the code below for bonus chapters, book recs, giveaways, and more!

Missed Jackie and Scott's epic romance?
Scan the code below to read all the hilarious yet steamy details.

ACKNOWLEDGMENTS

In case you're wondering, Deep Creek Lake is an actual, gorgeous lake in the mountains of Western Maryland full of fabulous "locals."

I vacationed there as a child, went skiing a few weekends as a teenager, and have been a handful of times with my husband. I even did a very brief stint at the Oakland Lowe's. It's really that lovely that we just keep going back.

Even so, it had been a while since I'd visited and I needed a little help from the community to make sure I got some the details just right.

Many thanks to the fine people of Deep Creek Lake (with a huge shout-out to Jessica Dijak!) who embraced this d-list author and pointed out all the glaring errors so that you, reader, could experience this story with authentic Deep Creek vibes.

BEFORE YOU GO...

My biggest thanks to you for taking a chance on an unknown, indie author (that's me, in case I'm being too vague). And since you've gotten through to the end, and then some with this little blurb as well, I'm hoping I can ask one more huge favor. Please consider leaving a review on Amazon, GoodReads, BookBub, or any other social media outlet you peruse in your spare time. Rave about how much you loved it, or tear it down and release whatever pent-up anger and emotions you've suppressed for the past decade or so - I'm grateful either way.

HAPPY READING,

Leigh Donnelly